Stealing
Lillian

Stealing Lillian

Tony Kenrick

David McKay Company, Inc.
New York

STEALING LILLIAN

To Freda
Sans musk and garlic.

Stealing
Lillian

Prologue

Whenever people start playing the "Whatever Happened to So and So" game it's usually only a matter of time before somebody comes up with the name Don Ray Bergstrom. And, as always, the question is followed by shrugs and blank looks. Don Ray popped onto the scene from nowhere in a barrage of publicity and then just seemed to disappear somehow. He had a wife, Jane, and a daughter, Sherrel Ann, and was immensely, fabulously rich.

Everybody knew that.

And everybody knew about Sherrel Ann and the multimillion-dollar kidnaps.

But what everybody didn't know was the truth about them. It was shortly after she'd made headlines a second time that Don Ray dropped out of sight.

Ella Brown knew what had happened to him, of course.

And so did Lillian.

And Lasky and Daniel and about twenty-five others.

Including Bunny Calder who knew better than anybody else.

What did happen to Don Ray Bergstrom?

There are quite a few people who are praying that nobody ever finds out.

Chapter 1

There are a lot of things that happen in the world that are left unfinished, and a lot that don't even make it halfway. But everything has some kind of beginning, some definite moment in time that you can point to and say, "That's when it started."

For Bunny it was without doubt the day he met Ella Brown.

It was a Monday, and it began like most other Mondays—slow and reluctant to get going, then picking up with a rush as it became undeniably clear that another work week had arrived. He took the same route to the office that morning that he'd been taking for the past six months: up Forty-sixth, where he had a studio apartment in one of the old warehousey-looking buildings just east of Second, past the steak joints on Forty-fifth, all of them appearing sleepy and hungover from the night before, on past the post office to the Pan Am building and the parade of secretaries pouring into it, down the side of the Roosevelt, down Vanderbilt and into the Chock Full O' Nuts on Madison. Before that, when he'd been in his chocolate milk shake period, he'd varied this route so as to arrive at the Stanhope Coffee Shop, which served, in his opinion, the best milk shake in the midtown area. But now that he was back on coffee and donuts he gave the nod to Chock Full O' Nuts, the best counter coffee in New York. The trouble was a lot of other New Yorkers had reached the same conclusion, so that at 8:45 on any weekday morning not only was every seat taken but the space behind each seat was also occupied—

by a hungry customer impatiently waiting for the diner seated in front of him to eat up, pay up and get out. This was one aspect of this otherwise excellent coffee counter that fazed some people. They claimed that they couldn't stand somebody breathing down their neck, mentally urging them to swill their coffee and gulp their Danish. But it didn't bother Bunny one bit. Other things bothered him—like sharks and runaway trucks and nerve gas—but people, never.

He went through the door, paused a moment, spotted his mark then moved toward him. It was a short fat man who was just sliding into a seat as its previous occupant was leaving. Bunny stood behind him and waited till the man had given his order, then leaned over and spoke to him.

"Sir?"

"Huh?" The fat man looked round.

Bunny gave him a smile. "I just wanted you to know, sir, that I'm not one of those pushy people. You just go ahead and enjoy your breakfast."

The man looked at Bunny for a moment, grunted something, then turned back to the counter where his coffee arrived a minute later. He picked it up, dumped sugar in it, stirred it and started to sip it as Bunny leaned over him again.

"Take all the time you want. Go ahead."

The man nodded without turning round and reached for the pastry that had come with the coffee. He was about to take his first bite when a hand on his arm stopped him.

"Bon appétit."

The fat man waited, then bit into the pastry. He only got time for a few chews.

"Just forget I'm even here," Bunny said.

The fat man sighed, picked up his coffee, gulped a fast mouthful and wrapped his unfinished pastry in a paper napkin. He picked up his check, fumbled some change down onto the counter and swung off the stool. "Here," he said tiredly, "take it."

"But you haven't finished," Bunny said, swinging himself onto the seat. The man went away toward the cash register, and Bunny looked down at the fifteen cents he'd left on the counter. With an easy movement he swept the money into his hand. The counter girl came up and ran a fast cloth over the counter surface; Bunny gave her a sympathetic smile. "I'm afraid he stiffed you."

The girl sniffed. "We get 'em all the time."

4

"Some people just don't appreciate service," Bunny told her. "Look, I don't want you to be out because of that guy," he put the money down on the counter. "I'll tip you for him."

"Come on," the girl said, surprised, "no call to do that."

"I insist. And could you bring me coffee and a donut? Pick out a good one for me."

"Sure thing." The girl hurried away, and Bunny turned to the man who'd just taken up a position behind him. "Good morning," Bunny said.

"What?" the man said uneasily. Only cops, muggers and tourists spoke to strangers in New York.

"I feel that it's only fair to warn you, sir," Bunny continued, "that I'm a member of the S.E.A."

"The what?" The man backed fractionally.

"The Slow Eaters of America. We chew every mouthful thirty-two times."

"Yeah? What do you do with scrambled eggs?" The man knew he was being conned but he moved away all the same. Bunny's coffee and donut arrived faster and fresher and hotter than anybody else's that morning, and he ate a leisurely breakfast, having only to shoo away two or three other hopefuls who were foolish enough to stand behind him. He got his check, put down his own tip, waved away the girl's effusive thanks, paid at the cash register and walked out onto the avenue. He turned south toward Forty-second, where he worked. It was a warm morning in the early part of July, which was fine with Bunny; he liked summer. Air conditioning, gin and tonics, the ball game blaring out of the bars, ice cream, salads, the beach on the weekends, daylight when you got up in the morning and daylight when you went home, and no heavy topcoats to slump around in. No coats to cover up the girls either. That was definitely one of the nicest things about summer: you could tell a girl without a score card. Like the one that was jiggling toward him now; no bra but lots of everything else.

"Have a good day," Bunny said to her cheerfully as she passed.

The girl, used to three or four propositions on her way to work, and twice as many on her way home, flicked cold eyes briefly at him, then came back for another look: warmer and much more interested. A lot of women took a second look at Bunny, he was what a lot of them had in mind when they went on singles weekends. For a start he was thirty-five and unmarried, always a nice thing on a singles weekend. He was medium tall, nicely coordinated in his movements, as if

5

he'd been an athlete in college—which he hadn't. But the slim, bony-shouldered figure gave that impression. He had fairish hair, dark eyes, a good, strong, open face with a touch of Robert Redford about it. Specially in the smile. A girl friend had once described Bunny's smile as his best side. Bunny used it sparingly and at the right times—for openers to hook somebody in, and for closers to clinch the deal. But, then, in Bunny's line of work a nice smile was very important; and if you didn't have a presentable image and a pleasant manner to go with it you wouldn't have been very successful. Bunny's profession was talking people into things. Most of the things he talked them into were legal enough, but his methods would have been frowned on by the Better Business Bureau and, as often as not, the police.

When he reached the corner he stopped, gave a tug to his jacket, ran a hand through his hair and set himself. He strode off at a faster pace. His own particular work week had officially begun.

He swung round Forty-second, passed a candy shop, a nut shop, a strudel shop and a hosiery store and went in through a door above which three stories of windows featured large letter cut-out signs, all of them promising to find you a job. Bunny mounted a flight of stairs, walked down a corridor and stopped outside a frosted glass door on which was lettered the words "Gemstone Jobs, Inc." There was a man waiting there for him.

"Hi," Bunny said. "Getting a jump on the competition?"

"What competition?" the man asked. "Wait till you see the book." He nudged the flat sample case by his side. He was a young man who looked like a series of moons—small moon face, large moon body. He had tangled, black, oily hair and a smooth, almost golden skin.

Bunny let them both in. "Have you been to us before Mr.—?"

"Mussolini. Angelo Mussolini. No, I ain't."

They entered a small outer office that featured a filing cabinet, a few nondescript chairs, a couple of Van Gogh prints in unpainted do-it-yourself frames and a large table with forms and ballpoint pens covering the top and chairs drawn up to it on either side.

Bunny indicated the table while he opened another door. "If you'd just fill out a form for our records, I'll be right with you. You're an art director, right?" The sample case could only have been an advertising portfolio, and seeing as how the copywriters in New York are Jewish and the art directors Italian, Bunny's guess was simple.

The young man looked at him as if Bunny hadn't yet gotten the message. "Not *an* art director. *The* art director."

"Uh huh," Bunny said. "Where are you now?"

6

"Kappel and Rike."

"What are you working on?"

"Frozen food, beer, you know."

"Be right with you," Bunny said. He let himself into the inner office, closed the door and went to the phone and dialed. He called a friend of his who ran an employment agency across town and specialized in the ad business. "Hello, Sam? Bunny Calder. How was your weekend?"

"Please, I have a wife, three kids and a mortgage in White Plains. How do you think it was?"

"Sorry," Bunny said. "Listen do you have anything for an A.D. heavy in frozen food and beer?" The description seemed to fit the man in the outer office.

"Talented?"

"He'd better be. His name's Mussolini."

"Yeah, I may have something. K and E just picked up some food business. Pays twenty-five. Let me check and I'll call you back."

Bunny hung up, crossed to the door, opened it and invited his client in. He took the portfolio from him, laid it out on the desk and unzipped the sides. He said to him, "Let's take a look at some of the winners, shall we?"

"They're all winners," the art director growled. "Six gold medals in there but for that awards jury. Bunch of aesthetic cripples."

Bunny flipped through the book. "You've got some nice stuff here."

"*Nice?*" Angelo looked as if Bunny had bad-named his mother. He gave the book a vicious backhand slap. "Show me another book in this town that's so nice. *Nice?*" he said again. "Listen," he thumped his finger into his breast in time with his words, "when you hire Angie Mussolini, you don't get just nice, you get fan*tas*tic."

Bunny tried to look impressed. "How old are you, Angie?"

"Twenty-two."

"How much are you looking for?"

"Thirty-two."

Bunny continued turning pages. "I may have something. I'm not sure they'll go that high."

"So I'll take thirty. Just as long as it's out of this town."

Bunny looked up fast. "You want to relocate?"

"Yeah. Bunch of gutless dummies here. I thought maybe Chicago."

"Chicago?" Bunny echoed. He sounded alarmed. Chicago was no

7

good; if Sam came up with the K&E job, and this guy got it, that would mean 50 percent of a very nice little commission, plus whatever else he could con out of shy little Angie. And Sam only handled New York jobs; he had to keep the art director in town. He said, looking very concerned, "You mean they haven't told you about Chicago?"

"What about Chicago?"

Bunny slipped easily into the argot. "It's death, man. A real hernia. No business, no budgets, no talent. I mean they treat ads like dry cleaning there—in by nine out by five. They slap a piece of copy on a spike file and ring a bell for you. A paste-up boy in the bull pen here gets more respect. And the city . . . wow, it's filthy, crime-ridden, dangerous, polluted, no restaurants, no shows, the rents are through the roof, and when it isn't raining, it's snowing. The worst ads in the country, the worst town in the country. It's the bottom of the barrel, man. Zilch, *nada,* nothing."

The phone rang and Bunny picked it up.

"Bunny? Sam. Hey, I goofed on that job. It's not K and E, it's Burnett in Chicago."

Bunny thanked the man, hung up and faced his client, a thoughtful look on his face. He leaned back in his chair and said tolerantly, "On the other hand, there's a lot to be said for Chicago, too."

Bunny showed the ad man out, told him he'd be in touch, then turned to the young woman who was sitting fidgeting on a chair. "Good morning. Are you registered with us?"

The girl shook her head.

"Well, I'll tell you what," Bunny said. "I have to slip out for a few minutes, so why don't you just go ahead and fill out a form and I'll be back with you in no time."

The girl looked doubtful. "I don't know if I want to wait. I really need a job, and maybe some other place . . ."

Bunny was smiling and pointing at something framed on the wall. It was a blow-up of a small-space newspaper ad. It said, "We'll get you the job you want, at the salary you want, in the business you want. We guarantee it. Gemstone Jobs." Then, underneath that, the slogan: "We're batting one thousand."

"Our ad means what it says," Bunny told her. "What kind of job are you looking for?"

"Airline secretary. Shorthand typist, really."

"You're kidding," Bunny said. "I got one, just came in. It's perfect for you." He was moving past her. "I'll tell you all about it in just fifteen minutes, okay? Just fifteen minutes." Then he was out of the door and running down the stairs. He came out onto Forty-second, hurried down the block and turned into an entrance several doors away. The small storefront window was full of travel posters and model ships and airplanes, and some multicolored streamers radiated down from a top corner. The sign on the window said, "Haverstraw Travel."

Bunny crossed the floor and went busily in behind the counter to a desk. It was a tiny office and there was only one man in it. Bunny greeted him. "Good morning, Mr. Haverstraw."

Mr. Haverstraw, thin, fiftyish and much put upon by the world, looked up from the ticket he was writing, glanced tiredly at his watch and said, "Mr. Calder, are you superstitious about arriving on time, or what?"

Bunny moved things round on his desk. "Sorry I'm late, but there was this sweet little old lady who spilled her shopping bag coming out of the Bohack, and somebody booted her Wonderbread. Naturally, I ran in to get her another loaf and I've never seen such a check-out line in all my life."

His boss went on looking at him and Bunny said, "They were having a dented can sale."

The other man nodded and blinked at that and said thoughtfully, "Do you make these things up the night before or are they all off the top of your head?"

Bunny was saved from having to turn that question aside by the sound of the front door opening.

"A customer," Mr. Haverstraw said. "Go ahead, tell her one of your stories. See if you can sell her a world cruise."

Bunny gave him a painful grin. He crossed to the counter and started to say, "May I help you," when he got a good look at the customer. He lowered his voice and spoke a little slower. "May I help you?"

The girl was terrific, and she had a smile and a voice to match. She said, "I was staring at that poster in your window, the one with the beach. I have some time coming up next week and I'd like to get some sun and salt water, but I don't really have any place in mind."

Bunny jumped right in. "I do. I've got just the place. Absolutely ideal. Fabulous sunshine, uncrowded beaches, superb food, great night life, hotel rates half those of other fashionable resorts . . ."

The girl looked interested. "Where is it?"

"New Zealand."

9

She laughed. "Oh no, I'm on a budget. It'd have to be something a little closer to home."

"Closer to home?" Bunny snapped his fingers, dug under the counter and came up with a brochure which he flipped open to the center spread and held up for her to see. "Now tell me, have you ever seen a beach like it? Ever seen water that clear? And the food at this place is fantastic. Off-season hotel rates, too."

"It's beautiful," the girl said. "Where is it?"

"The Great Barrier Reef."

She shook her head. "Still too far. I thought maybe someplace in the Caribbean."

"Great idea," Bunny said. He delved underneath the counter again and came up with another brochure. He showed her a picture of a palm-fringed island. "Is that what you have in mind?"

"Beautiful. Where's this one?"

"Hawaii."

"Hawaii's in the Pacific."

Bunny regarded his hands. "Technically, yes. But it's got everything you want—great sunshine, fabulous food . . ."

The girl was starting to pick up her pocketbook. "Thanks all the same, but . . ."

Bunny had another brochure on the counter before she got any further. It was the one he always saved for when he worked back from New Zealand. "Saint Martin," he said, "just a short hop from Miami. Half French, half Dutch. Great food. Bouillabaisse on one side, rijstafel on the other. It's exotic, off the beaten track but close to home. You'll love it."

The girl put her pocketbook down again. "Now, that's more like what I had in mind."

Bunny piled it on. "Believe me, it's a piece of heaven. A fabulous place. There's only one spot I know that you'd like any better."

"Where's that?"

Bunny whipped out another brochure. "The Fiji Islands. Look at that lagoon. Have you ever seen water . . ."

"Tell me more about Saint Martin," the girl said. She reached for the brochure that Bunny had dropped on the counter. She said it politely but firmly, and Bunny saw that he'd better settle for the Caribbean. He gave her a few facts and figures, then did a little exploring. He noticed the lack of any ring on her finger, not that that meant much these days. He said casually, "Will you be traveling with your husband?"

10

"I'm not married."

"Your roommate, then?"

The girl was engrossed in the brochure. "I live alone. I'll be going by myself."

"Splendid," Bunny said. He meant it, too; he rarely got a piece of luck like this first thing Monday morning. When she looked up at him, puzzled by his reaction, he smiled and reassured her. "I mean, a pretty girl like you, you'll have a great time down there."

"Oh." She smiled back and folded the brochure. "Well, look, I'm going to think about this. Can I call you later on?"

"Sure thing." Bunny produced a card and handed it over. "My name's Calder. You just call me anytime, and if I've stepped out for a moment just leave your number and I'll get right back to you."

She thanked him for his help and said good-bye, and he watched her as she walked out of the door. She looked even better moving than she did standing still. He wondered where she lived and what her apartment looked like. Again he marveled at such luck coming along so soon in the working week. Which reminded him that he was still working and had a girl waiting for him at the job agency. He went over to his boss, but Mr. Haverstraw beat him to the punch. "Well," he said, "what did you finally sell her, a bus tour of Chinatown?"

"The West Indies. She hasn't said yes yet but I think it's a sale." Bunny paused, then said carefully, "Oh, er, Mr. Haverstraw . . ."

Again his boss pre-empted him. "No need to say it; you didn't get time to have breakfast this morning and could you just pop out and grab a fast bite."

"I'll only be five minutes, sir."

Mr. Haverstraw sighed. "Calder, I see my dentist more regularly than I see you." He waved a tired hand, defeated. "Go. Go."

"Thank you, Mr. Haverstraw. I'll be right back."

Bunny walked out of the door then broke into a trot, ran up the street, turned into the doorway and took the stairs two at a time. Sometimes keeping two jobs going could be a mite harrowing. Still, he reminded himself, you had to hustle if you wanted to get ahead in this world.

He burst in through the frosted glass door. "Sorry to keep you waiting. Something important came up."

The girl pouted. "I was just about to leave."

"And walk out on the job of a lifetime?" He took the card from

11

her and read off some details. "Let's see now, Diane Kresge, currently with Eastern."

"I'm supposed to be there now."

Bunny read on. "Shorthand typist and you'd like to switch jobs but stay in the business." He looked up at her. "For the travel deductions, huh?"

The girl confirmed it.

"Miss Kresge, I'm going to go into my office and work a little magic, all right?"

The girl looked at her watch, worried. "Maybe I'll stay with Eastern."

Bunny was challenged. "Miss Kresge, no other personnel agency in town operates the way we do. We're the only ones who'll guarantee you the job you want. You came to me for an airline job, and I'm going to see that you get one. Now you just give me three more minutes." He slipped into the inner office and closed the door, sat down at the desk and opened a filing cabinet. He took out a brown manila envelope and the list inside it—several pieces of paper stapled together. At the top of the list was the letterhead of the Appleton Employment Agency. Bunny had lifted it from a previous job. When Old Ma Appleton had fired him for double feeing (never proved), he'd photostated their placement records and brought them with him. He turned a page to the airlines section and ran his finger down the names and dates. He stopped at one and read it out. "Janet Walker, TWA. Placed three months ago. She'll do fine." He dialed and asked to speak to her.

"Hello, Miss Walker? Good morning, my name's Brubaker, at the Appleton Agency. I'm new here . . . that's right. Look, something's come up that I wanted you to think about. There's a great job going for a shorthand typist at Lufthansa, but they only want to hire somebody from that secretarial school you went to. What's the name of it again . . . ? The Brogan School, of course. Well, this guy at Lufthansa swears that the Brogan girls are the best typists he's ever had and he won't take anything but. Now, I know you've only been in your present job a short while, but the thing of it is Lufthansa's willing to pay an extra fifteen a week for a Brogan girl, and, well, we thought we'd give you first refusal. What do you think?"

The voice on the phone was hesitant. "Gee, I don't know. I certainly could use the extra money."

"You crazy about your job over there?"

"It's okay."

12

"Well, I know that Lufthansa's an awfully nice place to work. And this guy's supposed to be a real sweetie. I took the liberty of mentioning you to him, and he wants to hire you."

"You mean without even seeing me? No interview or anything?"

"Nope. The fact that you're a Brogan girl is good enough for him. If you want it, the job's yours."

"Well," the girl said, "I sure could use the money . . ."

"I think you'd really be happy there, Miss Walker. Incidentally, what's your boss's name?"

"Mr. Gabor."

"Miss Walker, far be it from me to push you into anything, but why don't you walk in and tell Mr. Gabor you're quitting."

"No, I'd have to think it over before I'd do that. I'm on the bowling team over here and—"

Bunny broke in on her. "I quite understand. You give it a think and I'll get back to you in a couple of days. Okay?" They said goodbye and Bunny replaced the phone and frowned at it. A couple of days was too long to wait for Miss Walker to make up her mind; he'd have to help the decision along a bit. He picked up the phone and dialed TWA again. "Mr. Gabor, please."

A man's voice came on the line. "Gabor here."

Bunny went to a heavy German accent. "Herr Gabor? Kleinmuller here, Lufthansa. You haf on your staff a Miss Valker, ya?"

"Miss Walker? Yes, she's with us."

"Is Miss Valker a goot verker?"

"Is she a what?"

"No funny business mit der boys at der vater cooler?"

"What is this in reference to, please?"

"Routine check. Auf Wiedersehen, Mr. Gabor." Bunny replaced the phone, sat back and constructed the scene cross town. He said, trying to get the timing right, "He's looking at the phone in his hand, he's putting it down, he's thinking about it. Now he's sending for Miss Walker . . . here she comes. Miss Walker, I just had a call from Lufthansa checking on you. Are you thinking of leaving us?" Bunny answered the question in a lighter voice. "As a matter of fact, Mr. Gabor, I am. I'm sorry, but it pays more." His voice lowered again. "In that case, Miss Walker, seeing you're going to a competitor, I suggest that we waive the usual notice and that you leave today." Again the lighter voice. "Oh, I see." And the drop. "We'll miss you, Miss Walker." Bunny picked up the phone and dialed again and asked for Mr. Gabor again.

13

"Mr. Gabor, my name's Calder at Gemstone Jobs. Look, I have a very good shorthand typist here with airline experience who I'm trying to place, and I'm calling round the airlines on the off chance that there might be a vacancy coming up soon. . . . Really? Why, that's wonderful. . . . Yes, very good girl . . ." He reached for the card in front of him. "Name's Diane Kresge. Used to be with Eastern. . . . Sure she can start today. I'll send her right over. . . . Okay, fine. Oh, and you might tell your accounts department that I'll bill them at the end of the month. . . . Fine. Nice talking to you, Mr. Gabor." Bunny hung up, scribbled on a piece of paper, leapt out of his chair and went into the outer office. "Miss Kresge," he said, "how does TWA starting today grab you?"

"You mean it?" The girl was amazed. "Just like that?"

Bunny jabbed a finger at the ad on the wall. "We're still batting a thousand, Miss Kresge." He handed her the piece of paper. "Here's the man you have to see and the address. He's expecting you." He walked her to the door. "Oh, incidentally, don't worry about paying my bill right away if it's a struggle."

Miss Kresge's smile lost some of its sparkle. "I thought the employer paid. I thought these were fee-paid jobs."

"Normally they are," Bunny answered, removing a speck of dust from his lapel, "but not TWA. It's a policy of theirs. Matter of fact, they're a little touchy about the whole subject so I wouldn't bring it up if I were you. Now off you go and knock 'em dead."

He smiled her out of the door and off his hands, then marched back to the inside office and phoned TWA for the fourth time. When he was put through he said, "Miss Walker? Brubaker at the Appleton Agency. Listen, you haven't resigned yet, have you . . . ? Oh no! Miss Walker, I'm afraid that job at Lufthansa fell through. . . . I know how you feel. . . . I know you can't ask for your job back, but what I'm trying to say is you don't have to. I know for a fact that Gemstone has a good one"—he picked up Diane Kresge's card—"at Eastern, I believe. . . . That's right. So why don't you call them? Gemstone Jobs on Forty-second. I think the guy's name is Calder. Call him in half an hour. . . . Absolutely. You won't miss a day's pay, Miss Walker. Sorry about the mix-up. Bye, now."

Bunny hung up and performed a mental heel click. He couldn't remember a better Monday: he'd moved two girls around, which meant four fees; there'd be another one and a half if Angie, the boy art director, got that job in Chi, and a whole wad of dough if that luscious chick decided to take a vacation. He checked the time, bolted into the outer office and almost knocked down the girl who was coming in. "Stick around," he said. "I'll be right back."

She started to say something but Bunny beat her to it. He pointed to the wall. "Fill out a form. We're batting a thousand," he said, and vanished through the door. He pounded down the stairs and back to the travel agency.

His boss was waiting for him, phone in hand. "Why, Calder," he said. "How nice of you to come back and see the old gang."

"Sorry, Mr. Haverstraw. I ran into an old college chum."

Mr. Haverstraw said with a touch of triumph, "You told me you never went to college."

"I didn't," Bunny said smoothly, "but my friend did."

Mr. Haverstraw, his eyes closed, thrust the phone out. "Here. Somebody calling for you."

Bunny said hello into the phone. It was the luscious chick.

"Mr. Calder? I was just talking to you a little while ago about Saint Martin."

"Oh sure. Hello, there."

"I made up my mind on my way to the office. I'm going to do it. Do you think you could go ahead and book me into a hotel, etcetera?"

"I'd be happy to. When do you want to go?"

Bunny took some particulars, the last of which was her name and address.

"Brown," the girl said. "Ella Brown. Apartment four, three fifteen West Sixty-eighth."

"No kidding. I live just round the corner. Hey, I'll tell you what, I'll have your tickets and vouchers for you tomorrow afternoon. Why don't I drop them off myself?"

"No need to go to all that trouble. Just mail them."

Bunny said, "It's surer this way. Sometimes the rain or the snow stays those couriers. What time do you usually get home?"

"About five forty-five. Six."

"Then why don't I meet you outside your apartment house tomorrow night about that time? Would that be inconvenient?"

"That'd be fine. But I could drop by one lunch hour . . ."

"Oh no. We run a personal service, Miss Brown. It's the only way we can compete with the big guys. I'll see you tomorrow evening."

They swapped a few more words, then hung up. Bunny set to work immediately; this was one booking he wanted to nail down. For the next fifteen minutes he busied himself calling airlines and hotel reps

15

and writing up vouchers. He looked again at the address he'd just written off a record sheet. Three fifteen West Sixty-eighth was probably one of those old rambling brownstones, the kind that were broken up into big apartments years ago. He could get real good money for something like that if the ad pulled. Which reminded him: he'd forgotten which name he was using this week. He slid out a bottom drawer and took out a folded newspaper. It was a two-day-old copy of the Cleveland *Plain Dealer*. He took a fast look and made sure his boss was otherwise occupied, then turned to the classifieds. He ran his eyes down the Travel Section till he found his ad. Oh yes, Campbell, Hotel Americana. He put the newspaper away. That ad had proved a gold mine in the past. And now with this girl going to—girl! There was one waiting for him at the agency.

He jumped up and went over to his boss. "Sorry to trouble you, Mr. Haverstraw, but could I ask you a question?"

The other man looked up surprised. "Good heavens, Calder. You've been at your desk a full fifteen minutes. What happened, you pass out?"

"Mr. Haverstraw, you've got me all wrong. I'm not about to play hooky in our busiest time of the year."

Mr. Haverstraw looked a bit disconcerted. "You're not? You mean you actually plan to spend some time here today?"

"Of course I do. I sold that West Indies ticket for a start. I have to follow that up. And there's that honeymoon in Miami, and that guy I talked into going skiing in New Guinea. I've got a lot of work to do."

Mr. Haverstraw was visibly moved. "Why, I don't know what to say, I er," He coughed, embarrassed. "What was it you wanted to ask me?"

"Okay if I take my coffee break now?"

16

Chapter 2

While Bunny, with a fabulous variety of excuses, continued to shuttle back and forth between the employment and the travel agencies that afternoon, New York was very much occupied with enhancing its reputation as the busiest, richest, rudest, toughest and, in spite of some of these qualities, most visited city in the world. On that particular July Monday a grand total of 186,247 people entered the town that the Dutch had bought from the Indians for twenty-four dollars and change. Although now there was a growing body of New Yorkers who felt that the Dutch had been taken. But of all the visitors that day the ones who would have interested Bunny most—had he but known it then—were the four men who arrived at Kennedy on the Air France flight from Paris.

Because, later on, some friends of those four men had a very good try at killing him.

Not knowing about those four, Bunny wasn't expecting them.

But there was another group of people who did know about them and were most definitely expecting them.

Or somebody like them, anyway.

There was nothing out of the ordinary about their arrival; the DC-8 floated along its glide path, touched down with a small hop, ran on and swung smoothly into an exit ramp. It taxied up to the terminal, the stairs were run out and the passengers filed into busses that took them a hundred feet to the terminal doors. Nobody was taking any chances. Then a ground crew ushered them into the Immigration Room, a drab, functional room, an American flag and a picture of the President its sole decoration. A row of glass-fronted booths formed a barrier across the floor, uniformed men and women sitting behind them. There were booths for U.S. passports, booths for alien passports. A group from the Midwest that had been traveling together went through chatting, animated, glad to be home and speaking English. The people lined up at the alien section were silent, respectful. On their best behavior.

Thirty minutes later, the last passengers cleared, the three immigration men who'd been processing the foreign passports went into an office in the rear of the room. Inside, their chief sat with another man. He was dressed colorlessly in a gray suit and dark tie, an ordinary-looking man in his mid-forties, short and slight, totally unremarkable except for a habit of adjusting his old-fashioned half-rim glasses before he spoke. He did it now as he put a question to the three men. "Nothing?"

The three men shook their heads. "They didn't come to me," one of them added. The man looked at the floor for a moment then over at the chief. He said in a quiet voice, "I don't understand it."

The chief thought it was pretty clear. "Wrong flight, that's all."

The man looked back at the three immigration officers. "Was there anybody you took a second look at?"

"I had one guy that came close," said the first man.

"Me too."

The third man said, "I had two guys. Close but no cigar."

"You're sure? You're absolutely positive they couldn't've been the ones?"

"Not unless they had face jobs."

"Not even then. Those two I processed had similar features, sure. They looked like the guys in the photographs. But they weren't them."

Their questioner looked at the chief again. "I don't understand it," he said a second time. "We're expecting four men and we get four men. Only they're not the ones we're expecting."

"Coincidence," the chief replied. "You know how many people we get through here."

"But our info was that those men boarded that plane."

"Then the info was wrong. It wouldn't be the first time."

"It would for this particular source." The exchange broke down and was replaced by a thin silence.

18

The chief, slapping both hands down onto his thighs, broke it. "Then they parachuted out, and we know they didn't do that. That plane's been searched top to bottom by now. Even the freight's been checked. And we had two men in the ramp crew. Everybody who was on that plane came through those doors outside. Those guys didn't, so they weren't on it. You can't take off for New York and not get off in New York. They've got to be coming on another flight."

The man with the glasses took them off this time, breathed on the lenses and began to polish them with a Kleenex. He thought about what he'd just been told. The chief was a good man; a lot of experience, a lot of years on the job. His argument was based on sound logic and good common sense. He couldn't for the life of him see how he could possibly be wrong.

But he knew that he was.

And he knew that they were in deep trouble.

Chapter 3

That Monday, the 3:45 Carey bus from Kennedy—the one that had connected with the Air France flight—had been diverted from its usual route owing to an accident in the Midtown Tunnel and had to take the Queensboro Bridge into Manhattan. And in doing so it had passed within a block of Bloomingdale's and Ella Brown, another person who was due to become very, very aware of the friends of those four men. Ella worked at Bloomingdale's, and so was employed at a very special place; Bloomingdale's, if not numerically the most popular store in the city, has got to be the emotional favorite. Probably because it manages the difficult trick of combining the attributes of many of the other department stores. Like Macy's and Gimbels, it sells just about everything, but with a lot more ambience than those huge, drafty warehouses, good as they are. It has the chic of Bonwit's, the flair of Lord & Taylor, and the busy, captivating personality that Altman's tries for. Maybe the glassware at Jensen's is just as good, and the cookware at La Cuisieniere and the luggage at Mark Cross, but then you can't go down into the basement of any of those stores and buy Brie from Merlun, paté from Strasbourg and frozen pompadoms from Bombay.

But as good as each department is, the one that's probably the biggest draw, and contributes more to store traffic than any other, is Interior Decoration on the fifth floor. It's on the same floor as the furniture, naturally enough, but instead of being confined to just a small corner, it runs almost the complete length of three walls, advertising itself in a series of dazzlingly furnished model rooms, which provide a showcase for all that furniture. Next to an Early American living room might be a maharaja's shooting lodge in Bangalore, which is butted up against a pop star's bedroom, which adjoins a salon in an English castle. And so on. People come up there and stroll around to get ideas for their one-and-a-halfs in Queens, although the best idea you can get is how to get your hands on the twelve hundred dollars that that adorable sofa costs, and another seven hundred for the matching chair. But there's no charge for looking, which makes it one of the best free shows in New York.

Of course, not everybody comes for a freebee, and a lot of people have the money and taste to buy their furniture there. And when some of them went whole hog and had the store handle their decor as well, they found themselves talking to Ella Brown, who advised them about rugs and carpeting and wallpaper.

It was natural that she had a pretty fabulous apartment herself: not only did she have the eye and the flair and the knowledge to put it all together but she got a decorator's discount in the stores that sold only to the trade, which meant she could snap up a bargain when she saw one.

After three years of collecting, adding, changing, improving, she had one of the great apartments on the West Side; so good, in fact, that *House & Garden* was coming to photograph it for an upcoming issue. It was in an old brownstone—Bunny had been right—which had been kept in fine condition: the front doors still had their original leaded glass and the monumental stoop had been retained in all its sculptured glory.

The following day, Tuesday, just after six, Bunny was standing on the lower step watching Ella Brown walk toward him. She was still thirty feet away so he had time to take a really good look at her. She was wearing a plain-colored shift, no make-up, no jewelry, as if she reserved all the decoration for the apartments she designed. But then, Bunny thought, girls that looked like she did didn't need much embellishment. She had a kind of fifties figure—not the tall, angular look of the present day, but shorter and a lot curvier; the kind of figure that never goes out of fashion with men. Her hair was a deep brown, almost black, framing high cheek bones and a wide, full mouth, large dark eyes. Lovely.

"Hello there," she said. The smile did nice things to her face.

Bunny greeted her. "Hi, neighbor."

21

"I hope I didn't keep you waiting."

"Not at all. I just got here." He tapped the folder he held in his hand. "You're all set. Tickets, reservations, vouchers and a guide to the island."

"This is really very kind of you, Mr. Calder. Going to all this trouble."

"No trouble." Bunny waved a vague hand behind him. "Like I say, I'm just around the corner."

The girl moved by him. "Come on up and I'll give you a check. I wish I could offer you a drink but I have to go straight out again."

Bunny pooh-poohed the idea. "I wouldn't dream of imposing." They started up the steps together and Ella opened her pocketbook and fished out some keys. Bunny reached out a hand. "Allow me." He let them in the front door and they climbed a flight of stairs, Bunny telling her about the great seafood they had on the island. When they reached the apartment door Bunny bent to unlock it and opened it. Immediately his face clouded over. He sniffed. "Do I smell something burning?" He sniffed again.

"What . . . ?"

"Maybe the kitchen," he said quickly.

Ella rushed ahead of him into the apartment. She was back a minute later. "The stove isn't on and I don't smell anything . . ."

Bunny wrinkled his nose and checked again. "You know, neither do I now. It's gone. I'm sorry, must have been all the talk about food."

"Forget it," she said. "I'd rather have a false alarm than a real one. Come in and I'll get you that check."

Bunny stepped inside, handed her the keys, then stopped dead when he saw the apartment he'd just entered. He took it all in slowly. "I have never in my life. . . . It looks like a shot from *House and Garden*."

Ella laughed. "As a matter of fact they're coming in a few weeks' time. When I get back from Saint Martin."

"I don't wonder," Bunny said. He moved farther into the room. "It's the Taj Mahal."

The physical proportions of the room were striking enough—huge; long and wide, with twelve-foot ceilings and sash windows recessed into an alcove at one end. But the way it had been furnished and decorated was staggering. It was a copybook example of the eclectic look —modern and period blending in perfect harmony. Bentwood, Bauhaus, Louis, there wasn't a single piece that wasn't a classic of the

22

furniture-maker's art. The wallpaper, the floor coverings, the drapes, the pictures, the wild, unexpected ornaments, the place was alive with ideas; cluttered but uncluttered, it was a miracle of interior design.

Bunny couldn't get over it. "Did you do all this?"

Ella told him that she was in the business and that it was a lot easier for her.

"Yes, but still . . ." Bunny pointed around him. "And there's a bedroom off?"

"Uh huh. And a bathroom off that. The kitchen's through there."

"Fantastic," Bunny said.

Ella sat down at a small mahogany desk, beautifully traced and inlaid with different kinds of wood. She scribbled a check and handed it to him. "That's correct, isn't it?"

Bunny barely looked at it. "Right on the button." He took another glance round then came back to the girl in front of him. "Well, I won't keep you any longer."

They moved toward the door. She said, "I feel awful, turning you out without a drink."

"Never mind. Next trip."

They stopped at the door and regarded each other. There was a pause. They were getting on beautifully. Bunny shook himself. What was he thinking of, this was one chick he couldn't afford to get involved with. He put a hand on the gold-embossed doorknob and gave her the smile. "So," he said. "Have a great vacation. And don't forget your suntan oil."

It was a lame exit line but it got him out of there. He waited till he was on the street and halfway down the block before he took a look at the wax impression he'd made of her keys.

It was as clear as crystal.

Chapter 4

The racket that Bunny worked with other people's apartments was extremely simple. Being in the travel business, half the day anyway, he knew exactly when people were going to be away and when they were coming back, seeing as how he booked their trips himself. So it was an easy matter to rent their apartments while they were gone. His modus operandi was very much the same as the one he'd followed with Ella: he'd book the client a trip, and, after making sure the client lived alone, would offer to deliver the tickets personally and find an excuse to get the client's keys in his hand for thirty seconds. Then he'd have duplicates cut by a locksmith he knew who charged him twenty dollars and no questions asked. Then he'd find somebody who wanted to rent an apartment for a couple of weeks, or however long his client would be away. He'd found that the best and easiest way of doing this was to run an ad in the Cleveland paper, the area being a rich one for potential visitors to New York. He'd use a return name and address which he constantly changed so that he could never be traced afterward. When somebody in Cleveland answered his ad he'd contact them and set things up. The folks from Ohio never knew about the con, of course; they thought they were getting a genuine summer vacation rental. When the owner returned, and was outraged to find that somebody had been sleeping in his bed, there was nothing he could do about it. All that the super or the doorman could tell him was that the people had had a key. Who knew their names or where they were from? And Bunny was safe because nobody ever connected that nice friendly travel agent with the deal.

It was a sweet little racket and it worked well because he never invited trouble. He was always careful in his choice of people to whom he rented. If any kids with electric guitars and smokers' cough turned up from Cleveland, or a couple of shop girl amateurs who were planning to turn pro for a few weeks, they were out. But for the main part the applicants were solid, upright midwestern citizens who were coming to the Big Apple to see the shows, eat a little French food and get away from the kids for a while.

And that's exactly the impression he got of Mrs. Cronkite when he called her from the lobby of the Hotel Americana the next day. He'd gone there on his lunch hour and told the desk clerk that his name was Campbell and asked if there was any mail for him. Bunny had found that a hotel would always receive mail for you as long as you had a reservation. Bunny never used the reservation but he always made one. The clerk had handed him three letters. The first two people he'd called couldn't make the dates. The third one, Mrs. Cronkite, could. He described the apartment to her and the woman said it sounded marvelous. They agreed on a price and Bunny arranged to meet her and her husband in a week's time when they came to New York.

The call completed, Bunny was tempted to call Ella at Bloomingdale's and ask her out to dinner, but he resisted it. With the racket he was working it was best to have as little as possible to do with the apartment owner; it was best to keep a low profile. Still, when he thought about Ella's profile, specially her allover profile, he kind of regretted his policy. So he told himself to forget it; he didn't want to screw things up now that he was doing so well. With that apartment all set up and ready to go he was free to concentrate on the job agency. Free, that is, as long as he could keep Mr. Haverstraw off his back, which meant coming up with some more excuses.

As he left the hotel and turned south he wondered idly if his boss would buy his mother's malaria again.

Bunny met the Cronkites in the lobby of the Americana the day Ella Brown left for the Caribbean. Jack Cronkite was a big-boned, square-jawed man, broad shouldered; a tummy on him. He looked to Bunny like a college football player who'd parlayed a moderate amount of success on the gridiron into a profitable little real estate

25

business in a nice middle-class suburb of Cleveland, or a small town nearby.

As it turned out, they were from Hiram, Ohio. His wife, dressed neatly and atrociously in a floral-pattern dress, had a perpetually smiling face and punctuated the start of every sentence with a sharply drawn breath and a half-raised hand. Bunny could picture her back home, in an immaculate, stiffly starched apron which she'd sewn herself, making pickles for the church bazaar.

Bunny gave them a big hello and helped them with their bags out of the lobby and into a cab. "You come to New York often?" he asked in the way of openers.

"First time," Mr. Cronkite said. He had a deep, muscular voice. "Been meaning to for years, but somehow we always ended up at the lake."

Mrs. Cronkite sucked in a breath and raised a hand up and down. "Actually," she said, "we're with three other couples. But they're staying in a hotel and paying the earth."

"You made a wise choice doing it this way," Bunny reassured her. "It's far more convenient having your own place. No lining up for door keys, no crowded elevators, no waiting on room service. Wait till you see it, Mrs. Cronkite. It's won awards all over the country."

"I'm so excited," she flapped. "It sounds marvelous." She pronounced it "morvelous."

"It's your apartment, is it?" Mr. Cronkite wanted to know.

"No, I'm renting it for a friend. Her name's Brown. Oh, and incidentally, the super doesn't know anything about this so if you run into him or anybody just tell them you're friends of Miss Brown. Reason we have to do it this way is because there's no sublet clause in the lease. You understand."

The Cronkites understood.

The cab whisked them through the park and dropped them outside the brownstone. Bunny let them in the front door and led the way up the stairs. When he opened the apartment door and stood aside for them to enter, Mrs. Cronkite couldn't believe it. With a sharp intake of breath, and a hand that rose and fell as if she were under oath, she said, "I don't believe it. I just don't believe it. It's simply morvelous. Look at it, Jack, isn't it morvelous?"

"Very nice," her husband allowed in his tight, flat voice. "A little fancy but very nice." He looked suspiciously at the Japanese silk canopy that hung from the wall over the matched-print sofa.

"I knew you'd love it," Bunny said as he led them over the pale

26

lemon broadloom. "The bedroom's through there, bathroom off. Kitchen through there. The place has got everything and it's all ready to go."

Mr. Cronkite had his wallet out and was counting money. He handed it to Bunny, who handed him back a set of keys. "Just slip them into the mailbox when you leave," Bunny told him. "And you will be out by the twenty-fourth, won't you? That's when Miss Brown gets back, and you wouldn't want to be on top of each other."

"Have to be," Cronkite said. "We're holding return tickets for the day before." He took another look at the silk canopy as if he wished the return tickets were for two hours' time.

"Then I'll leave you with it." Bunny held out a hand and Cronkite killed it with one squeeze. "I know you'll look after it."

"Heavens," Mrs. Cronkite said with a quick hand raise, "of course we will. Don't give it another thought."

And Bunny didn't.

But he was going to.

Chapter 5

The immigration man had lost a lot of sleep thinking about those four men who hadn't been the four men he was after, and by the time he'd come up with a wild idea and checked with the airline and found that the idea wasn't so wild, it was too late to do him any good. The basic idea was so simple he kicked himself for not thinking of it sooner. After all, there were only so many ways you could get into the United States. Those men had fooled him by choosing the one that had never occurred to him.

But they'd probably held reservations on a dozen previous flights, canceling each one as it became necessary. Not because of subterfuge but because of the weather. They needed to fly on a day when the weather report included extremely high westerly winds, winds that often made it necessary for eastbound planes, bucking them for hours, to make a fuel stop at Gander, which, as the airline had confirmed, that particular flight had done. What happened at Gander he could only surmise, but he still had a pretty good idea. The four men who, no doubt, had received a transatlantic phone call the night before would have stationed themselves on the airport's observation deck. One of them with binoculars. When the flight had landed, the passengers had been taken into the transit lounge to wait out the refueling. Nobody would have noticed that four of those passengers were of the same age and nationality as the four men who'd watched them arrive. Or that they were dressed in dark, almost identical, suits.

Nor would anyone have noticed, or cared, that those four passengers each had his ticket in his top jacket pocket, the seat number showing. Forty-five minutes later, the refueling completed, all the passengers had been ushered out of the transit lounge and guided toward the waiting ramp busses. It would only have been a short walk, perhaps no more than sixty feet. It's not hard to get down onto an airport ramp if you're really trying. Nor to get by one ground stewardess busy supervising an entire plane load. The passengers would have been counted, but only after they were back on board and in their seats. The count would have tallied—it was a heavy flight; there were 164 people.

But only 160 of them had been on board before.

From there on it would have been plain sailing. While Gander is one of the world's largest airports, it's nowhere near one of the busiest. It doesn't even rank in the first ten in Canada. So when a flight has come and gone, things can relax for a while.

The men would have slipped out of the washroom where they'd hidden and out through a service area. They'd have walked to the parking lot and found a car whose owner had made the mistake of leaving the ticket inside, broken into it, jumped it and driven out of the airport. The first left would land them on the Trans Canada Highway. They'd followed it through the green lakes and pines of Newfoundland to Port aux Basques and the overnight ferry to Nova Scotia. Then down the long, curving roads of New Brunswick to Quebec, and into an early-morning Montreal, with maybe a few hours' sleep in a motel. Then Ontario and down the Four Oh One to Toronto. They'd probably bought a few things in Toronto—football sweaters and jeans—something American. And got themselves another car. Then down the Q.E. Highway to Niagara Falls and the Peace Bridge. There, lined up to go across, Ontario tags on the car—the football sweaters, the hockey club decal on the windshield—what were they? Four young Greeks or Italians, maybe; Toronto had a big Greek and Italian population. Then the border. You didn't have to show your passport on the Canadian border, not if you were Canadian. The question at the bridge, "Where were you born, please?" would have been answered by a single rehearsed word: Toronto. Pronounced, "Ta-*rown*-oh." And then the fast wave through.

Sure, that's how those men had done it. They'd made it into America because everybody who comes from Europe comes by plane or by boat.

But nobody comes from Europe by car.

When the immigration man went to Washington and told his boss what he thought had happened, his boss agreed with him. "It's your baby," he said. "The standard approach didn't work. What are you going to try now?"

The other man pushed at his glasses, resettled them on his nose. "Something smarter," he said.

Chapter **6**

All in all, the Cronkites had had a good time in New York, if a little mixed. They'd seen three musicals and two hit plays, both of which Mr. Cronkite had slept through, visited the Statue of Liberty, been to the top of the Empire State, toured the U.N.—even though Mr. Cronkite didn't hold with the U.N.—tapped their toes in time with the band at Radio City, which, as Mr. Cronkite had pronounced, was "more like it," eaten in four French restaurants—Mr. Cronkite ordering steak each time—and bought a large Oriental-style rug for the living room at a store on Fifth Avenue that had been holding a going-out-of-business sale for the last seven years. Mrs. Cronkite thought that New York was just like Hiram, only bigger, although she'd been shocked at the brashness of the hookers in the theater district, while Mr. Cronkite had gritted his teeth at the sight of all those "damned pansies" in Times Square and claimed that the city should do something about them. They'd also toured Grant's Tomb, the World Trade Center and the Bowery, Street of Forgotten Men.

The friends they'd come to New York with, who were all staying at the Taft, had had a mixed time as well. The men all agreed that the Metropolitan and the Museum of Modern Art had been frankly disappointing as had P. J. Clarke's—hell, it was just a bar. But they gave the nod to the Baskin-Robbins ice cream, the clams at the King of the Sea and the haircuts. Specially the haircuts; they were awfully expensive but good. Mr. Cronkite had had three so far.

As far as the girls were concerned the highlight of the trip was when they'd gone to see that handsome Fred Bottleberry in person at ABC-TV. The boys had gone over to Forty-second street and paid five dollars each to see a movie called *Lash of Velvet* starring a young lady named Hillary Pillory. They all solemnly agreed that it was jam-packed with redeeming social values.

On their last day in town the couples decided to splurge. They had an early lunch at the Oyster Bar at Grand Central—Bloody Marys all round then the oyster stew, which all the ladies said was delicious but pushed away after two mouthfuls—then gone up to see the Indians play the Yankees. The men had all drunk numerous beers and, because it was a hot day and because Cleveland was beating the pants off the locals, the ladies had a couple, too. After the game they'd returned to the Taft and gone into the bar to celebrate the victory then separated after agreeing to meet for pre-dinner cocktails at the Top of the Six's. From there they went on to Mama Leone's for a long, loud dinner punctuated with many chianti bottles and free anisettes which were pressed onto them with the espresso. They'd got a cab down to the Village to the Red Onion for some good, old-time Dixieland and some good, old-time bourbon. After a while they were doing more drinking than listening. When the Cronkites invited everybody back to their rented apartment for a final drink, the other men insisted on buying bottles of Jack Daniel's to bring along.

When they arrived at Ella's apartment they all had a little trouble climbing the stairs. By the time they'd finished the whiskey they would have had no trouble falling down them. The wives had collected in a drunken little group in one corner, smiling stupidly at each other, their mouths as crooked as their eyes. They were very happy. By contrast, their husbands had gone past the happy stage and were well and truly into the doldrums and fast approaching the belligerent phase.

The four men—Jack Cronkite, Wally Sims, George McCormick and Charlie Walworth—had split into two factions. Jack and Charlie had gone to Ohio State, while Wally and George had graduated from the University of Michigan. And while they were all pretty good friends, there was always that little rift between them; the old rivalry that came out now and then, particularly when they'd been drinking. It was further exacerbated by the fact that all four of them had played on their college football teams and faced each other on the field. That year, Michigan had pipped Ohio State by three points.

Jack Cronkite groped for the whiskey bottle and tried to top off his drink. The bottle was empty. Cronkite shook it to make sure, then tried the other empty bottles. The others watched the bad news sourly. They all looked at each other, one faction suspecting the other of having grabbed the last drink. The rift was becoming a vast crevasse.

It was Cronkite who started it. He looked blearily at Wally Sims and said, "We were always better'n you guys. Would've waxed your ass hadn't fumbled."

"Bushwah!" Wally said to a point two inches to the left of Cronkite's right ear.

"Beaten by s'perior team, is all."

George McCormick seconded the opinion. "Goddamn right." It wasn't more than a mumble; George was having trouble getting his mouth to move.

Charlie Walworth snorted. "S'perior? Buncha plumbers." He brought his glass up to his mouth, missed it and tipped the last of his drink over his chin. Charlie was in a bad way.

George got part of his mouth working this time so that his mumble was more distinct. "Beatcha then," he said, lifting a heavy finger and bludgeoning the air in front of him, "beatcha now."

Jack Cronkite leaned forward in his chair and fell off it. "You couldn't make five yards on us."

Wally Sims leaned forward too, eyes struggling for focus. "Wanna bet? Take you on ri' now."

With varying degrees of success, the four men got to their feet. They stood swaying in a circle and clumsily began to struggle out of their jackets.

"Show *you*," Wally said to a lampstand beside Charlie Walworth's head.

"Ball. Need a ball," Cronkite said, looking round as if he expected to find one in the middle of the Venetian glass collection arrayed on a sideboard. He moved unsteadily down the room and into the dining area where there was a table outside the entrance to the kitchen. There was a large bowl of fruit on it. Mrs. Cronkite had gone to the market early that day to replace the coffee and cornflakes they'd used during their stay, and by way of a thank-you to the apartment owner had bought a sack full of fruit and some luscious melons. Cronkite picked up one of the melons and weaved his way back to the group again.

"Awright," he began. "Our goal line the bay windows. Your goal line the hall closet. Walls are outa bounds. Ten count before a rush. 'Greed?"

" 'Greed," the other three chorused.

George had a question. "Ev'body el'gible?" It was a tough phrase to say with a mouth that wouldn't move.

They all agreed that everybody was. Then they moved shakily and unsteadily to the center of the room where they stood swaying like radio aerials in a high wind.

Cronkite fumbled a coin from his pocket. "You guys call."

"Tails," George said.

Cronkite flipped the coin high into the air and four pairs of unfocused eyes rolled up to follow its flight. Ten seconds went by and the eyes were still looking upward.

Charlie Walworth said, "You see it?"

"He didn't toss it," George said.

"The hell I didn't," Cronkite answered. "It's up there somewhere."

Wally Sims looked down. "Hey," he mumbled. He reached out both arms, hooked them round George and Charlie's shoulders and with intense drunken concentration started to raise his knee, his foot rigidly extended. The other three men peered at the coin that glittered on his shoe top.

"Heads," Cronkite cried triumphantly. "Our ball."

He put the melon down on the yellow carpet and the men separated into two teams. George and Wally chose to defend the hall closet, moved in that direction and held a defensive huddle. George told his teammate to play back and to watch for the long bomb, but in George's frozen-mouthed mumble the last part came out as "oshor da bom bom." Wally agreed anyway. At the other end of the room Jack Cronkite and Charlie Walworth were huddling too. In the corner the wives had become dimly aware that something strange was happening; the men were whispering in two groups, and was that a melon lying on the carpet?

In the Ohio State huddle Cronkite was calling a play. "Off left tackle for starters. On two."

Charlie, staring dully down at his feet and breathing heavily through his mouth, cried, "Yah!" and tried to smack a fist into his hand in the traditional manner of the offensive team breaking from the huddle. He missed his hand, belted himself in the ribs and went down. His teammate immediately called a time-out. Michigan protested. "C'mon, we ain't on TV," Wally said. "S'matter with him, anyway?"

34

"Shaken up on the play," Cronkite explained.

When Charlie had recovered, Cronkite trotted unsteadily to the melon, crouched down over it and glared into the face of George McCormick, who was set opposite him. Charlie staggered up behind Cronkite and looked woozily over the defense. Wally, one eye closed and arms spread wide, was playing safety man way down the end of the room underneath the Japanese canopy. The four of them were all big men, roughly about the same size and weight, so they were pretty evenly matched. Cronkite began barking signals. "One, two." He hiked the melon into Charlie's waiting hands and drove his shoulder into George's body. Charlie, pounding after the block, made three yards before Wally came up fast and crookedly and nailed him at the start of the sofa. Everybody went down with a crash. Then they got up slowly. Underneath the melon carrier was an Indian coffee table crushed beyond recognition. George absently brushed it aside and said, "Second an' seven." The wives, by this time, had realized what was going on. When you're brought up in the Midwest you recognize a football game when you see one. They quickly separated into two factions as the men had done, all of them having attended the same colleges as their husbands, where they'd met and married.

Charlie's wife got to her feet as if she were lifting somebody on her shoulders. "Yeh, Buckeyes!"

George's wife made two attempts to rise, which was one less than Wally's wife had to make. "Go get 'em, team."

Mrs. Cronkite stayed seated. Something was bothering her. She peered at the scene through an alcoholic haze, waved a leaden hand, and said, "Careful the furn'ture."

Back in the huddle Cronkite called an end sweep, which was exactly what they got on the second play when they swept a Steuben punch bowl and twelve glasses off the end of a bookshelf, and on the third down when they upset an endtable.

"Fourth 'n four," Wally crowed.

"Goddamn it," Cronkite said to his teammate, "we'll have to punt."

He centered the melon and crouched over it. Wally went deep to receive, down near the hall closet. The two Michigan wives were jumping up and down on an Empire sofa. "Block that kick! Block that kick!"

At the count Cronkite snapped the melon back to Charlie, who had retreated to the window. It was a good snap and, surprisingly, Charlie caught the melon. He held it out in front of him, let it go, and swung a heavy size eleven up to meet it. The melon shot up into the air, shattered the crystal chandelier, and mashed itself all over the ceiling. George stood underneath it, watching it. Cronkite and Charlie joined him. Slowly a large piece of the melon began to unpeel. It curled bit by bit away from the ceiling and, when the force of gravity proved too strong, dropped off and fell. It landed in George's waiting arms, and the entire Ohio State team jumped onto him.

"No runback. No runback," Cronkite chortled.

George, slightly concussed, got up in stages and staggered back to consult with his partner.

"Bastards," Wally said. He was really gone. "They rung in an unnerinflated ball."

Cronkite went to the dining table, selected another melon, and brought it back.

Then the other team took over. Wally, who'd been a fair quarterback at college, whispered into what he suspected was George's ear. "Flair pattern, stop 'n go in the left flat."

George, who'd played on the line and was trying to get both eyes pointing in the same direction anyway, said, "Hell's the left flat?"

"Near that desk thing."

They broke up and groggily approached the melon, while Cronkite warned his partner to watch for the draw play. George counted and hiked the melon to Wally, who back-pedaled crazily as if he were being pursued by every linebacker in the NFL. George faked Charlie out of position, stepped off his right foot, and rushed into the clear on the other side of the room. With his hands up and his head turned looking back for the pass, he ran straight into an exquisite art deco sideboard and broke two doors and three of its legs off.

But Wally had already released the melon. He still had a good arm and, because he didn't want to risk an interception, really stung the melon, which zipped through the space where George's hands should have been, smashed two signed lithographs and splattered all over the embossed wallpaper.

"Incomplete," Cronkite shouted. "Second 'n ten."

Charlie's wife was greatly encouraged. She scrambled up excitedly on a Siamese balsa chest and waved her arms through the air. "Drive 'em back, drive 'em back, waaaay back!" The Siamese chest splintered underneath her.

Opposite, on the silk cushions of the sofa, Wally and George's wives were jumping up and down in time to their rhythmic chant. "We wanna *touch*down! We wanna *touch*down!"

"Careful the furn'ture," Mrs. Cronkite warned her kneecap. Her head was lolling like a stalk. "Not our 'partment."

Her husband went to the table and chose the ripest melon he could find, a piece of strategy that almost backfired on him. Once again Wally went to the air, but this time, when George was taken out of the play by a lacquered Chinese screen, Cronkite was ready. He leaped for the pass, a high arcing lob, but the melon slipped through his hands and burst against the top of his head. He scooped some of it up and was gamely trying to run it back when he stepped on a piece. His feet went from underneath him and his wildly flailing hand smashed a thin support post which brought down the entire Japanese canopy. It fell like a tent over all four players. When they climbed out from underneath it it was discovered that Wally was also clutching a piece of melon. He claimed that Cronkite had lost the melon when he'd fallen and that he'd recovered his fumble. When Cronkite loudly disputed this and pointed to the piece he held, an argument followed. However, when both pieces of melon were measured and Cronkite's found to be the larger, he and Charlie took over at the sideboard. With a less ripe melon this time. Their first play resulted in three yards and a cloud of dust when Charlie demolished an incredibly old, incredibly fragile Javanese wood carving. Their next play, a run around right end, was good for four yards, two porcelain lamps, a Bentwood rocker, a nineteenth-century brass telescope, and a superb copy of a Hepplewhite escritoire that had cost five hundred dollars and three days of haggling on Third Avenue.

Fifteen minutes later, when the game was called by an irate neighbor from downstairs, the score was Michigan 15, Ohio State 12.

History had repeated itself.

Chapter 7

In his twenty-five years as a lawyer, Herb Smathers had seen a lot of angry people in his office, but nobody as mad as Ella Brown was that morning. She paced up and down in front of his desk, crossing the floor in quick, furious steps as if unable to make up her mind which direction to travel in. Her teeth were clenched shut and her eyes boiled with anger and she kept throwing her arms into the air. "You should see the place. I mean, you should just *see* it."

Smathers, a slim, graying man, sharp eyes moving in a serious face, stepped bravely into the opening. "What's it look like?"

"What's it look like?" Ella stopped and fixed him with a death ray from her eyes.

"It looks like King Kong walked in and stepped on a roller skate."

The lawyer raised his eyebrows. In his profession he was used to hyperbole but it still clashed with his respect for a factual account. "Ella, could you be a little more specific? Describe it to me."

Ella proceeded to, at two hundred and fifty words a minute. "The walls are coated with fruit cocktail, the drapes look like used bandages from the Civil War, and the carpet, once a faultless sea of gold, is now the color of a gas station ramp. And the furniture—my God! It's either leaning, lying, or completely smashed. Sixteen pieces and not a single one with a right angle. Vases smashed, pictures broken, the sofa ripped . . ." She stopped pacing and whirled around.

"*House and Garden* is supposed to be coming next week. In its present state the place wouldn't even make the *Police Gazette*."

Smathers fiddled with the silver water jug on his desk. "Ella," he said, "have some Holland water. It'll cool you down."

"I don't want to cool down. Three years it's taken me to get that apartment together. I ate spaghetti for six months to buy that Hepplewhite. The most beautiful, elegant desk I've ever seen. You should see it now—it looks like a hat rack."

Smathers swiveled his chair, came round his desk and took her hand. He spoke soothingly to her. "Come on now, Ella. Sit down."

"If I sit down, I may explode."

"You may explode anyway. Now, calm down and tell me about it. I have to have some good solid facts if I'm going to help you, and all I've got from you so far is a lot of wild descriptions."

Ella closed her eyes, took a deep breath and let it out slowly. "Okay," she said. "Okay." She allowed herself to be led back to the desk and lowered into a chair. Smathers returned to his own and watied a moment before he began to speak quietly and carefully. "Now, what happened? Were you turned over? Burglars?"

"No burglars," Ella said. "I would have welcomed burglars." She threw her hands in the air again. "I would have welcomed the Seven Samurai and their horses. Anything but what I got."

Smathers was used to playing the straight man; it was part of his job. "What did you get?"

Ella got a grip on herself. "According to Mr. Kastner downstairs, the night before I got back he heard the most godawful racket coming from my apartment. He went up there when it got too much." Ella stopped, ran a tongue round her lips, and said as evenly as she could, "Four men were playing football."

Smathers heard correctly but didn't understand it. "Football? But this is the baseball season."

That did it. Ella shot to her feet, back to maximum volume again. "I don't care if it's the hopscotch season. Those men ruined my apartment."

It took the lawyer another five minutes to get her calmed down and sitting still in the chair. Smathers said, "Got back from where? Where were you when all this happened?"

"The Caribbean." The last outburst seemed to have drained her. She spoke in a crushed, sadder but wiser voice. "I was down there on vacation. Somebody stayed in my apartment while I was away."

"You know that for sure?"

Ella nodded unhappily. "Mr. Kastner met them coming into the building a few days after I left. They told him they were friends of mine. Since they had a key he believed them."

With very little movement, Smathers flicked open a notebook and got a pen into his hand. "This Mr. Kastner, did he say what kind of people they were? Their names, where they were from?"

"Ordinary, middle-aged couple. They didn't tell him their name. They were from Ohio someplace."

The lawyer's pen moved swiftly over the pad. "Ohio. Well, that's something." Then he murmured under his breath as he wrote: "Four men . . . playing football . . ."

"And their wives."

Smathers' pen stopped dead. "Their wives were playing too?"

"Mr. Kastner says they were doing a snake dance on the sofa."

Smathers put his pen down and tapped his hands together slowly. "They were all drunk I assume . . . ?"

Ella gave a bitter laugh. "I would say so. Mr. Kastner manages the house, so he has a key to the apartment. When he went up there and let himself in he was run down by a man carrying a melon."

"A melon," Smathers repeated. He coughed and tapped the notebook. "This man, the one with the melon, did he say anything to Kastner?"

Ella nodded. "I believe his exact words were 'Oops, sorry, ref.'"

Smathers absorbed this piece of information thoughtfully, then picked up his pen again. "Okay, let's see what we have to go on. The fact that these people had a key means they didn't just chance upon an empty apartment. They knew you were going to be away. Or somebody told them, more likely. How many people knew you were planning a trip?"

"That's the crazy part, Herb; this was a spur of the moment thing. I hardly had time to tell anybody except my boss and Jerry, whom I work with, and one or two girl friends. Certainly nobody who'd do something like this to me."

"Did you cancel any door deliveries? Newspapers, groceries, that kind of thing?"

"No, I don't have any."

Smathers mulled it over. "That still leaves a lot of people who would've known you were going away. And when. The airline people, for example. Anybody who could get a look at an airline computer would know your departure and return dates. They could get your address from the phone directory."

Ella sighed. "That's probably how it happened."

Smathers pressed his teeth into his lower lip and canceled his previous suggestion. "But that still doesn't explain how they got hold of your keys. Did you have them out of your possession at all, leave them where anybody could get them?"

He got a sad, negative headshake for an answer.

"Did you book this trip yourself or through a travel agent?"

"Travel agent."

"Then that's another person who knew when you'd be gone."

It was clear that Ella thought the questioning was pointless; she'd been shafted and there was nothing she could do about it. The nameless couple from Ohio would be impossible to trace. All she could do was go home, have a good cry, salvage what she could, then start all over again. She was about to say as much to her lawyer when something he'd said clicked in her brain. Her next two words were barely audible. "Travel agent . . ."

"Pardon," Smathers said.

He didn't have any trouble hearing her the second time. A look of growing comprehension widened her eyes and she leaped up. "Travel agent! He came up to the apartment. Insisted on opening the door. He said he smelled something burning. I rushed into the kitchen, checked everything then came back. He had maybe thirty seconds. Would that be enough time?"

Smathers told her it would be plenty.

Ella closed her eyes and grimaced as if arrows were hitting her. "Ooooh, the rat," she said. "The rotten, miserable crumb! I wondered why he insisted on bringing those tickets himself." She planted both hands on the lawyer's desk and jutted her chin at him. "He's going to pay for this, Herb. He's going to pay in blood."

Smathers was wearing his impartial attorney's expression. "That may be a little difficult, Ella."

"Difficult? The man was responsible for ruining my apartment. How can it be difficult?"

"For a start, what proof do we have?"

"My apartment, the Super Bowl, remember?" She started pacing furiously again, her earlier despondency sunk without a trace. "Just wait till I get my hands on him. I'm going over there and tear down his undershirt back. I'm going to—"

"Hold on, now, Ella. We don't know that he did it and we can't prove that he did it, although he sounds like a likely suspect. It would appear that he took an impression of your keys, had them cut, passed them on to that couple, and pocketed the rent they paid him. But that's just a guess. Now, if we could trace those people in Ohio, which we can't, and they agreed to identify him, then we'd have a case. But as it is we don't have a legal leg to stand on."

Ella was only half listening, coming up to the boil again. "I'll get him. I'll pay him back in kind. I'll find out where he lives, rent a man with a cement mixer and pave his entire apartment."

Smathers reached for a phone and started to dial. He said, "If he's working a racket, he has to have some way of contacting the people he rents to. I'm just wondering—" He broke off and said into the phone, "Hello, Susie? Herb Smathers. . . . Fine, thank you. Look, does Joe still get those out-of-town newspapers? . . . Uh huh. Would you have one from Cleveland, a recent one? Thanks." He put a hand over the mouthpiece and spoke to Ella. "If those people were from Ohio, he's probably running an ad there. He'd pick a Cleveland paper to get the biggest readership. That's my guess anyway but I may—" He broke off a second time and took his hand from the phone. "Fine. Now turn to the Classifieds, the Travel Section. . . . Right. Now tell me if you see an ad that mentions anything about renting an apartment in New York, something like that." He spent the time it took to get an answer watching Ella grow more and more impatient. "No," he said into the phone. "No . . ." Then, "That could be the one. Could you read it to me?" His pen scribbled for a minute. "Perfect. Exactly what I was looking for, Susie. I owe you some flowers . . . sure. Say hello to your boss for me. Good-bye." Smathers hung up, smiling. "Well, I only wish all my guesses were that good."

"You find something?"

Smathers picked up the notebook and ran his eyes over what he'd written. "Do you remember that travel agent's name?"

"Caulfield. No, Calder! That's it, Calder."

"Listen to this: 'Coming to New York? Why pay high hotel rates? Rent an apartment while owner is on vacation. Write Campbell, Hotel Americana, New York City.'" Smathers looked up from the notebook. "I'm willing to bet you a lobster dinner that Mr. Campbell is your Mr. Calder."

Ella reached for the book, and Smathers chuckled as he handed it to her. "You know, in a funny way you have to admire this fellow."

"You have to *what* this fellow?"

"No, I mean it. The ad's so cheeky. Rent an apartment while

42

owner is on vacation. Notice he doesn't mention anything about the owner knowing about it. An honest advertiser, for a change."

That was too much for Ella. She tossed her head in a gesture of bewildered resentment. "Herb, come on, now. You just told me you admire him and now you're claiming he's honest. We're talking about the guy responsible for the rape and pillage of my apartment. A beast, a monster, a defiler of furniture. What's got into you?"

The lawyer swung his chair round a few degrees and regarded her thoughtfully. There was a different expression on his face, as if he were considering something unconnected with the present business. He said slowly, "Tell me about this man. Describe him."

"A red suit, long tail and horns."

"Please. Is he young, old, what?"

Ella was exasperated by the questions. "I don't know. Mid-thirties, I guess."

"Presentable looking?"

"Oh sure. All part of the con, you know. Nice build, good-looking. It's all there, all right, the rat."

"Nice manners?"

"Don't worry, very polite. The fink."

"Fast on his feet?"

Ella rolled her eyes upward. "Ho, ho, a forked tongue of silver."

"A good actor, would you say?"

"Olivier could take lessons. Herb, you can see the beast for yourself if you want to take a cab ride to Forty-second." She rummaged in her pocketbook and tossed a ticket folder onto his desk. "There's the address."

Smathers picked up the folder but didn't look at it. He was still looking very intently at the girl in front of him. He slowly rubbed a hand back and forth along his jaw.

"Herb," Ella said, "for heaven's sake . . ."

The lawyer snapped out of it. "Sorry, I was thinking." His voice was crisper. He seemed to have reached some kind of decision. "Ella, I think I have a way of settling this to everybody's satisfaction without going through the usual legal channels."

"If you're thinking of taking out a contract on him, I'm all for it."

Smathers got up and came round the desk, put his arm round her shoulder, and moved her toward the door. "I want you to go away now and come back at, say, five forty-five. But promise me you won't go near Calder."

"Can't I go see him for just ten seconds? Just long enough to bite his nose off."

"No, you'll stay right away. We'll fix him but we'll do it my way. I'll tell you about it this evening." He opened the door. "Now off you go and let me make a few phone calls. Make sure you're back here at a quarter of six. And try to stay calm." He saw her out of the office then came back and picked up the phone and the ticket folder. He called the travel agency.

"Hello? Is Mr. Calder there, please?"

Mr. Haverstraw's tired voice answered him. "No, I'm sorry. Mr. Calder only works here."

"He works there or he doesn't work there?"

"It's hard to tell. Can I help?"

"Thank you, but this is a personal matter. Would you know where Mr. Calder is right now? I'd like to get hold of him."

"He won't be in till ten thirty. His mother's had another malaria attack."

"Malaria?" Smathers' trained legal mind couldn't resist following that one up. "How does anybody's mother get malaria?"

"According to Calder, she was an army nurse at Guadalcanal."

"Uh huh. Well, if he's due in at ten thirty suppose I call back at ten forty?"

"You could try," Mr. Haverstraw answered, "but he'll probably be on his coffee break then."

"Then how about ten fifty?"

"No good. He'll be at lunch."

"Perhaps I could leave a message . . ."

"Sure, just let me get a pen and—hold it, his mother must have pulled through. He's walking in the door right now. I'll see if I can grab him before he leaves."

A few moments later Bunny came on the line. "Hello?"

"Mr. Calder, my name's Smathers. I'm a lawyer, Mr. Calder, I wanted to see you about a matter. It seems there may be some money coming your way."

"Money? For me?"

"That's right. Would it be convenient to come and see me this evening, a little after six at my office? I'm on West Fifty-eighth."

"Well, sure. But what's all this about money? Whose money? Is this a gag?"

"I'd prefer to go into it when you get here, Mr. Calder. Smathers and Partners, four West Fifty-eighth. Have you got it?"

44

"Yes, but—"

"See you this evening then. And I'm glad to hear your mother's recovered."

Smathers jabbed the phone button down, released it and dialed another number. When it was answered he asked for a Mr. Lasky.

A man's voice came on.

"Bill, Herb Smathers. I'm calling about that little matter we discussed the other day."

The man the lawyer was talking to, a short, slight man with the habit of pushing at his glasses before he spoke, said, "What about it?"

Smathers picked up the notebook and leaned back in his chair. "I think I may have something for you," he said.

Chapter 8

At five forty-five Ella was back in Smathers' office being told that Bunny would be arriving soon and being made to promise to behave. "Not one word, Ella. Just 'Hello, Mr. Calder,' and that's all. This has to be handled carefully, and I don't want it to dissolve into a barrage of name calling on your part. Is that clear?"

Ella, who'd stopped off at the supermarket on her way over, shifted the grocery bag off her knee and down onto the floor. "All right. But don't think it's going to be easy. And you still haven't told me what you're planning."

"All will be revealed very shortly. An associate of mine will explain everything. He'll be here any minute."

"Herb," Ella said, "I've never known you to be so secretive."

Smathers looked away from her eyes and examined his nails. "It's because this solution I have in mind is of a delicate nature."

Ella was stopped from exploring any more by the phone that buzzed on the lawyer's desk.

"Thanks, Miriam," Smathers said into it. "Send him in, would you, and then that's all. See you tomorrow." He replaced the phone. "Calder's on his way in, Ella. Now remember, not one word."

The door opened and Bunny entered the room. "Mr. Smathers?" he began. He didn't get any further; that's when he saw Ella, and when Ella saw him. "Why, Miss Brown," Bunny said with a puzzled smile. "Hello there."

The sight of him coming toward her, smiling, confident and without the slightest trace of guilt, was too much for Ella. She jumped to her feet and said sweetly, "Hello, Mr. Calder." Then she kicked him on the left shin.

"Yaa!" Bunny cried, clutched his leg and hopped up and down.

Ella kicked him on his right shin, and Bunny cried out again and changed legs. Still not satisfied, Ella grabbed the nearest weapon she could find, which happened to be a salami she'd just bought at Gristede's. She whipped it out of the shopping bag and slugged him over the head with it.

"Ella!" Smathers barked. "Stop that! You promised."

She whirled round at him. "I promised I wouldn't say anything, and I didn't."

"Ella," Smathers said forcefully, "drop that salami." He came round the desk and took it away from her, grasped her firmly by one elbow and marched her across the floor. "Out!" He propelled her through the door. "You wait outside till I call you, young lady." He closed it after her, locked it and came back to Bunny, who had collapsed into a chair and was rubbing his two throbbing shin bones and trying to figure out what had happened.

Smathers, embarrassed, cleared his throat and frowned. "I'd like to apologize for your reception, Mr. Calder. People coming into my office are usually met a little more cordially."

"My God, I should hope so," Bunny said. "Beaten about the head and shoulders with a Hebrew National . . ."

Smathers placed the offending salami on his desk, walked round and slid into his chair. He put his fingertips together and spoke in his best legal manner. "Mr. Calder, if we could put aside that unfortunate occurrence for a moment . . ."

Bunny went on massaging. He said, ruffled, "I don't think I'm quite ready yet." He looked round at the door, then back at the lawyer. "Is she a feminist or something?"

Smathers wasn't diverted. "Let us review the circumstances that have brought you here."

"You said something about money coming to me."

"Correct, and in doing so I'm afraid I was guilty of, what we call in the legal profession, telling a great big whopper."

Bunny stopped massaging. "You were kidding? There's no money coming to me?"

"Not a cent. I only told you that to make sure you'd come."

Bunny spread his arms. "Hell, Mr. Smathers, you didn't have to do that. I would have come for the two broken legs alone."

The other man pressed on. "Mr. Calder, finding Miss Brown in my office as you did must have been quite a surprise for you."

"Yes, indeed." Bunny rubbed tenderly at his head. "And it got even more surprising."

"Then you're not denying that you know Miss Brown . . . ?"

"Of course not. She came in to see me at the travel agency I work at. I booked her into a hotel in the West Indies."

"And you have no idea why she greeted you the way she did just now?"

Bunny looked bewildered. "Maybe they gave her a room on the back."

"I see." Smathers was watching him closely. "Tell me, does the name Campbell mean anything to you?"

"Sure. Tomato soup." Bunny made an open gesture of looking at his watch. "Mr. Smathers, if you don't have any money for me, and you're all through with the questions, I'd like to get on home and put some witch hazel on my broken body."

"Just one more question before you go, Mr. Calder." Smathers shot it at him quickly. "How much did you get for her apartment?"

"Her apartment? You mean Miss Brown's?" Bunny looked puzzled by the question. "I'm in the travel business, not real estate. What are you talking about?"

The lawyer studied him for a moment then opened a drawer and took out a manila file. He opened it, looked at the blank tax form that was inside it and executed a perfect bluff. "Mr. Calder, I told you I wouldn't ask any more questions. Instead I'm going to make a statement. Eleven days ago you rented Miss Brown's apartment to a couple from Ohio, the same couple who contacted you at the Americana Hotel. During their stay they got friendly with one of Miss Brown's neighbors, so we have their name and address. We could easily fly them back here to identify you but I don't think we need to go to all that trouble and expense, do you?" Smathers tapped his forehead in exaggerated forgetfulness. "I'm sorry, I said I wouldn't ask any more questions."

During the last half of the lawyer's statement Bunny's hands, which had resumed rubbing his shins, had moved slower and slower. Now they stopped altogether. His puzzled expression had been replaced by one of sad acceptance.

"Oh," he said, flatly. "That do make a difference."

48

"It do, don't it?" Smathers replied.

The atmosphere in the room had changed. The heavy smoke screen that Bunny had thrown up had been quickly and efficiently dispersed and there was nothing he could do now except sit there and wait for Smathers to start cracking the whip. Smathers, with a captive audience now, took his time about it. "Mr. Calder, I've known Miss Brown a long time, been a friend of the family's for years. And I can tell you that she's a girl with exceedingly high principles and a great respect for what some people might call the old-fashioned values. Like honesty and fair play. And she thinks that what you did—invading her privacy and renting her apartment to strangers for your own personal profit—was a despicable thing to do. And so do I."

Bunny grunted. "Yeah, but you didn't kick me."

"But what has really put the icing on the cake is the fact that those people wrecked her apartment and all the furniture in it. Furniture that she's been collecting for years."

Surprised, Bunny said, "You're kidding. Those people? But they seemed just folks. You know, down for a day on the steam cars."

"Solid citizens, huh? Well, solid citizens drink too. Sometimes a little too much."

"You mean they got looped and threw plates at each other?"

"They got paralyzed and played football. With three other couples."

"Believe me, Mr. Smathers," Bunny said slowly, "I didn't count on anything like that and I'm truly sorry. I'll be glad to pay for the damage or replace whatever's been broken."

"You can't replace the law, Mr. Calder, and that's also been broken."

"I get it," Bunny said tightly. "You want to nail me."

"That," Smathers said, stretching the words to twice their length, "depends."

He rose, excused himself and went out of the door. He found Ella in the reception room flipping rapidly through a magazine. The pages were taking a beating.

"Well," she asked, "does he admit it?"

Smathers affirmed it.

"Too bad, I was hoping we'd have to use torture."

"Now listen, Ella, we're going back in there now and I don't want a repetition of before. I know you're mad at him and I can understand it. But you're going to have to keep a lid on it. So you keep your hands strictly to yourself, is that clear?"

49

"Perfectly clear."

"Very well, then." He opened the door for her and Ella walked in, marched straight to Bunny's chair and yelled in his ear. "You dirty rotten cheaty rat-schmuck worm!"

"Rat-schmuck?" Bunny said.

Smathers glared at her. "Ella, you promised."

"I promised not to attack him physically and I haven't."

"You haven't?" Bunny couldn't believe it. He shoved up both pants legs and pointed. "What do you call these?"

Ella glanced down and said disdainfully, "Socks with holes in them."

Smathers, refereeing, waved both hands at them. "Please, please. We have serious business to discuss here."

Something buzzed on his desk, and the lawyer, with a last admonition to Ella, left them and went into the adjoining office. He greeted the man who'd just come in.

"Hello, Bill. They're both here." He very quietly opened the door a crack. "Take a look."

The other man crept to the door and peeked in. He adjusted his glasses before he spoke. "The girl looks okay, but the man. . . . Is he wearing shorts with a suit jacket?"

"No, he's showing her his legs."

The man closed the door softly. "In my day," he said, "it was the other way round."

He looked at Smathers. "You really think he can do it?"

"I'm sure of it. He's a damn good actor. I threw him questions that most men would have buckled under, but he sailed right through them. He's smart, he's fast on his feet and he doesn't crack under pressure. I think he'll do."

"And the woman?"

"I've known her for years. She's a little hot tempered at times, but she's got a good head on her and she's one hundred percent reliable."

"Very well, better introduce me. But, Herb"—he stopped the lawyer with a hand on his arm—"I hope you're right."

They entered the room together. Ella, elaborating on her earlier description, was telling Bunny exactly what she thought of him. Smathers tried to stem the flow. "Ella . . ."

She ignored him and kept on at Bunny, who was trying to apologize about the apartment. Smathers picked up the salami and banged it down on his desk like a gavel. "Ella. Please!"

50

She stopped and turned her head to him and Smathers took advantage of the pause.

"Ella, I'd like you to meet an associate of mine, Mr. Lasky. This is Ella Brown. And this is Mr. Calder."

Everybody nodded to each other, and Mr. Lasky took a long look at the salami that Smathers had dropped back onto the desk. It seemed to him a very curious paperweight. Smathers motioned him into a chair and sat down himself and began.

"Mr. Lasky is with a branch of the U.S. Immigration Department."

"My God," Bunny said, "they're going to deport me."

Smathers said, "At this point in time I feel that some kind of explanation is in order, particularly to you, Ella, and I think I can best explain what this is all about by telling you something about myself that I doubt you know." Smathers was incapable of putting more than two sentences together without sounding like he was summarizing a case in court. He stopped, coughed, and took his time before beginning again. "Over the years I've handled dozens of immigration cases, and in doing so I got to know the people in Immigration pretty well. So it was just a short jump from dealing with them as a lawyer to working with them as a lawyer, in which capacity I've been employed for some time now. This in turn has made me privy to classified information, and when Mr. Lasky told me in passing last week that they were faced with a particular problem, and needed a particular kind of person to help them out, I promised to keep my eyes peeled. I must admit that I thought that I could be of very limited help, but that was before you came to me, Ella, and told me about Mr. Calder here."

Ella, a note of alarmed uncertainty in her voice, said, "Herb, I told you about this man so he could be hung, buried, dug up and shot. You sound like you're getting ready to offer him a job."

Bunny didn't like the things Smathers was saying either. He said, "I already have a job. Two, in fact."

Lasky spoke up. "Perhaps I'd better fill them in, Herb." He edged forward on the chesterfield, and they swung their attention to him. Sitting there in his drab gray suit, his face empty of expression, the glasses slightly magnifying the pale eyes, he was a very unprepossessing figure. His voice was hardly a deep baritone, either. Nevertheless, when he spoke, they listened.

"A few weeks back four men entered this country illegally. Where they came from doesn't matter. Nor does their nationality. What does matter is that these men are very dangerous people and they slipped by us. We want to get our hands on them." He forestalled Bunny, who was getting set to ask a question. "Let me finish, Mr. Calder. You were probably going to ask how this concerns you. I'm getting to that. I want to tell you about these men first. We know quite a bit about them. Formerly, they were all members of a liberation group which they found too plodding and not extreme enough. So they broke away and formed a splinter group, taking with them a number of recruits who felt the same way they did—a need for action on a larger and more vigorous scale than the parent group was prepared to consider. But when they branched out on their own they ran into a problem. Financing. No doubt they'd counted on getting funds from the same foreign country that's supplying the parent group. But they were wrong. They were ignored, and that must have hurt. So they've decided to finance themselves."

"Then they've come to raise money?" Ella asked.

"They've come here to steal money," Lasky replied.

Seeing Ella had been allowed to ask a question, Bunny asked one too. "Why here?"

"Because America is still the country with the most money. And New York's its richest city. London, Paris, Zurich, you name it; there is still far more available cash here than anywhere else in the world."

"Then you figure they'll raid a few banks, go on home and buy some guns."

"Not guns, no. These people are after recognition, remember. They want to do something that'll make everybody sit up and take notice. Earn them credentials, if you like." Lasky paused, which gave his next words greater emphasis. "According to our information, which we're pretty sure is correct, they're planning to buy themselves a fighter bomber."

It was so unexpected it stopped them for a moment. Then Ella spoke. "Can they do that? I don't know anything about these things but I wouldn't have thought you could just buy something like that."

"You can buy one just as easily as you or I can buy a used car," Lasky told her. "All the major countries are in the armament business, a lot of the smaller ones, too. Models are superseded by newer models, which creates a big second-hand market. A lot of it's legal, a lot is illegal. All you need is money."

"But a fighter bomber," Bunny said. "How much would one of those run you? Even an old one?"

Lasky made a small iffy movement with his hand. "Fifteen, twenty million."

Bunny whistled. "Well, they're not going to find that kind of money lying around, even in this town."

"Exactly," Lasky said. He moved forward on the chesterfield another inch. "You can't steal twenty million in one or two tries even in New York. Amounts of that size do exist in certain vaults around the city, but even if these people succeeded in getting into one of them they'd never succeed in getting out. It's only a matter of time before they realize this, which will only leave them one alternative."

"Which is?"

The government man traded a fast glance with Smathers before he answered. "A kidnap."

A change came over Bunny's face. He seemed to remember that all this preamble had something to do with him and he didn't see where the connection could possibly be. He said as much to Lasky who told him what he had in mind.

"We're going to set a trap for them. We're going to offer them a kidnap victim."

Bunny pointed an amazed finger at himself. "Me? Who'd pay twenty million for me?"

"Who'd pay twenty cents?" Ella said.

"Not the victim, Mr. Calder. The victimized. If this thing works out, they're going to be sending you a ransom note for twenty million dollars."

Ella was too surprised to comment this time, but she wasn't as surprised as Bunny.

"Mr. Lasky, I'm embarrassed to admit it but I don't have twenty million in my bank account right now. It's been a rough month."

"You will have. That is, we can make it appear that you do. Let me explain." He nudged his glasses up and down and picked up the tempo. "These people that we're dealing with know that it's useless kidnapping embassy or consular staff, for example, because most governments won't encourage terrorism by buckling under to ransom demands. A business firm might, if one of its executives was taken, but not to the tune of twenty million. But once emotion is involved, then policy flies out the window. But the only kind where emotion is involved are private kidnaps. Which is the kind we've decided to arrange. The problem then became where to find the rich man, somebody rich enough to be able to be hit for a multimillion-dollar ransom. Naturally, that was impossible. We couldn't ask a real millionaire to help us out. That would be going beyond the call of duty. So we realized we'd have to create one of our own."

Bunny was looking at Lasky as if he thought he was crazy. "And you're thinking it's going to be me."

"Precisely."

Ella said, "Supposing you can make all this happen; what are these people supposed to ransom?"

"Mr. Calder's daughter."

Bunny started looking at Lasky as if he knew he was crazy. He said, "I have an ex-mother-in-law they can have for free. But I don't have a daughter."

"We'll arrange that, too."

Bunny climbed out of his chair. "Well, it all sounds like a lot of fun and I'm sorry I'm going to miss it, but, um, bomb-throwing terrorists and me, we don't have too much in common."

Ella's eyes flashed at him. "No? You should see my apartment."

"So if you'll excuse me . . ." Bunny started to move round his chair. Smathers took over. "Mr. Calder, eleven days ago you obtained a key to a private apartment and had it cut for an illegal purpose. There's a strike against you for a start. Then you used it to obtain entry without the owner's permission. Technically, that's breaking and entering."

"And vice versa," Ella said.

"Then you rented the apartment to those people, no doubt claiming that it belonged to an acquaintance. That's misrepresentation and actual fraud. And you contacted those people through an advertisement which you placed interstate, which makes it a federal offense. I would estimate the possible cumulative sentences to be somewhere around—"

"I get it." Bunny dropped wearily back into his chair. "But why me, that's what I want to know?" He looked at Lasky. "Why not one of your own people?"

Smathers answered, "Because this is a very delicate matter, Mr. Calder. As it is, if this thing comes off, certain people might accuse us of entrapment. The less government people involved, the better. Especially in the part you're going to play."

Bunny blew out a miserable breath and sank down deeper in his chair.

"It's not all that bad, Mr. Calder," Lasky offered. "There'll be compensations. We'll pay you for your time, of course."

Bunny brightened. "Oh? How much?"

Lasky looked at Smathers, who looked at Ella. "Ella, how much would it cost you to put your apartment back as good as it was?"

"If it were possible, and at today's prices, maybe six or seven thousand."

"Seven thousand dollars," Smathers said to Lasky.

"Seven thousand dollars," Lasky said to Bunny.

Bunny closed his eyes and kneaded the bridge of his nose.

"And don't forget," Lasky continued, "you're going to be one of America's richest men. That can't be all bad."

"I'll probably be one of America's deadest men, too."

"Oh no. Believe me, there won't be any element of risk as far as you're concerned."

"As far as *I'm* concerned? Then who?"

"The daughter," Ella said softly. "The little girl."

Lasky didn't look happy. He said formally, "We're planning to minimize the risk to almost zero."

Ella asked him where they were going to get a child from, and Lasky told her that they'd already got one.

"How old is she?"

"Nine."

"And she knows what she's getting into?"

Lasky nodded. "She knows exactly what she's getting into."

"Nine years old." Ella shook her head. "The brave little kid."

"So," Lasky said, rising and going over to the window, "we have the father and the daughter." He turned and looked at Ella. "All we need now is the wife."

"Do you think you'll be able to—" Ella stopped. Smathers was looking at her, too. And like Lasky, in a curious way. Comprehension dawned slowly. "Oh no," she said, then repeated it much more definitely. "Oh no. No sir-ree, Bob. If you're thinking of me for the part, you're going to have to think again. Boy, are you going to have to think again." She jabbed a finger in Bunny's direction. "I wouldn't for one instant be associated with this man in any way, shape or form."

"It'd only be for a week or two," Smathers said. "You'd only have to see him now and then."

Ella's voice rose. "I can't stand seeing him now, let alone then. I'm sorry, Herb, but you're asking me to do something I just couldn't do. He's a cheat, a liar and a crook."

"Just a second now," Bunny said.

"Ella," Smathers began. "Look at it this way . . ."

"I'm not going to look at it any way. Nothing would induce me to even consider it. Believe me, Herb, I'd like to help. But with him part of the deal, it's no deal." She clamped her mouth shut, folded her arms tightly and glared straight ahead. She made it quite plain that wild horses couldn't make her change her mind. But Smathers had something better than horses. He said, "Very well, Ella. I understand how you feel and I won't try to sway you." He was shuffling some papers on his desk and seemed to discover something. "Oh. You were asking about the child. Here's a picture of her."

He held out a small black-and-white print which Ella reached for. A thin-faced little girl looked out of it. She had a sprinkling of freckles over a turned-up nose, brown hair cut short and worn with a straight-across fringe. The dark eyes stared at the camera as if she were a little afraid of it, but the firm line of the mouth and jaw showed that she wasn't going to let anybody know it.

"Look at her," Ella said. "The poor little kid." Her head came up, angry. "What kind of parents would let their child volunteer for something like this?"

Smathers, playing it beautifully, looked down at his hands. "There are no parents."

"No parents?"

"The child lives in a Home."

Ella's face drew in on itself as her expression changed. Her eyes went back to the print.

"What did you tell the administration?" Bunny asked.

"The truth."

"And they still let you borrow her?"

"Mr. Calder," Smathers said levelly. "Many of the places that are called Homes are anything but. The children are fed and clothed, but there's no love."

A small choking sound came from Ella's direction.

Smathers locked eyes with Lasky for a brief instant then poured it on.

"Consequently, they'll agree to allow their charges to do things that a mother wouldn't even consider."

"It's inhuman," Ella said.

"It is tough, Ella, I agree. But what can we do? We have to catch those men now, and this plan has an excellent chance of succeeding. But it requires a child." Smathers gave a tiny disappointed sigh. "We had hoped that you'd go along with us, to look after the child while she was in our care. We would have felt better having someone like

yourself around to be with her if she . . . if she needed somebody."
He shot a fast glance at Ella to see how he was doing. He was doing
fine. "It's too bad. It's too late to find somebody else. The little girl
will be all on her own now."

"Herb, will you stop, please?" Ella was blinking hard. She looked
back at the photograph Smathers had been careful to leave in her
hands. She took a deep breath. "All right," she said quietly. "All
right."

Smathers and Lasky broke into smiles.

"But"—the smiles shortened—"tell Attila, here, that this is a mar-
riage in name only. I don't want to even catch sight of him unless it's
absolutely necessary. No being together, no talking together, no nothing together unless it's unavoidable. And if he puts one hand on me,
even to help me out of a cab, I'll scream the place down. Is that
clearly understood?"

Smathers and Lasky nodded solemnly.

Ella swiveled her head toward Bunny, who was listening and
watching with an inscrutable expression on his face.

"And you, Mr. Calder, you rat. Have I made myself one hundred
percent crystal clear?"

"One hundred percent."

Ella looked around the three men's faces then shook her head in
wonder. "Amazing," she said. "I came here to see this man get his
electric chair and one hundred lashes and instead I'm getting married
to him."

Bunny began to smile. He'd apparently seen something humorous
in the situation. And something promising. He said, "Miss Brown,
I'm sure we'll be very happy."

Ella almost went for the salami again.

Chapter 9

Two days after the meeting in Smathers' office Bunny and Ella were
sitting with Lasky in the rear seat of an unmarked government car
that was fighting traffic on the Long Island Expressway. As unmarked government cars seldom ran to air conditioning, it was no
cooler inside the car than outside—outside being a sticky July evening. But while the temperature inside was decidedly warm, the atmosphere was decidedly frosty. Ella hadn't as much as acknowledged
Bunny's presence, never looking at him and choosing to gaze out of
the window whenever he spoke. Lasky, who'd diplomatically sat himself between them, would have preferred a more congenial relationship between them, knowing that it would have made his job a lot
easier. Not that it would have been a piece of cake under the best
conditions; there was a lot these two had to do, and they had to be
perfect at it. Again he hoped that Smathers had been right in his
choice.

Since picking them up half an hour before, Lasky had been slowly
filling them in on the plan in general, giving them just the bones. Now
he started to flesh it out a little. He began with an apology.

"I'm sorry this has been so fast. If we hadn't needed to move
quickly we'd never have disrupted your schedules like this."

Ella said, "I'm surprised my boss didn't scream when he heard I
wouldn't be around for a while, coming off of a vacation."

"No problem there. I told him very discreetly that you were on government service and asked him to keep it quiet. He wasn't mad; he was impressed."

"How about my boss," Bunny asked, "Mr. Haverstraw? What did he say?"

Lasky stalled behind a small cough. "He, er, he said he'd just think of you as being on a coffee break."

"That's my boss," Bunny said. He got a pang when he thought about the possible apartments he'd be missing out on. Not to mention the double fees he wouldn't be getting from his other business. He'd had to put a vacation sign on the door. All in all this crazy little venture he'd been roped into was going to cost him quite a bit of money. Still, he couldn't have made money in jail, either; and as Smathers had said, there had to be compensations in his new status, however temporary it was going to be. Maybe he could even come out of it ahead. They were going to make him a multimillionaire, weren't they? Which reminded him that Lasky still hadn't told him just how they were going to accomplish that. He asked him now and Lasky touched his glasses and resettled them, but he did it faster and with less fuss than previously. In fact, as they left Manhattan farther behind, the mannerism grew less and less. Lasky was obviously a man who was bothered by pressures.

"It won't be that difficult," Lasky said. "Creating an impression of wealth never is. A poor man who can borrow a Rolls Royce for a day immediately appears rich. Which is what we've done for you only on an enlarged scale."

"How large?" Bunny asked.

"Very. We want to make this thing as tempting as possible for these people, so instead of making you just another millionaire, we're making you extremely wealthy. To look it you'll need all the trappings—the house, the yacht, the plane, the cars—and we've been able to induce a few authentically rich people, whom we've taken into our confidence, to lend us some of those things."

"How about all the cash? Who's lending you that?"

"Oh, you won't need cash. After all, the super rich don't use it much themselves. They transcend mere currency. It's all done with paper, which is why you're so rich incidentally."

"Before you explain that part," Bunny said, "answer me this. If I'm so rich, why doesn't anybody know about me? Where have I been all these years?"

Lasky told him that they'd anticipated that. "The answer was simply to make you a publicity-shy recluse who'd previously gone to painstaking lengths to stay out of the public eye. It's not without precedent, there are quite a few rich men who are like that. They like to keep out of sight. Perhaps it's a throwback to the days when people were taxed on appearances, I don't know. But shunning the limelight is very believable behavior for somebody worth six hundred million dollars."

Even Ella couldn't help but look surprised. Bunny said, "That's how much I'm worth? Six hundred million?"

"I told you we wanted to make it tempting," Lasky said blandly.

"Six hundred million," Bunny repeated. Then he had trouble with it. "But how about the money boys, Wall Street and the financial books and the IRS? Won't they see through it? It can't be possible to keep money like that secret."

"Mr. Calder, before I transferred to Immigration I was with the Treasury Department. You'd be surprised just how much money is kept secret. A little over a year and a half ago somebody sold two hundred tons of gold on the London exchange. It was rumored to be an American sale; illegal, of course. But nobody knew that was around and that was a billion and a half dollars' worth."

"Yes, but that's gold. I'm talking about cash and securities. I think I am, anyway."

"Take either of them," Lasky replied. "There is something like nine hundred billion dollars' worth of securities owned in this country, so there's plenty of room there. And as far as cash goes there's seven hundred billion on deposit in banks alone. And as for the cash we don't know about," Lasky raised a hand, "for the last couple of years the largest bill printed has been the one hundred dollar bill. And in bills over that size there is still more than four hundred and fifty million outstanding. And it's not in banks, it's in people's pockets. So believe me, nobody's going to wonder where your money came from."

"I guess you're right. It's a rich country, isn't it?"

"Very."

"Okay, next question. How do people find out about me and my riches? That is," he glanced at Ella and tried an exploratory communication, "us and our riches?"

Ella snapped open her pocketbook, took a Kleenex out and daintily blew her nose. Bunny got the message.

"We've lined up a press conference. Newspapers, magazines, TV. They'll be out in force tomorrow. By the day after everybody will have heard about you."

"Are you sure you'll get that kind of coverage?"

Lasky was positive. "Kings, queens, movie stars, millionaires—newspapers love that kind of copy because they know their readers will lap it up. A rich man from nowhere is just the kind of thing they'll pounce on."

Ella frowned at that. "We're going to be fooling an awful lot of people."

"True," Lasky admitted. "But it's a harmless enough deception. Nobody will be adversely affected by it except, we hope, our guerrilla friends." He watched the traffic sliding by on the highway for a moment then spoke again. "By the way, how many people would you say would recognize you instantly from a photograph? Parents, for example, people who wouldn't have the slightest doubt. Miss Bown, how about you?"

"There's my mother and father, they'd know, of course. Some girl friends and the people I work with. One or two ex-boyfriends."

"No current boyfriend?" Lasky asked.

Bunny turned his head at that, interested in the answer, and Ella saw it.

"Not at the moment." It riled her to have to admit it in front of him.

"Better call your parents tonight," Lasky said. "Tell them as little as possible, but tell them not to get excited when they see your picture in the paper." He turned to Bunny. "How about you, Mr. Calder?"

"There are some people, sure. A couple of buddies, some business contacts and," he added casually, mainly for Ella's benefit, "about eight or nine girl friends."

"How about parents?"

"There's my mother. I'll call her." Bunny wrinkled his brow and said, again for Ella's benefit, "I think I've got the number somewhere."

The eloquent little sniff that Ella gave said that she knew he was the type who never called his mother.

Lasky allowed that there wasn't much they could do about their friends or business associates and that they'd just have to let them wonder. "If they ask about it, when you go back to being yourselves, you'll just have to tell them it's a look-alike. It shouldn't be that difficult, newspaper shots don't reproduce that well and we'll make sure the lighting for the TV is less than it should be. With a little luck nobody will blow the whistle on you."

"You haven't told us who we're going to be," Bunny said.

"Mr. and Mrs. Bergstrom. Don Ray and Jane. We thought that Don Ray Bergstrom had a nice ring to it for a rich man. You have an entire background, of course—family, where you're from, how you made your money etcetera—which is all contained in the press release we've prepared. I'll give you both a copy tonight so you can bone up for the reporters tomorrow."

"When does the little girl arrive?" Ella asked.

"You'll meet her tonight."

"What's her name?"

"Lillian. Lillian Phelan."

"Lillian," Ella repeated. "The poor little kid."

"As your daughter her name will be Sherrel Ann. It struck us as the kind of cute name overindulgent parents might call their child."

Nobody had any more questions for the moment, and Lasky decided to reserve more information till later on, and the three of them sat back as the car swung off the highway and took them through East Norwich and into the town of Oyster Bay. They followed the road that skirted the edge of the harbor and came to a high fieldstone wall that fronted tall green maples and elms. The wall went on for a couple of hundred yards till it was broken by massive wrought-iron gates, a small stone gatehouse in back. The car slowed, turned into the gates, and went smoothly over a red pebble drive. The drive curved in a slow sweep through high cypress pines and trimmed hedges, then straightened up and revealed the house it led to.

Bunny and Ella were both stopped by the sight. Incredulous, Bunny said, "This is where we live?"

"I've read about this place," Ella said.

The car stopped at the bottom of a flight of marble steps that spilled down from the entrance and they got out and took a better look. The main section of the house, the center part, was built in three distinct layers: an elegant row of arches formed the base and supported a dozen slim Corinthian columns, each thirty feet high, which in turn held up a flat ballustraded roof. Twin rows of double-sash windows were set into the wings of the house which extended grandly on both sides for a hundred and fifty feet, each wing ending in a smaller version of the center section. The house was magnificent; monumental, but at the same time breathtaking in its classic proportions.

Ella couldn't get over it. "A Palladian mansion. You usually have to go to England to see one."

62

"That's where the original of this is," Lasky said. "It's an exact copy of Heveningham Hall. The grounds are way smaller of course, only twenty acres, but the house is almost as big. Besides the main rooms there are two libraries, a gallery, a great hall, two ballrooms, a billiard room, and, upstairs, something like thirty-two bedrooms. When it's fully staffed there are twelve people on the payroll." He turned to Bunny. "We thought it was the kind of place a man like you would buy."

"Mr. Lasky, I rent a studio with a leaky air conditioner and a woman who does two hours every Wednesday. It may take me awhile to get used to all this."

"I can understand how you feel, but those reporters will be here at eleven in the morning so you're going to have to acclimatize fast. Shall we go in?"

Lasky dismissed the driver, asking him to return after dinner, then led the way up the staircase and through the center archway. He produced a key, opened the paneled door and stepped aside for them. The entrance hall was a glowing stretch of brilliant black-and-white marble; a superb double staircase seemed to grow out of it as it climbed to the first floor, curved gracefully round and swept down to the other side of the hall. At the top of the stairs, on the landing, twin columns supported the ceiling, and the Palladian motif was repeated in long, scooped wall niches. The walls were hung with oval portrait plaques and oil paintings in huge baroque frames. If Bunny and Ella were beguiled by the room, they were stopped by the gallery that Lasky led them into. The floor, as wide as a highway, was a gleaming expanse of parquet that ran the entire length of one wing, Chippendale and Sheraton furnishings flanking it on either side. The walls rose up and melded into the ceiling which formed a soaring parabola of decorated plaster, fluted moldings and corner pieces like icing on a wedding cake, twin chandeliers tumbling down like a waterfall of frozen crystal. The ceiling design was reflected in brilliant oranges and yellows and pinks in the incredibly huge carpet that covered the center of the room.

In an awed voice Ella said, "It's Robert Adam, isn't it?"

"It's after his style," Lasky said. "It's only a copy, remember, although the furniture is genuine Georgian."

Bunny, peering up at the ceiling, asked Lasky who owned the house.

"A man named Bernie Silverman."

Half to himself, Bunny said, "I wonder if he takes vacations."

63

It was lucky for Bunny that Ella was too engrossed in the house to hear him. They walked through into a living room and Lasky continued the guided tour.

"The house was built in nineteen twenty-seven by Colonel Compton. His wife had the money, her father owned a couple of rubber plantations in Brazil and got out before the bust. Long John Silverman bought the place ten years ago."

"Long John Silverman? What is he, one of those business pirates?" Bunny asked.

Lasky denied it. "Oh no. They call him that because he manufactures underwear."

Bunny halted beside a gigantic Chinese vase. "You mean jockey shorts bought all this?"

"Not really. That was just his start. He made his first real money in barbecue aprons then went on from there."

"Barbecue aprons," Bunny said, taking in the fifty-foot Chinese rug. Ella had wandered away for a closer look at a marble fireplace. "And tell me," Bunny continued, "did the underwear king lend you this place just like that?"

Lasky gave him an ambiguous look. "In a manner of speaking. We merely had the IRS point out to him what could be construed as a slight oversight in his last tax return and he was more than happy to move into his Manhattan apartment for a week or two."

"You guys sure have a way with people, don't you?"

Lasky parried the remark by not hearing it. "Come on, you can see the rest of the house later. I'll show you round the grounds."

Ella declined Lasky's invitation and they left her dreamily walking round the room, lost in it. Lasky led Bunny through a series of equally splendid rooms and out through a side door. The path here was made of the same fine red gravel as the drive, and they followed it beside a lawn that was almost as even as the rugs inside.

Bunny said, "Did you say it takes twelve people to run this place?"

"That's right. A butler, a chauffeur, a valet, a housekeeper, four maids, a chef and his assistant and two gardeners."

Bunny looked round him contentedly. "I think I'm going to like it here."

Lasky, a touch of hesitancy in his voice, said, "They're not all here now."

"They're not?"

Lasky fiddled with his glasses, and Bunny saw the gesture and wondered about it.

"No. You see, as Mr. Silverman isn't going to be here for some time he's given them their vacation now."

"You mean we have to run this mansion by ourselves?"

"No, no. Not by yourselves. There's a chef who'll cook for you and also look after anything else you need."

Bunny felt better. "A private chef. Not bad."

They'd reached the rear of the house which was almost as grand as the front, having a similar façade but without the columns and the roof statuary. Lasky stopped outside an enormous expanse of door and pressed a switch in the wall. There was an electric hum from somewhere and four garage doors slid up and rolled silently back on their runners. The sight that they presented drew a soft exclamation from Bunny.

"This is the garage," Lasky said.

"I guess you could say that."

In front of them, lined up in a shining row, were eight automobiles. As they walked slowly down the line Lasky introduced them. "Ferrari Daytona, Aston Martin DBS, Maserati Bora, Citroën SM, Rolls Royce Silver Wraith, Lamborghini Espada, Thirty-six Hispano-Suisa, Mustang."

Bunny frowned at the last-named car. "How did that get in there?"

"That's Mr. Silverman's car."

"The others aren't?"

"No. Mr. Silverman only owns two cars and we didn't think that was enough for Don Ray Bergstrom so we borrowed some more."

"From people who are bad at arithmetic at tax time . . ."

Lasky didn't deny it.

"Did you borrow that, too?" Bunny was pointing at an old dilapidated pick-up parked against a wall. The body was a mass of dents and scratches and the upholstery was patched and sprung. The bank was full of fertilizer sacks, boxes of plants and small potted trees, tags tied to them. One headlight was missing.

"Forty-eight Ford," Lasky said. "No, that's the gardener's. Let's borrow it. I'll show you the estate."

Bunny tapped the hood of a car that looked like a steel and glass bullet. "Wouldn't we be more comfortable in this?"

Lasky already had one foot on the running board. "This is more practical."

Bunny postponed the bullet car till later, climbed into the pick-up, brushed some seed packets off the seat and banged the door closed three times before it stayed that way. The truck started with a roar that never quieted, and Lasky eased it out of the garage, onto the drive and over the softly rolling lawns. The tailored grass stretched away on either side of them, broken by ordered rows of flower beds and topiary trees clipped in animal shapes. They passed a maze made from high hedges and a formal walk which led to a wrought-iron gazebo. There were fish ponds and fountains and stone statues and monumental urns; a Japanese garden, a Roman garden and an English garden in which four white swans paraded.

"Beautiful, isn't it?" Lasky said. "He's supposed to be the best gardener in the country."

Bunny jounced up and down in his seat and shouted over the roar of the engine. "He sure ain't the best mechanic." He pointed to a large, hangar-like building. "What's that over there?"

"The sports complex. Swimming pool, tennis courts, squash courts, gymnasium, bike track. The golf course is on the other side. It's only a nine-hole pitch and putt, naturally."

"Naturally," Bunny said. He pointed in another direction. "Is that the outdoor pool?"

"That's the sailing pond. Colonel Compton was a model-boat fan. He owned a model of the Constitution that fired a real broadside. He'd invite people to sail their models on the pond then he'd blow them out of the water."

"Colonel Compton was a nut," Bunny declared. "What's that building next to it?"

"That's the indoor sailing pond."

Bunny got his mind around that. He said, "The Colonel certainly didn't believe in cutting corners."

"Don't forget," Lasky answered, "when he built this place they still had the old tax structure. I doubt you could build a place like this today."

"Unless you were Don Ray Bergstrom."

Lasky's mouth slanted in one corner, which was what he called a smile. "Good," he said, "you're getting the idea."

They drove past a screen of cypresses, bumped round a hillock and found a glittering blue harbor spread in front of them. Lasky stopped the pick-up. "That's something else we borrowed." Two hundred yards out, an enormous yacht rode serenely at anchor.

"Did Cunard make a tax error, too?" Bunny asked.

"That's J. K. Jones' boat, one of the largest privately owned yachts in the world. It used to be a Mediterranean car ferry. It cost him as much to convert as it did to buy."

"This J. K. Jones, how did he make his money? Break it to me gently."

"You're not going to like it," Lasky said.

"I'm going to hate it. How did he make his money?"

"Novelties."

"What kind of novelties?"

Lasky sighed. "I think his biggest account was the prizes in the Cracker Jack box."

Bunny sat back in his seat hard. "I can't stand it. Jockey shorts, aprons, popcorn prizes . . . whatever happened to all the railroad barons, the shipping magnates, the newspaper publishers, the rubber kings like Colonel Compton? Aren't they rich anymore?"

"Times have changed, Mr. Calder." Lasky chunked the Ford into reverse, backed up and drove back the way they'd come. He raised his voice above the clatter of the truck. "You have to realize that industries like those aren't owned by single individuals anymore."

"But candy give-aways," Bunny said. "Don't tell me that'll buy you a yacht like that."

"Of course not, but it starts them on the road. They find a product, market it successfully, diversify into other areas and get themselves a nice little company going. They build it up fast and when the growth curve looks good enough they go public. If the stock catches on and they've been smart, they're made."

"What do you mean, smart?"

"Retained sole ownership of the company. They recapitalize, offer several million shares, retain four or five million for themselves, and when the issue's subscribed they're suddenly members of the super rich."

"But their money's mostly on paper, isn't it?"

"Sure, but it's still purchasing power."

The truck hit a bumpy section, and Bunny hung on as he jounced around, then continued his questions. "Is that how Don Ray made his money?"

"Something like that. You got your start in real estate. It's all in the press release I'll be giving you. Certain kinds of real estate deals can be almost untraceable so if anybody gets nosy about the source of your wealth they won't get very far. Then you bought huge blocks of stock in most of the blue chips. You bought them through a numbered bank account in New Jersey. Again, that's untraceable."

"How about this house and that yacht? They must both be pretty well known. How come I suddenly own them?"

"You offered Silverman and Jones a price they couldn't turn down. When this thing is all over it'll be put out that they bought them back for a song when you took a blood bath in the market. That's why you'll drop out of sight again."

The news of the impending disaster seemed to shake Bunny more than the truck was doing. He looked at Lasky, dismayed. "But I'm fabulously rich. It can't be possible to go broke that quickly."

"Mr. Calder," Lasky said patiently, "in nineteen seventy, in one single day, one of the super rich lost almost as much as Don Ray Bergstrom's worth. You have to think big, Mr. Calder."

That shook Bunny, too. He couldn't see how losing half a billion dollars in a day was thinking big.

Lasky steered the truck into the garage and switched off the engine, which seemed to groan with relief as it died. Bunny followed him out of the garage, through a side door and down some stairs. They emerged in a huge brightly lit kitchen, the walls and floor made entirely of blue and white Spanish tiles. The place shone with polished copper and stainless steel, and Bunny counted three electric ovens, an open fireplace with a series of spits running through it, a microwave assembly and an oil-fired cooking stove as big as a pool table.

"The chef must have stepped out for a minute," Lasky said, "but you'll meet him later."

Bunny marveled at the kitchen. "He's got to be a cordon bleu." He moved toward a freezer against the wall. It was as long as a supermarket cabinet and crammed just as full. Stacked and labeled in their own sections were grouse, pheasant, partridge, pigeon, ortolan, suckling pig, legs of lamb, barrons of veal, crown roasts, Porterhouse steaks and Châteaubriands. Bunny opened the tall, commercial-sized refrigerator that stood next to it. One half was stacked very neatly and efficiently with sixteen ounce jars of Iranian caviar. The other half was packed just as competently with two-pound crocks of pâté from the Périgord. Reverently, Bunny closed the doors.

Behind him Lasky said, "Mr. Silverman's something of a gourmand."

"Yes, I'd say he qualified," Bunny replied. He walked to the end of the kitchen to a wide frosted pane of glass set into the wall. He wiped it with a sleeve and peered in. Row upon row of wine bottles looked back at him.

"They're the whites and the champagne. The reds are through here." Lasky preceded him through a door. The bottles nestled in metal shelves that stretched from floor to ceiling. There were three rows of them running the entire length of a room that was twice the size of the kitchen.

Bunny walked down an aisle reading off the labels. "Chambertin, Romanée Conti, Richebourg, Nuit Saint George, Beaune, Corton . . ." He crossed into another aisle. "And will you look at the Bordeaux . . . Château Latour, Margaux, Lamarque, Kirwan, Grand-Puy-Ducasse . . ." He stopped. "Mr. Lasky, I think you chose the right man after all."

Lasky suggested that they join Ella, and they went back upstairs. They found her admiring the paneling in the billiard room. The room contained a pool table, a billiard table and a snooker table and one whole wall was taken up by a parade of cues fitted into a mahogany rack. On the other walls were gilt-framed oils of Victorian hunting scenes.

Ella turned to Lasky as he came up to her. "It's staggering," she said. "I've been over the entire ground floor. I've never seen so many fine pieces outside of a museum."

"Wait till you see the rest of it," Bunny said. "Swimming pool, tennis court, bike track. And you won't believe the cars. Or the yacht. And the kitchen and the wine cellar . . . we even have a French chef."

It was Lasky who replied; Ella didn't give the faintest sign that Bunny was even in the room. "Not quite, Mr. Calder. Hartley's American. From New York."

Bunny waved the disclaimer away. "Some of the best chefs are American—Julia Child, Michael Field. Better than a lot of French chefs. I'm getting hungry just thinking about it."

Lasky consulted his watch. "Dinner should be ready shortly. You'll meet Hartley then."

They moved together into an adjoining room whose central feature was a circular bar the size of a small carousel. The bottles, inverted and fitted with pouring spigots, ran round the interior of the bar in three unbroken rows. Bunny reacted to it in much the same way he'd reacted to the cars.

"Will you look at this," he said, walking round it. "A drunk's candy store. Not one brand repeated twice." He ducked under the counter and came up on the other side. "How about a drink before dinner? What's your pleasure, Ella?"

Ella looked as though her pleasure would be for Bunny to drop dead.

"Oh, I wouldn't touch anything there, Mr. Calder," Lasky said. "That's Mr. Silverman's personal bar."

"Oh." Bunny looked a little put out. He ducked under the counter and rejoined them. "Where's our bar? I'm dry as a bone."

Lasky fiddled with his glasses. "I'm afraid there isn't one."

"Only one bar?" Bunny was surprised. "That's too bad. I was kind of counting on a vodka martini." He brightened. "Tell you what, why don't I run into the village and pick up a bottle. Only take me a minute."

"Sorry you have to trouble."

"No trouble, I'll just tool in in one of the cars. Where do you keep the keys?"

"The key's in it," Lasky answered.

"In what?"

"The pick-up."

The smile on Bunny's face shrank somewhat. "Well, er, I thought I'd try one of the others. The Lamborghini, maybe."

Lasky shuffled his feet and looked uncomfortable. His glasses bothered him again. "Mr. Calder, those cars are really only for show. For when the reporters get here tomorrow. After all, they aren't our property."

"Neither is the pick-up," Bunny said.

"Yes, but the pick-up gets a lot more miles to the gallon than the Lamborghini." Lasky was saved from having to expand on that by the buzz of a telephone. He excused himself, picked it up, spoke into it briefly then replaced it. "That was Hartley. Dinner's ready. Shall we move into the dining room?"

On their way there Ella asked Lasky what time the little girl was due to arrive.

"Sometime after dinner. Even though the newspeople aren't due till tomorrow morning, we thought it best if you all spent the night here just in case a couple of eager beavers get here early."

"You still haven't told us anything about the plan. How it's supposed to work and why."

Lasky said that he'd held off on purpose. "I'll go over everything in detail in the morning with the three of you. I want you all together." He led them through double doors into a room that was a kind of annex to the enormous dining room that opened off it. In the center of the smaller room a table had been set for three. As they seated themselves a soft chunking noise announced the arrival of a dumb-waiter set into a wall.

Bunny crossed to it and brought back a silver tray. There was a large covered serving dish on it and a bottle of wine wrapped in a napkin and lying in a pouring basket. He set it all down, closed his eyes and sniffed at the steam rising from the dish. He picked up the bottle, carefully keeping the napkin over it, and poured a little into his wine glass. He said, "Do you mind if I try to identify it? Just to see if I can get close."

Lasky watched with some interest. Ella examined the curve of the table legs. Bunny brought the glass to his nose. "Fine bouquet. Very delicate." He sipped, ran the liquid round his mouth and swallowed slowly. "A Burgundy, I think. Too full for a Bordeaux." He sipped some more. "A little nervous at first but it's quite brave on the back of the throat. Definitely a Burgundy." He took another sip and looked deep into the glass. "It has that slightly spicy taste of the Côte de Nuits. A Musigny perhaps. A Grand Cru without doubt. Probably from one of the larger vineyards. So in that case," he crinkled his eyes and tried the wine again, "it could be a clos de Vougeot, or a Bonnes Mares. Yes, I'd say it's a Bonnes Mares. And I'll take a wild guess and say it's a sixty-two. I'm probably way out," Bunny said, although he didn't for a moment think so—when he'd toured the cellar he'd seen a bottle of the wine he'd just described out of the rack, and he figured it for the dinner wine. Smiling, he lifted the bottle and unwrapped the napkin and looked at the label. A cherubic little man dressed in lederhosen and playing an accordion smiled cheerily back at him.

"*Italian Swiss Colony?*" Bunny's expression was a lot less happy than the accordion player's. With a horrible suspicion building inside him he reached for the serving dish lid. He stared at what was on the dish, then said very softly, "Knockwurst and beans." He looked up at Lasky, his face a mask of noncomprehension. "What is this, the Army? What happened to the pheasant and the grouse and the Château Latour? I mean, what is this?"

For the first time Ella addressed him directly. "It's dinner. And if you don't mind, I'd like some, please."

Bunny was too dazed to comply and Lasky served the food. "Mr. Calder," he said, "perhaps I'd better finish what I started to explain before. I'm the only government man concerned with this affair that you've met so far. That's because we thought it easier if you only had one contact. But there are about thirty people involved in this behind the scenes, all of them drawing salaries, which makes this a very expensive operation. Naturally we have a budget and it's pretty tight so we have to cut down where we can."

Bunny was looking morosely at the food on his plate. "So we have knockwurst instead of filet and an old Ford instead of a Ferrari."

"You won't lack for anything." Lasky searched for a nice way of putting it. "It's just that you won't be able to do any actual splurging."

"And that yacht out there, that would be actually splurging, wouldn't it?"

"If you used it, yes. It'll have to stay just anchored there."

"Grand," Bunny said. "Just grand."

Heavy footsteps sounded behind them.

"Ah, Hartley," Lasky said, glad of a respite. "This is Miss Brown and Mr. Calder."

The man who'd just walked in brought a stubby finger up to his forehead and flicked a salute at them. The muscles in his thick forearm bulged. "Hi," he said. His voice was like the rest of him, big and heavy. He wore a stained white tee shirt and an equally grubby apron that spread like a sail around the ample bulge of his stomach. He had short grizzled hair, and the battered face of an ex-wrestler. A chewed toothpick hung from the corner of his mouth.

"I'm happy to meet you, Mr. Hartley," Ella said.

The toothpick fluttered. "Likewise."

"Hartley knows all about the set-up," Lasky explained. "He's one of us. He's a judo expert and a specialist in hand guns. We don't think for a moment that you'll be in any danger from those men but just to be on the safe side Hartley will be in the house at all times. He's doubling as cook and will also see that you have anything you need."

Bunny prodded a knockwurst with a fork. The knockwurst resented it. "Where did you learn to cook, Mr. Hartley?"

"Army."

Bunny said, "Well, I got the wine wrong but I was right on the button with the food."

Ella gave him a withering look and said to the big man, "It's a very nice meal, Mr. Hartley."

His rugged face lit up like a lottery winner's. "Cookin's my hobby. The guns, the judo, they're okay, but a guy like me, he needs a creative outlet, you know?"

"Yes. Well, thank you, Hartley," Lasky said. "You can send up dessert anytime you're ready."

"Sure thing, Mr. Lasky. I made it myself," he confided to Ella. "Guess what it is."

Bunny, his head in his hands, said two words in a voice of doom. "Strawberry Jello."

"Hey, that's right," Hartley said. He lumbered out of the room, surprised by the accurate guess.

Lasky's hand started toward his half-rims, changed direction toward his fork, then finally settled for picking up his wine. "Hartley has a few rough edges but he's a dead shot and a black belt. You'll feel safe with him around."

Bunny moodily watched the beans congealing on his plate. "I'll feel hungry with him around."

After the Jello had arrived and everyone had finished, Lasky offered to show them the upstairs. As they climbed a wide carpeted staircase and moved under the arched ceiling of a long hall, Lasky told them that both wings of the house had been closed off, which had made the sleeping arrangements a little cramped. Although he didn't say then how cramped. They stopped outside a door, Lasky opened it and switched on a light. "This is where Lillian will sleep."

The room was an eighteenth-century masterpiece; four-poster bed, wall tapestries, Aubusson carpet, velvet drapes.

"She'll love it," Ella said. "The kind of room a little girl dreams about."

"Your room's through here." He led them into an adjoining room which was much bigger but furnished in the same manner.

Ella ran her hand over the silk canopy. "I'm running out of superlatives."

Lasky glanced uneasily at Bunny. "I'm afraid your accommodations aren't quite as spectacular, Mr. Calder."

Joking, Bunny said, "Don't tell me. I have to bunk in with Hartley."

"Amazing," Lasky said. "You were right about the Jello, too."

Bunny exploded. "You're kidding!" He threw a wild arm around his head. "Four people rattling round Buckingham Palace, here, and two of us have to double up?"

Lasky spread his hands. "I'm sorry, but we thought we'd have a married couple for this job. I don't know why it just seemed they'd be easier to get. So Mr. Silverman only opened two bedrooms up here and one in the servants' quarters. The rest are all locked up tight."

"I wish Mr. Silverman was locked up tight. Only two bedrooms . . ." Then Bunny got an idea. He lowered his voice and

73

looked as if he was ready to do everybody a big favor. "You know, this room's way big enough to share. I guess I don't mind curling up in that dressing room over there."

Ella turned to Lasky. "Give Mr. Calder this room. *I'll* bunk in with Hartley."

It was finally decided that Bunny would sleep on a sofa downstairs until another bedroom could be opened for him. But this was found to be impossible. All the furniture, being delicate antiques, was made for either sitting or reclining; nothing was made for sleeping. The only thing he could find that was long enough and wide enough for him to stretch out on was the snooker table. He and Lasky stood looking at it, both a little dubious. "If you put cushions down, I guess you'll be okay. We'll find something better for you for tomorrow night."

"Oh?" Bunny said. "You have one with a canopy?"

Mr. Lasky coughed, embarrassed. "Mr. Calder, I realize that since you've been here you've had a few, shall we say, surprises."

"Shall we say bitter disappointments?"

"Disappointments, then. And believe me, I'm truly sorry about them. We appreciate what you're doing for us and I wish you were happier about things."

"Just as long as they're all over. I don't want any more surprises. And they are all over, aren't they?"

"Well, er, there is one other thing I think you might want to be prepared for."

Bunny gave him a sick grin. "Hartley's been locked out and we have to share the snooker table."

Lasky was stopped from denying this by the swish of tires rolling over the gravel drive, and Ella's hurried entry into the room. "Will that be Lillian?"

Lasky imagined that it would be and led them through the house to the front door.

Out on the drive a station wagon had pulled up. A severely dressed, hatchet-faced woman got out and was followed by a small girl who moved quickly away from the car and ran up the steps toward them.

Ella smiled at her warmly and said, "Hello, Lillian. I'm so glad you're here."

The little girl answered in a harsh crackly voice. "Me too, I'm busting for a piss. Where's the john?"

It took Ella aback. "Er, through there and to the left."

74

Lillian brushed by her and as she trotted over the marble floor, took a quick look around her. "Holy Christ," she said, "Place looks like a Texas whorehouse."

Stunned, they stared after her. Then Bunny drew the government man aside.

"Mr. Lasky. That extra little surprise you were going to tell me about." He pointed a finger down the hall. "That's it, isn't it?"

Mr. Lasky reached for his glasses.

Chapter 10

As rich and splendid and influential as Oyster Bay is, it still has to line up for the sunrise. Fire Island is the first piece of land the sun touches before it sails across Great South Bay and wakes up Lindenhurst and Babylon, surprises a few early morning drivers on the Southern State Parkway, gets Farmingdale out of bed, warns Syosset of another day, another dollar, steps politely into Oyster Bay, then tiptoes across the Sound to break the news to Connecticut. But that particular morning the sun arrived in Oyster Bay with an unceremonious thump. Its slanting rays speared through a break in the cypress pines, crashed through the billiard room windows and hit Bunny in the eye. He groaned, rolled away from the treacherous light and dozed off again. Two hours later he began to dream that he was lying shipwrecked on a beach. A mermaid had put a golden apple in his hand but a fisherman had caught his hand in a net and was trying to land the prize. He woke out of it to find that his left hand had fallen into a pocket of the snooker table. He pulled it out and found that it was clutching a red ball. Bunny brought it up close to his face and tried an early-morning focus. When he recognized what it was, he remembered what he was sleeping on, the house in which he was staying, and the people with whom he was sharing the place, which brought forth another groan. He rolled off the table, swung his feet to the floor and blearily ran his tongue round his mouth.

"Coffee," he said.

He hitched at his pyjama bottoms, padded over the floor and found the door that led below stairs. Hartley was in the kitchen dressed in the same stained white outfit he'd been wearing the evening before. He greeted Bunny with a gravel-voiced "Hi." The toothpick that wagged in his mouth looked like the same one, too.

"Morning. You wouldn't have a cup of coffee on you, would you?"

"Sure thing." Hartley reached for a pot, poured a cup and handed it over. "How did you sleep?"

"God only knows." Bunny drank the coffee in three gulps, put the cup down and massaged his hand. Hartley waved the coffee pot at it.

"What happened to your hand?"

"Somebody snuck down in the night and sunk it in a side pocket." The coffee was starting to have its usual regenerative effect, and as he offered his cup for a refill he started to feel better. He said to the big man, "You always get up this early?"

"Bein' a chef ain't easy," Hartley confided. He picked the lid of a saucepan with a giant hand and tipped in a package of instant oats. "It's a demanding art." Brows puckered, concentrating, he began to stir the oats. "Anybody awake upstairs yet?"

"I don't know. I just got off the table."

"You meet the little kid last night?"

"Yes, indeed," Bunny said.

"What's she like?"

Bunny shrugged. "Like any nine-year-old marine."

"Tough little cookie, huh? Well it's a tough job she's got."

Bunny drained his cup and got to his feet. "Mind if I shower in your bathroom? I'm supposed to look like half a billion dollars for those reporters today."

Hartley told him to go ahead, and Bunny padded over the kitchen floor and went into the servants' quarters. The bathroom was small and cramped, and for some reason the hot water wasn't running and Bunny had to suffer a cold-water shower and shave. Then he dressed in the only place available: the closet in which his clothes had been hung. Thirty minutes later he was on his way upstairs, still feeling the effects of a rotten sleep, a painful shave and the bang he'd given his elbow pulling on his shirt in the closet. But he resolved not to let it show; if he was going to charm Ella—and he was going to do that or die trying—it wasn't going to be with a long face. He'd given it quite a bit of thought lying awake half the night on the snooker table. She was mad at him, hated him maybe. Okay, but that was now. But she was a woman and most women could be got around sooner or later.

And the sooner he got around her the sooner he could move off the table and into that nice comfortable bed in the master bedroom.

He found her in the breakfast room. "Good morning," Bunny said. She and Lillian were sitting at the table and Hartley was lumbering around putting down breakfast things in front of them. Ella was making an attempt to get acquainted with the girl; there hadn't been much time for that last night. After Lillian had arrived and found the john, Ella had shown her to her room and Lillian had gone straight to bed. Lasky had left the house soon after with a promise to be back early in the morning before the newspeople arrived.

Bunny gave the girls his number-three smile. "Everybody sleep well?"

Lillian, without taking her eyes off the corn flakes she was lapping up, said, "Hi," in a flat, disinterested voice. It was one more word than he got from Ella, and Bunny sighed inwardly and mentally plumped up the cushions on the snooker table.

Ella went on telling Lillian what an adventure it all was. "One minute I was choosing drapes at Bloomingdale's, the next I'm living in a millionaire's mansion."

Lillian stayed with the corn flakes; she didn't seem too interested. Looking at her, Bunny saw that the photograph Smathers had shown them had been a recent one. The short, fringe-cut brown hair, the freckled nose, the thin, expressionless face, it was all there. The rest of her was on the thin side, too. The skin on her face and arms was pale and clear and although the morning was already warm, she looked cold. She was dressed in sneakers, jeans and a yellow tee shirt; the clothes were neat but drab and a little too big for her. She wore nothing that could have been called an adornment unless you counted the colored Band-Aid high on her upper arm.

Ella tried again. "Well," she said brightly, "I think you're just about the bravest little girl I know, volunteering the way you did."

Lillian reached for her orange juice and said nothing.

Bunny tried to help out. He sat down at the table, winked at Lillian and said, "And I think you're definitely the bravest little girl I know." He gave her a pat on the knee.

Lillian's hand moved quickly and slapped Bunny's away. She snarled at him, "Watch it, Mac!"

Bunny was flabbergasted. "What did I do?"

"You know damn well what you did, you pervert."

Ella stared at him frostily. "What did you do to this child?"

78

Bunny appealed to the unjust gods. "Aw come on now. All I did was give her a friendly pat."

Lillian slitted her eyes at him. "You try to feel me up again and I'll cut your water off."

"Now just a second, young lady. You're going to have to learn the difference between a feel-up and a pat."

"I know the difference. That was a goddamn feel-up."

The relationship was saved from a major blowup, and a possible end to the whole charade right there and then, by Hartley, who swiftly intervened.

"You want some more corn flakes, kid?"

Lillian left off glowering at Bunny and looked up at Hartley. "Uh uh. But that was good."

Hartley modestly brushed some crumbs off the tablecloth. "You gotta understand corn flakes."

Lillian dug into her jeans, came up with a pack of cigarettes, stabbed one into her mouth and lit up.

"Lillian!" Ella said.

"Yeah?"

Ella immediately softened her voice, trying to make up for the admonishing tone she'd used. "Well, that cigarette . . ."

Lillian blew out a lungful of smoke. "It's okay. It's a filter." She stuck it back into her mouth and from a back pocket produced a newspaper and a pencil. Ella grabbed the chance to get friendly again. "Is that a crossword? You like crosswords?"

Bunny was watching them warily, nursing his wounded reputation.

"It's a scratch sheet," Lillian announced from behind the paper.

Hartley, coming round to take her plate, peeped at it. "Hey!" He'd seen something. "Burgundy Blue in the fifth."

Lillian squinched her eyes against the cigarette smoke. "Yeah, but look who's up—Rodriguez. He doesn't know his ass from a hole in the ground."

Bunny said, "Miss Brown, could I see you in private for a moment?"

She was about to ignore the request when she caught the slight nod of his head toward the little girl and the meaningful look he gave her.

"Would you excuse me, Lillian? I'll be back in a minute."

"Doughboy figures in the third," Lillian said.

"A shoo-in," Hartley agreed.

Bunny guided Ella across the floor and into a small drawing room. As soon as he'd pulled the sliding doors closed he started talking.

"Putting your personal aversion to me aside for one moment, we have a problem here."

Ella, all set to give him a withering burst, changed her mind. "I know we do."

Bunny pointed at the doors. "That kid's supposed to be worth twenty million dollars? A chain-smoking horse player with a mouth on her like a stevedore?"

"Look, there's something you must understand. That little girl's been brought up in an institution that I don't think gives a damn. She's had to get along by herself with nobody to lean on. Naturally she's a little hard-boiled. She protects herself behind a tough veneer in a tough world."

"And it's going to get tougher. Lasky must have been out of his skull choosing her. She's supposed to be my darling little daughter, the apple of my eye. She thinks I'm a sex fiend, for God's sake."

Ella bit her lip. "Maybe we should stop treating her like a nine-year-old. Hartley doesn't, and she seems to like him all right."

"Fine. Let Hartley play the millionaire and I'll fix the corn flakes."

There was a knock on the doors and they opened. "Good morning, I was told you were in here."

"Come on in, Mr. Lasky," Bunny said. "We were just talking about you."

Lasky saw by the expressions on their faces that he'd better close the doors. "You have a problem?"

"It's not going to work, Mr. Lasky. When you picked Lillian you cast for the wrong part. Machine Gun Kelly's daughter, okay. But a multimillionaire's? A man who could afford to send her to the best schools in Switzerland? Hire a duchess to teach her etiquette? Those reporters will laugh in your face."

Lasky waited till Bunny had blown himself out then quietly disagreed. "I think that little girl is a pretty good actress. No matter how she behaves now, I'm sure you'll find that when the time comes she'll be totally believable."

"I doubt that strongly. Isn't there some way we can keep her out of sight so the reporters know about her but don't get to meet her?" Bunny snapped his fingers. "I've got it. She's a hopeless diphtheria case, bedridden all her life."

Ella said, "That's sick. She's perfectly healthy and will respond like any other child given a little love and understanding."

"And a hot tip in the fifth," Bunny added.

Ella flared at him. "Your trouble is simple. If somebody proves immune to the big smile and your con man's charm you automatically put them down."

"She put *me* down. It was *my* hand she slapped away from her leg." Bunny looked at Lasky who was looking right back at him. "Wait. That's not as it sounds, Mr. Lasky, you see—"

Lasky waved away the explanation. "I wouldn't expect too much affection from her at the start, Mr. Calder. She's been in and out of foster homes all her life, so she's not likely to respond immediately to any new parental relationship. She's been burned too often."

"Exactly," Ella said. She gave a choked little sniff and blinked her eyes quickly.

Bunny looked uncomfortable. "Now, listen. I don't want to appear an unfeeling brute. I can appreciate her problem and I'm sorry about it. But I don't think she's right for the job, that's all."

Neither of the other two replied; they looked at him and let him stew.

"Hell, I like kids. I give to the Fresh Air Fund every year."

"Every nickel helps," Ella snapped.

Bunny charged in. "That's another problem with this setup, Mr. Lasky; the lady who's supposed to be my wife can't stand me. And it's going to show. And another thing: what happens when the newspeople find out that one of America's richest men sleeps on a billiard table? This thing isn't going to work in a million years."

"Mr. Calder"—Lasky chose his words carefully—"it may seem that we've gone into this thing in a rush, and to some extent that's true. But believe me, there's a lot of planning behind this and we feel that the idea is flexible enough for any contingency. You've read that press release by now so you know that we've made you a very eccentric person. If anything strikes those reporters as strange, they'll put it down to that."

"And when Lillian starts calling her bookie, that's supposed to be eccentric, too?"

"As I said, I'm sure she'll do a good job for us."

Bunny was still unconvinced, and he and Ella argued some more about it till Lasky told them that they didn't have any more time to discuss it. He led them back into the breakfast room, picked up Lillian and Hartley, and ushered everybody into the big living room. He waited till they were all sitting before he began.

"Before the newspeople get here I want to review the plan of action with you and also explain a bit more about what we expect to happen. Lillian and Hartley already know most of it, which only leaves

Mr. Calder and Miss Brown. So." He coughed and cleared his throat. "You know the basic idea—to give a barrage of publicity to a rich couple who think the world of their daughter, and, hopefully, tempt a certain group of people into kidnapping her."

Ella said, "You mean to attempt to kidnap her, surely."

"No, I mean the whole works." Lasky pushed at his glasses. "I must confess, Miss Brown, that I haven't been looking forward to telling you this, but for the plan to work, Lillian has to be actually taken by those men."

Alarmed, Ella looked at Lillian then back at Lasky. "But that sounds so unnecessary. Isn't it possible to arrest those people as they're about to take her?"

"To do that we'd have to have men close to her at all times and there's no way to make it look right. We'd run the risk of scaring those people off. The way we're setting it up we'll be able to follow them wherever they take Lillian, then move in when they think they're safe."

Bunny said, "But what if they spot you? They may panic. They may—" He stopped himself and flicked his eyes at Lillian, who was tapping the pencil against her teeth and frowning at the scratch sheet. She wasn't interested in what they were saying.

Hartley, his rocklike body incongruous in a Louis Quinze chair, was watching Lillian too. Ella hadn't taken her eyes off her.

"They won't spot us. We'll be following them from half a mile away. Lillian's going to lead us straight to them." Lasky crossed to her and pointed at her arm. "Miss Brown, what would you say this was?"

"A Band-Aid," Ella answered, wondering what he was getting at.

"Right. An ordinary, everyday Band-Aid covering a scratch or a cut. Only it isn't. This one's covering an electronic device that's glued to Lillian's skin. She's wired for sound."

Ella made a face. "Couldn't you have put it in her clothes?"

"Yes, but this is safer. Clothes can get lost. Besides, it didn't hurt, did it, Lillian?"

Lillian, still engrossed in handicapping horses, absently rubbed at the Band-Aid with her fingers. "No, but it itches like a bastard."

"Try not to scratch it, Lillian. It's pretty delicate." He said to Ella, "You'll have to watch that."

Hartley, admiration in his voice, said, "Tough as nails, that kid."

Lasky walked back to his chair and picked up where he'd left off.

82

"The bleeper sends a continuous FM signal that we can pick up and zero in on. This one's a new design and very powerful."

Bunny wanted to know its range.

"Three miles. Our receiver van is parked a quarter mile from the front entrance and picking up a signal right now. It's on a twenty-four-hour surveillance that's already started."

Ella received this with less than enthusiasm. Like a lot of people, gadgets confused her and so she tended not to have a great amount of faith in them. "There's no chance of anything going wrong? Losing the signal, maybe?"

"Not with the equipment we've got. The van's a British invention. Everybody has to buy a television license over there and they use these vans to track down license dodgers. It can pinpoint a TV signal exactly, not only the house it's coming from but which room in the house and which part of the room. It'll work the same way for us by tracking the bleeper. It's a very smart piece of machinery."

The explanation didn't cheer Ella any; she didn't trust machinery much, either.

Bunny raised a point that had been bothering him. "The recovery part sounds okay, but how about the actual grab? You're going to have to make it easy for them, but not so easy that they smell a rat."

"That's true. At first we thought we'd let them break into the house. There are no alarms on the gates, no dogs or anything, so they can get onto the grounds without any trouble. The house windows are all wired, but nothing these people couldn't take care of. But then we figured, why not make it even easier? Why not let Lillian simply ride a bike on the side drive? They'll obviously check the place out in the daytime—check exits and entrances etcetera—and if they spotted Lillian alone on the drive they'd be crazy not to grab their chance there and then."

"You don't think they'll figure that kind of luck is too good to be true?"

Lasky said no. "People welcome luck. Everybody likes to think he's lucky. Besides, they have no reason to suspect they're walking into something, and what could be more natural than a child riding a bicycle?" Lasky looked across the room. "How about it, Lillian, think you could handle that? A bike?"

Lillian stopped with the pencil point on her tongue. "What kind of bike?"

"What kind would you like?"

"Honda three fifty."

"Er, no. When I said riding a bike, I meant pedaling a bike. I think it would look more natural that way."

Lillian lowered the paper. "You want me to pedal a bike? All day?" The paper came up again. "Screw that."

"It wouldn't be for the entire day, Lillian. And you wouldn't have to actually pedal it all the time." Lasky looked round for help and Hartley did his best.

"Sure, kid, you could coast now and then."

"We'll get you one with gears," Lasky offered. "You'll hardly have to pedal at all."

Lillian shook her head. "Uh uh. No bike. I'll lose my cherry."

Bunny said to the ceiling, "It'll never work in a million years."

In an embarrassed half-whisper Lasky asked Ella if she'd have a word with Lillian later on. Then he resumed in his normal voice, glad to change the subject. "Now, the newspeople. They'll be throwing questions at you thick and fast, but if you've studied that news release there's nothing you won't be able to handle. Just remember to play up how devoted you are to your daughter." Bunny and Lillian swapped a distrustful look. "Her name is Sherrel Ann, remember. Miss Brown, they'll probably ask you questions designed for women readers, so you'll have to take care of them however you see fit. As long as you don't contradict any of the written facts, you're free to ad lib. Which should suit you, Mr. Calder."

Bunny wondered what he meant by that.

"There's only one thing more." Lasky stopped and his eyes swept over them and came to rest on Lillian. The other three followed his gaze. "Lillian," Lasky said gently.

"Yeah?"

"When the newspeople get here, you will watch your adjectives, won't you?"

The scratch sheet came down. "Huh?"

"I mean, you won't use any colorful descriptions . . ."

Ella came to the rescue. "What Mr. Lasky is trying to say, dear, is that you won't swear in front of the reporters."

"Oh, that." The scratch sheet went back up again. "Don't worry, I won't fuck up."

"Not in a million years," Bunny told the ceiling again.

84

Chapter **11**

By the time the newspeople started arriving an hour later, everybody was more or less ready. Bunny had taken another look at the background that had been written for him, Ella and Lillian had gone upstairs to change, and Hartley, at Lasky's tactful suggestion, had locked himself in his room. Even in his chef's outfit he looked too much like a bodyguard to be anything else.

Lasky had assembled the newsmen in the main library. There were about fifteen of them carrying a variety of cameras, tape recorders and notebooks. Two of them had back-pack video-tape cameras. Everybody was talking, and Lasky rapped against the door and tried to get some volume into his thin voice.

"Ladies and gentlemen, if I could have your attention for a moment." The hubbub died away. "I think we're all here now, so firstly I'd like to welcome you and thank you all for coming. My name is Lasky. I'm Mr. Bergstrom's lawyer and today I'm acting as his press agent, Mr. Bergstrom not having needed one previously." There was some polite laughter. "In a minute you'll meet Mr. Bergstrom and you may take your pictures and ask any questions you like. Then I'll introduce Mrs. Bergstrom and finally, to round out the family, their daughter, Sherrel Ann. You've all received releases so you know quite a bit about them, but no doubt you'll want to get the personal angle. So if I may ask you to be patient for just a few more minutes . . ."

He left them with that and went into the small drawing room where Bunny was waiting. "All set," Lasky said. "How do you feel?"

"Like six hundred million dollars."

"Fine. That's exactly the way I want you to feel. Don't forget, stress your money and talk Lillian up. That's why we're doing all this. Shall we go?"

Bunny gave a hitch to his chinos, smoothed down his polo shirt and followed Lasky into the library. The noise inside dropped away and Lasky said, "Ladies and gentlemen, it's my pleasure to introduce Don Ray Bergstrom."

Bunny smiled easily and said good morning, but his greeting was lost in the click of cameras and the sound of questions being thrown at him. Bunny took over immediately. He waved his arms and quietened them down.

"You'll all have your chance. I think it would be better if I signaled you one by one, okay?" He pointed a finger at a man on his left who had his pen poised all ready to go. The man asked the question everybody was planning to ask anyway.

"Mr. Bergstrom, how come you've hidden yourself away all this time and what has prompted you to come out of hiding now?"

"Well, for one thing I was very busy running my businesses and building up my personal fortune, which didn't leave me much time for anything else. But since then I've decided to ease up and enjoy my wealth. Hence I'm making my public debut, so to speak."

He glanced at Lasky, who looked pleased with the answer. Bunny pointed at another reporter but the man was beaten to it by a woman who spoke with the speed of a pneumatic drill.

"Any truth to the rumor about you and Jane Fonda?"

"I've never met Miss Fonda, but I think she's a fine actress." Bunny nodded at the reporter who'd been interrupted.

"Mr. Bergstrom, what's it feel like to be worth six hundred million dollars?"

"Secure. Next?"

"Do you intend to go into politics?"

"No. There are enough amateurs there already." Bunny didn't have to look at Lasky to know his reaction to that one. He pointed to another man, but the pneumatic drill jumped in again.

"Any truth to the rumor about you and Jackie Onassis?"

"I've never met the lady. Next?"

An intense-looking young man said, "Do you ever feel uncomfortable having so much money when the poor are starving?"

"Sure," Bunny answered. "But I'd feel more uncomfortable if the poor had my money and I was starving."

Somebody asked him the secret of his success. To square himself with Lasky Bunny said, "Long hours, hard work and an unshakable belief in the correctness of this country's foreign policy." He stabbed a finger at another man. "You?"

"Mr. Bergstrom, faced with sluggish stocks, lagging prices, underdeveloped markets and a weak dollar overseas, what do you recommend?"

"More exercise. Next?"

"Any truth to the rumor about you and Lita Lovegrove?"

For a wild moment Bunny was tempted to say that he'd been banging her blind for years, but instead he just shook his head and pointed to the next reporter.

"Mr. Bergstrom, do you number Howard Hughes among your acquaintances?"

Bunny saw a perfect opportunity to talk about his wealth as Lasky had asked him to.

"He's not what I'd call a close friend but we swap Christmas presents. A case of Scotch or an airplane maybe."

The pencils scribbled.

"Do you own a seven-oh-seven too?" somebody wanted to know.

"I did but it was too small. I traded it in on a jumbo. I took out the upstairs lounge and put in a putting green."

Again the pencils went at it. This was the kind of stuff they'd come for.

"How many cars do you own?"

"I don't know, five or ten. I'm not that crazy about cars."

"Which is your favorite, Mr. Bergstrom?"

"I like the fat English one, what is it called again?"

Fifteen voices said, "Rolls Royce."

"Right," Bunny replied. "But the one I use most is a Forty-eight Ford pick-up truck."

That was good for a number of surprised looks and an uncomfortable cough from Lasky's direction.

The questions switched to the house, and somebody asked how many people were on the staff.

"Counting the maid's maids, I'd say about thirty in all."

The same person asked where he'd found thirty domestics in this day and age.

"As a matter of fact, I get them all from this terrific personnel agency in New York. Gemstone Jobs. That's G.E.M.S.—"

He was interrupted by a reporter anxious to learn his favorite dish.

"My favorite menu is country sausage in pastry, fresh asparagus, lobster thermidor and chocolate mousse. But failing that, knockwurst and beans."

There were more surprised looks and another cough.

"Where's your chef from, Caravelle? La Grenouille?"

"No, before joining me Mr. Hartley was in Government service."

Fifteen pencils scribbled the words "Ex-embassy chef."

There was a fractional pause in the questioning and Lasky stepped in. "Perhaps this would be a good time to introduce Mrs. Bergstrom. I'm sure you'd like to ask her some questions, too. She's right outside." He left the room and returned a moment later with Ella. In a short, figure-hugging dress, and with her hair tied back, she looked marvelous. The cameras went into action again and when somebody asked for a shot of the Bergstroms together, Bunny readily obliged. He slipped his arm round her waist and pulled her close to him. Ella smiled for the cameras and went along with it and Bunny was the only person in the room who knew that what Ella really wanted to do was kick him in both shins again.

The questions started, led by some women reporters who'd been silent up till now.

"Mrs. Bergstrom, what do you think should be the woman's role in today's America?"

It had been decided that Ella should play the bland homemaker and leave the interest focused on Bunny and Lillian. Ella dished out the standard stuff.

"I think a woman should be happy to be a wife and mother but at the same time be free to pursue a career as well if that's what she wants."

"Who's your favorite dress designer? Is that a Bill Blass you're wearing?"

"No, I buy most of my clothes at Ohrbach's. A bargain's a bargain."

"Any truth to the rumor about you and Steve McQueen?"

Ella laughed. "The closest I've been to him is the sixth row back."

There were some more questions and then came the moment that Bunny was dreading. Lasky went out to get Lillian.

She must have been standing right outside the door because Lasky came straight back with her.

"Sherrel Ann Bergstrom, ladies and gentlemen."

There was a general murmur of "Ohs," and somebody said, "What a sweetie," as they crowded closer to take her photograph. It was lucky that they were concentrating on the daughter and not the millionaire, otherwise they would have caught Bunny staring at Lillian in astonishment.

She didn't look like Lillian at all. The sneakers, jeans and tee shirt had been replaced by a pink party dress tied in back with a bow, black patent leather shoes and white socks. And her hair, which previously looked as if it had been cut with a bread knife, had been shampooed and air-dried and flounced out prettily around her head. But it was her expression that surprised Bunny most. Lillian was actually simpering—coyly clutching a doll in her arms and simpering.

"Sherrel, what's it like being one of the richest kids in America?"

Lillian hid behind Ella and had to be coaxed out.

"Who's your favorite pop star, Sherrel?"

Lillian raised her eyes heavenwards and said in a sweet little voice, "Jesus is."

"What's your favorite thing in the world?"

Lillian, who was already holding Ella's hand, floored Bunny by grabbing his and smooching up beside him. "Mumsy and Daddykins."

"How about it, Mr. Bergstrom? She the apple of your eye?"

Bunny said something that sounded like "Wha?" and Ella quickly filled in for him.

"There's nothing we wouldn't do for her. Sherrel's our pride and joy." She kissed Lillian's cheek.

"Right," Bunny said, coming slowly out of his stupor. "Pride and joy."

"Would you say being a rich child has affected her adversely in any way?"

"Absolutely not," Bunny answered, back in the role. "Apart from giving her everything she wants, we've been careful not to spoil her."

"Actually," Lillian said in a Betty Boop voice, "Mumsy and Dadsy are very strict. They don't give me a single thing unless I ask for it."

Some of the newspeople swapped sour looks. One of them said, "Sherrel, is there anything you don't have that you really want?"

Lillian's face clouded and she looked ready to burst into tears. "My teddy. I want my teddy back." She tugged at Bunny's hand. "I think I left him on the drive."

Alarmed, Bunny said, "She's lost her teddy. I'll give five hundred dollars to the first person to find it."

Ella gave her a sympathetic hug. "Never mind, Sugar Plum, you've got fifty or sixty others."

Lillian began to cry. "I want that one."

Bunny crouched down beside her. "Don't cry, sweetheart. Tell you what, after all these nice people have left we'll drive into F.A.O. Schwartz and I'll buy it for you."

There wasn't a reporter in the room who didn't look ill.

Lasky spoke up. "If there are no further questions, ladies and gentlemen . . ."

The newspeople were glad to leave.

Lasky saw them out of the house, made sure they'd all left, then came back into the library looking very pleased. "Congratulations, everybody, you were all splendid. Lillian, that was a virtuoso performance."

Lillian, slumped in a chair, lit up a cigarette and blew a smoke ring.

Hartley ambled in. "It go okay? They buy it?"

"It went beautifully," Lasky told him.

Hartley beamed at Lillian. "I wished I could've been here."

"I wish you could have too," Bunny said. "They had you pegged as chef at the Caravelle."

"The Caravelle," Hartley breathed. His eyes shone.

"Hey, Hartley," Lillian said. "You want to shoot a little pool?"

"Sure, kid," he answered dreamily. He left the room with her, one of the finest chefs in the country.

Lasky was still tickled about the whole thing. "Miss Brown, you were exactly right. You too, Mr. Calder. That part with the teddy bear was a masterstroke. Although I must admit that I thought one or two of your answers a little too flip, but on the whole, it was a nice balance between rich man and eccentric."

Bunny nodded after the departed Lillian. "Sarah Bernhardt was the big surprise. After that teddy bear scene I thought she was going to announce her retirement."

"I hate to say it, Mr. Calder, but . . ."

Bunny held up both hands. "I know. I was wrong. She's a great little actress."

Ella rose suddenly from her chair. "She's also a child who's a lot closer to being kidnapped by a bunch of killers. Excuse me, please."

They watched her hurry from the room. Bunny said somberly, "She's not enjoying this one bit."

90

"You can't really blame her," Lasky replied. "She's a woman and she's bound to react emotionally. She thinks we're flirting with Lillian's life. You have to understand how she feels."

They were silent a moment, then Lasky said, "Anyway, the sooner this is over, the better all round. And I think we took a giant stride forward this morning. Tomorrow, everybody will know about the Bergstroms and their daughter. We'll be all set."

"Right," Bunny said. "All we'll need then are some kidnappers."

What Bunny meant of course, was "the" kidnappers.

But that's not what they got.

Chapter **12**

What they got was Syd and Errol.

Syd Reiner and Errol Breakstone.

Syd and Errol had never kidnapped anybody before, kidnapping being a little out of their line. Their line was the old fake accident shakedown. They'd go out to a suburban shopping plaza—any one would do as long as it was in a nice, respectable middle-class area—and look over the housewives as they maneuvered their station wagons into the parking lot and went in to shop for the family's dinner. They'd pick a woman who was either a nervous, unsure driver or one who looked as though she wouldn't accuse the butcher of weighing his thumb or complain about getting a wobbly buggy at the A&P. When the woman returned with her marketing Errol would have positioned himself unobtrusively beside a nearby car. Syd would be a few yards further away. When the shopper started her car and swung it out of the parking space a pedestrian would appear from nowhere and there would follow, in chronological order, a resounding thump, a squeal of brakes, a horrified lady driver, and Errol stretched out on the ground. This is where Syd came into the act. Rushing up to his partner, who'd be moaning and rolling around, he'd tell the lady in no uncertain terms that he'd seen "everything" and she was in deep trouble because his brother was a lawyer and what did she mean driving like a maniac and didn't she have any respect for human life and just look at that man. It was only a short step from there to where Errol, being helped shakily to his feet, would agree to settle out of court for twenty dollars, although it was frankly against Syd's advice, which was that these crazy speed fiends should be prosecuted and kept off the roads.

It usually worked like a charm, except for now and then when some busybody would call the police, which would effect a rapid improvement in Errol's condition. They'd been caught and hauled up for it a number of times but, by and large, their little act provided a fairly steady and remunerative employment for them both.

The contrast between them was considerable. Syd looked like a health-food addict on a diet, while Errol looked like an ex-light heavyweight, which he was. He had the fighter's thick neck and sloping shoulders, and a face that looked as if it had stopped every punch that had ever been thrown at it, which was very nearly the truth. A New Yorker by birth, he'd traveled the Midwest with a boxing troupe, playing state fairs and carnivals. The barker on the stage outside the covered ring would ask the crowd to send up a challenger to go three rounds with the pro pug ugly who, his hands taped and wearing a dressing gown, stood beside him looking mean and unbeatable. When Errol, claiming to be an upstate farmer or a downstate truck driver, would step forward and pick up the gauntlet the crowd would line up to pay their money to see if the local boy could do it. The crowd never seemed to be bothered by the fact that, when Errol stripped off inside, he was wearing Everlast shorts and boxing shoes. Errol was supposed to win, of course. The scenario called for Errol to go down under a flurry of blows in the second round, come to at the count of seven, gamely push himself to his feet and K.O. his opponent, thus demonstrating the kind of grit you were up against if you were foolish enough to tangle with a native of Nebraska or Kansas or Iowa or wherever.

The only problem was, Errol seldom survived the flurry of blows. No matter how brief it was or how lightly thrown, Errol, whose jaw was akin to the finest Waterford crystal, never could beat a ten count even when it took fifteen seconds. They tried switching to a body attack, but Errol proved to have glass ribs as well. Finally, with forty-three straight defeats under his belt—including two in the same night in Fulton, Missouri—the management threw a bucket of water over him, brought him around, and fired him. Errol had then drifted back to New York, where he'd met up with Syd and gone into a completely different line of business—the fake accident routine—although it wasn't that much of a change, seeing as how he still ended up dazed and supine.

Syd, on the other hand, had always made his living by brain rather than brawn. At five six, one twenty, Syd didn't have much brawn. He didn't have much brain, either, but what he had he used with quite a bit of imagination. Syd had sharp features, quick, darting eyes and looked a lot like a pet rodent that somebody had bought a suit for. Previous to meeting Errol he'd been active in charity and politics. With a collection box featuring the correct label, which a printer ran off for him for a large consideration, he'd collected for the Red Feather, The American Legion, The Lighthouse, The March of Dimes, The National Heart Fund, The Red Cross, The United Appeal, The Lions, Rotary, Republicans for Rockefeller, Republicans Against Rockefeller, The Chicago Seven, and, his own invention, The San Francisco Nine, which he claimed, when questioned by a cop, was the Giants. Between collection days he'd find a shiny new Cadillac left on a long-term parking meter, tie some bunting to the aerial, rest a hand-printed sign on the hood and raffle it off for the Childrens' Aid Society. Syd had finally been forced out of the charity game when he'd been caught selling a little booklet entitled, "The Ten Most Effective Prayers" in the terminal ward at Bellevue. He'd met Errol shortly afterwards and gone into his present line of work. Syd liked working with Errol because Errol let him do all the thinking, and it was true that he was marginally better equipped for it than his partner—while Errol's tent career had not exactly scrambled his brains they were definitely sunny-side up, and by anybody's count he was a slow thinker. Together they made a strange team—one of them big and dumb, the other small and not much brighter.

On the morning after the newspeople had made the trip out to Oyster Bay, Syd and Errol were sitting at their breakfast table eating Cheerios, Errol's favorite. They shared an apartment together in an old building on Twenty-eighth Street just west of Sixth, in that curious, nondescript area given over to small wholesale furriers and millinery supplies. Their apartment was old and tatty and the breakfast table was also the hall stand. Syd had a copy of New York's picture newspaper propped open in front of him and was deep in a feature article. Errol reached for the cereal box and winced.

"Ooh!" He rubbed a hand gingerly over his body. "No more Oldsmobiles."

Syd went on reading.

94

"Hey, Syd. How about I pick the car today? One of them little foreign jobs."

His partner was more interested in his paper. He flicked it with a finger.

"You read this in here?"

"What?"

Syd turned the paper around and pointed. "This bit here."

Errol reached for it. "Ooh!" He took the paper and pored over it for a long time. Then he looked up. "No, I didn't read it."

"Well? What do you think?"

Errol blinked at him. "Wait till I read it."

"Read it out loud," Syd told him. "I think we could make a bundle out of this." He leaned back in his chair, clasped his hands behind his head and concentrated. "Go ahead," he said, his eyes mere slits.

Errol began to read heavily and slowly, nodding as he successfully navigated the double syllables. " 'Bil-lion-aire comes out of hid-ing. Today Don Ray Berg-strom franzencroy as one of the rich-est men in America. Franzencroy he had hid-den him-self—' " His partner cut in on him.

"Hey, Errol."

"What?"

"What's with all the franzencroys?"

Errol pointed to the article. "Hard word. It's easier to say franzencroy."

Syd accepted that. "Well, listen, get to the part about that guy's daughter. Just read that part."

Syd resumed his former position, his whole being concentrated on pure thought. Thirty seconds later he said, "Go ahead." Then, after another thirty seconds, "It's near the bottom."

Shortly after that, Errol began again. " 'Their daughter, Sherrel Ann, is, as Mr. Bergstrom franzencroys it, "The apple of our eye. We would do anything for her.' "

"Get to the bit about the teddy bear," Syd urged.

Errol plodded through the newsprint and found it. " 'Mr. Bergstrom was so upset by the loss that he offered fifty, no five hundred for its re . . . for its re-franzencroy.' "

"That's it. That's the part." Syd tilted his chair forward with a bang and stared at his partner intently. "You get what I'm thinking?"

Errol began to smile. He liked the idea. "We go out there and find the teddy bear."

"Better than that. If that guy would pay five hundred bucks for the little kid's toy, what do you think he'd pay for the little kid?"

Errol checked the newspaper. "She lost too?"

Syd shook his head. "Not right now. But what if she got lost? What if somebody snatched her? How much do you think he'd pay to get her back?"

Underneath Errol's scarred eyebrows a light flickered and finally went on. "More than five hundred bucks."

"A lot more. Maybe a million more."

"Think of it," Errol breathed. "A million five hundred."

Syd was starting to get excited; he could practically taste that money. No more hustling; no more collecting for the Police and Firemen's Widows Fund. No more bullying rattled housewives out of a lousy couple of sawbucks. A fast, simple job, and it was Florida for the rest of his days.

"It's worth a try, Errol," he said, the excitement building. "It's worth a try." The excitement was building in Errol, too.

"It sure is, Syd. It sure is."

Syd's right index finger knifed the air as he made an executive decision. "We'll go out there and take a look this afternoon."

Errol's expression changed. *"We're* going to do it?"

"Errol, I want you should go out and get us a car. Something ordinary. A Chevy maybe." Syd let his lids lower. "We're going to make ourselves a million dollars."

"A million . . ."

Syd leaned across the table, enjoying the moment. He held his hand out. "Deal?" he asked. "Fifty-fifty?"

His partner nodded. "Deal," he said. He stretched out his hand. "Ooh!"

Chapter 13

"Ooh!" Bunny moaned. He disentangled the blanket, climbed down, and put a hand to his aching back. He dimly remembered turning away from the sunrise again and rolling off the cushions, which meant he'd slept for hours with nothing under him but hard green baize. He massaged his spine. It was incredible: here he was, the star of the show, fresh from a triumphant press conference, forced to sleep for a second night like a drunk in a pool room. Lasky had apologized profusely, claiming he'd clean forgot about it, what with the reporters and everything, and he'd promised faithfully to get another bedroom opened the next day. So it had been back to the snooker table, Ella and the master bedroom still being as much out of the question as ever. Perhaps more so.

With a hand pressed to his lumbar regions Bunny made his way down to the kitchen, where Hartley was sitting at the table, newspapers spread in front of him. When he looked up, the expression on his face seemed to say that he'd found the meaning of life, which was the exact opposite of what Bunny's seemed to say.

Hartley said, "Paris."

Bunny lowered himself carefully into a chair. "Coffee," he replied. Then a moment later, "Pardon?"

Hartley pushed at the papers. "It's in here. About me." He was in a daze. "Ex-chef at the U.S. Embassy in Paris."

"Congratulations. Coffee?"

Hartley came out of it and pushed his thick frame out of his chair. Carefully, delicately, he unscrewed the top of a Maxwell House jar, dug a teaspoon in, tipped it into the coffee cup in front of him, reached for the kettle, poured water on with a flourish, stirred it just so, and presented it to Bunny as if it were first prize at Dijon.

"How is it?" Hartley wanted to know, anxious.

"Three stars."

Hartley looked down at his hands, spread his fingers, and turned them over, marveling at them. "It's all in here."

The second cup of three star opened Bunny's eyes enough to check the papers. They'd made page one in the *News,* and page three in the *Times.*

"Good shot of Ella," Bunny said. "And will you look at Lillian? She's scuffing her toe in the carpet." He skimmed through the articles. "It's all in here—the house, the cars, the jumbo jet. Lasky should be pretty happy."

Hartley said, "You made the TV news last night, too. And we got *Time* and *Newsweek* to come."

"Hey, the *Times* did a profile on me. Listen to this: 'Trim athletic figure, a nice smile and a ready wit.'" Bunny grinned up at Hartley. "Wait till Ella sees that." He read on further then looked up again. "Did you see this? About lobster thermidor being my favorite dish?"

Hartley gave him a big smile. "Yeah, I saw that."

Bunny looked over at the pots and pans arrayed on the stove. He asked hopefully, "What's for lunch today?"

"Your second favorite dish."

Bunny closed his eyes and massaged his spine again. He thought of the leaky shower, the cold water shave and the tiny closet that awaited him. And of the army lunch after that. And of the army dinner. And, if Lasky slipped up again, of another night on the rack. He sighed and said, "Hartley, old man, I've been rich and I've been poor, and believe me, poor is better."

"Ooh!" Lillian said. She stepped painfully off the bike she'd been trying to learn to ride for the last half hour and let it fall to the drive. "Jesus, my coozy's killing me."

"It's just that you're not used to it," Ella told her. "You're saddle sore now, but it will be all gone tomorrow."

Lillian kicked at the handlebars. "If it ain't, I'm going to be all gone tomorrow."

Ella picked up the bike for her, and Lillian reluctantly mounted it

98

again. She pedaled unsteadily away. "That sonofabitch Lasky," she said for the fifth time.

Ella heard footsteps coming toward her but didn't look around. The tread was too light for Hartley and too heavy for Lasky which meant it had to be Bunny. Which meant she wasn't interested.

Bunny had come out of the house in a bad mood. His back still hurt, he'd cut himself shaving, and banged his ear on a coat hanger in the closet. But when he saw Ella his mood changed. A lovely girl on a lovely day, how could you be glum? She was wearing khaki pants and a white blouse that tapered down tight. The pants hugged her body, too. Bunny envied the pants. He stopped, tugged at his shirt, and reset his face in a smile. Today was a brand-new day, and if he played it right, maybe tonight could be a brand-new night. Hell, he'd approached this the wrong way; you couldn't rush a girl like Ella; she was the type that took a lot of wooing. Maybe something old-fashioned would do the trick. A picnic maybe. A picnic . . . not a bad idea. Get old Hartley to whip up some knockwurst sandwiches, drive someplace in the country, birds in the trees, a rippling stream—a long, slow drive back, dinner someplace nice on the way, then maybe a nightcap when they got back. Resolved, he stepped up to her. He followed her gaze, which was riveted on Lillian a little way up the drive, and said, careful to strike a note of concern, "She doesn't seem to like it much."

Ella, edgy and worried about the child, rounded on him fast. "Would you like it if you'd never ridden a bike before and had to ride one all day every day for goodness knows how long? Why don't you try a little sympathy for a change, or is that expecting too much?"

Bunny put a stop order on the knockwurst sandwiches.

Lillian was riding shakily toward them.

"Don't look down, dear," Ella called. "Keep looking straight ahead."

"Way to go, Lil. You're riding like a champ."

"Up yours," Lillian growled as she wobbled past.

Bunny shook his head. "I don't know, Lillian and I just don't seem to be as close anymore."

Ella, watching the girl, didn't choose to hear him. Bunny asked her if she'd seen the morning papers.

"I saw them," she said through tight lips.

"Good picture of you and Lillian."

No reply.

99

Bunny bent and picked up some pebbles off the drive. He buzzed a few at a nearby tree. "Did you, er, see the profile on me?"

"I saw it."

Bunny chuckled. "Honestly, some of those reporters . . . all that stuff about me being athletic, good-looking, a ready wit . . . I thought that was a bit exaggerated, didn't you?"

"I thought it was a downright lie."

Bunny threw all the pebbles at the tree. "Okay, back to work. Come on, we'd better leave her. She's doing fine."

"I'm going to stay for a while."

"Ella, remember why she's riding that bike. She's supposed to be alone out here."

The girl swiveled her head around, her eyes suddenly anxious. "They won't come today, will they? It's too soon, surely?"

Bunny shrugged. "Who knows? The news has broken. It's possible."

Ella held her gaze for a moment then looked back down the drive. The bike was wobbling less now, and Lillian seemed to be getting the knack. She pedaled past a line of trees heading toward the side gate and disappeared around a bend. There was something very symbolic about it.

Chapter 14

Errol got back to the apartment around two that afternoon. "I got one, Syd."

Syd threw down a magazine and jumped up. "Something ordinary?"

"A Chevy."

They locked the door behind them and went down the stairs and out onto Twenty-eighth. Syd looked up and down the street. "Where'd you park?"

Errol pointed to the car standing at the curb in front of them. "Right here." It was a mid-sixties Impala with white sidewalls and red cotton baubles running all around the windows. Hanging from the rear-vision mirror were two pairs of baby shoes, four crosses, two Saint Anthony medals, an outsize pair of dice, a two-foot rubber skeleton, and a hula girl whose pelvis was a bottle opener. Mounted on the dash, in ornate metal holders, were three religious pictures and two bunches of artificial flowers in plastic vases, while lining the bench beneath the rear window were four embroidered red velvet cushions. The seats had been upholstered in tiger-striped nylon, and the body had been painted with a four-inch brush and two gallons of Dutch Boy Flamingo Pink Supergloss. The suspension had been lowered so that the car was barely six inches off the ground, and the twin aerials had been raised and extended so that they soared over the car like fishing poles on a Chris-Craft.

Syd looked from the car to his partner. "You call this ordinary?"

"You said a Chevy."

"I didn't say this Chevy."

"The keys were in it," Errol said defensively.

His partner said that it would have to do and got in on the passenger side. Errol slid in behind the wheel. Lasky had been careful to give the address of the house in the news release and the *News* had mentioned it in passing, so with a copy of the newspaper beside them, they set out for Oyster Bay.

The traffic was light to moderate that afternoon, and apart from a Caliente that offered to drag them at a red light in Woodside, and a GTO that buzzed them on the Expressway, the trip was pleasant and uneventful.

Swinging into Oyster Bay Road and continuing past the wall of the estate, they were surprised to find a minor traffic jam outside the main gates. A uniformed policeman was standing there waving the cars on.

"Hey, Syd," Errol said.

"What?"

"Some other guys got the same idea."

"Naw. Hicks come out to take a look where the millionaire lives is all."

They rolled up to the car ahead and inched forward in a slow line past the gates. "Let's go. Let's go," the cop was saying. Most of the cars did a U-turn and crept back on the other side of the road for one more look, then sped off.

Syd's eyes narrowed, his brain smoothly ticking over. "There's gotta be another entrance to a place this big. Maybe a couple. Let's see what's up ahead."

They kept going till the wall turned a corner. They made the turn and followed it, but the wall ran all the way to the water without a break.

Syd suggested they try the other side and they retraced their route and passed the main gates again, then turned down the lane where the wall ended. The road was the exact twin of the other, except this one led to a break in the wall; a side gate of the same rococo design as the main ones, but smaller and not as grand. Errol swung the car around and drifted up to it.

"That's it," Syd said.

"Yeah. Looks like it."

Syd made another observation. "You can see part of the house through the trees there."

Errol squinted for better vision. "Where?"

"On the left. Just past that kid on the bike."

"I see it. Yeah." Errol offered an observation of his own. "Them gates, they don't look so tough."

"If they are," Syd proposed, "we could go over the wall and climb down that tree."

"Which tree?"

"The one that kid on the bike's standing under."

"I see it," Errol said. His eye was drawn to the kid. He frowned. "Hey, Syd."

"What?"

Errol thought better of it. "Nothing."

Syd studied the layout, his keen, rat-like eyes taking in every detail, committing it to memory.

His partner was still bothered by something. He picked up the newspaper and took a look at the picture of the millionaire's daughter. He looked back at the kid on the bike. "Hey, Syd."

"What?" Syd was busy estimating how much rope they'd need for the wall.

"That kid on the bike," Errol said. "She look like someone to you?"

Syd shifted his attention to her. "Yeah," he said slowly. "Your brother's kid, Alice."

"You know who else she looks like?"

"Who?"

"The kid on the bike."

"No, I mean, who else she looks like."

"This kid in the paper here."

Syd took a look at the newspaper. "Naw," he said. "She looks more like Alice." Then he took a second look and wasn't so sure anymore. He reached for the door handle. "Come on, we'll find out. Bring the newspaper."

They went cautiously up to the gate, unlatched it, and crunched up the drive toward Lillian, who'd stopped riding and was watching them approach her, a blank expression on her face.

They stopped in front of her and consulted the paper. They looked at the photograph and back at Lillian, still unsure. Syd ran his finger down the column of type till he came to her name which he read out loud.

103

"Sherrel?"

"Yeah?" Lillian said.

Errol plucked her off the bike, put a hand over her mouth, tucked her under one arm, and started walking for the gate. Syd trotted ahead and opened the car door. Errol put her on the rear seat and got in beside her while Syd slid in behind the wheel and took the car away fast. With the windows rolled up, and the car whipping along the main road, Errol released her.

Lillian closed her eyes and sank back into the blissful comfort of an upholstered seat. "Thank Christ," she muttered.

"She say something?" Syd asked.

"Praying," Errol said.

Flaked out in a bergère chair, his head on his shoulder, his arms dangling, Bunny was catching up on some of the sleep he'd been missing when the phone on the coffee table beside him buzzed and went on buzzing. His eyes opened fractionally as he groped for the phone and brought it up to his ear. Hartley's raspy voice told him that Lasky was calling on an outside line. There was a note of urgency in his words that Bunny hadn't heard before and it brought him fully awake. He climbed out of the chair and crossed the room to the outside phone.

"Hello? Mr. Lasky?"

Lasky's voice was quicker, too. "Mr. Calder, I'm calling from one of our cars. They've got her, Mr. Calder. We're tailing them now. We're about a quarter mile behind them going toward Manhattan."

"Wow. They didn't lose any time."

"That's all right with us. I just wanted you to know the position."

"Everything going okay, then?"

"Perfect. We're picking up a good strong signal. As soon as we get Lillian clear I'll call you. And I'd tell Miss Brown. Break it to her gently but assure her we're on top of things. I'll talk to you later."

Lasky rang off and Bunny put the phone down, thinking about it, wondering about the best way of telling Ella. When he turned around he saw he wouldn't have to. She was standing in the doorway watching him, her face tight. She spoke before he did.

"They've got her, haven't they?"

"Yes."

Ella didn't say any more, just stood there looking at the carpet, and Bunny went to her.

104

"Lasky says it's working perfectly. They're right behind Lillian and he figures they'll have her out in no time."

Ella said softly, "Damn stupid idea . . ."

Bunny brought his hands up to take her shoulders then dropped them again. He said, a little helplessly, "Ella, it's okay. Lasky's got a whole raft of men with him. Lillian will probably be back here in a couple of hours. Maybe less. Lasky said he'd call the minute she's safe."

The girl nodded her head and went over to the chair by the phone. She locked her hands together in her lap and sat back to wait.

The van was short, high, box-shaped. From its roof a circular aerial projected, which revolved slowly. Inside the van a man sat in front of a lighted console that was a riot of buttons and switches. He watched a screen and called directions to the driver in front of him. The van turned off Seventh into Twenty-eighth and rolled slowly on, paused outside a shabby apartment building then moved on again and turned up Sixth.

Ten blocks away, and traveling fast, Lasky, a phone to his ear, repeated an address. "One fifteen West Twenty-eighth, second floor front on the right. Got it." He picked up a radio mike and spoke rapidly into it.

At that time of day the traffic was beginning to pick up on Twenty-eighth, the rush hour well under way, people in the street, some trucks making late deliveries. Nobody paid much attention to the eight men who arrived on the street at thirty-second intervals. And nobody noticed the short-barrel shotguns under their jackets. Nor did anybody give a second glance at the man with half-rim glasses who walked round the corner from Sixth and stopped to look in a store window opposite a rundown apartment house. He seemed engrossed in the display of felts and fabrics; so much so that he didn't seem to notice the man who came out of the store and stood looking into the window next to him.

"All set," the man said to the glass. "They're clearing the second floor now. It looks right into that apartment."

"Right," Lasky said. He drifted away from the window and went into the store entrance and climbed the stairs. The first floor was divided into several showrooms, and the staff was being politely herded into an inner office at the back. Lasky walked to a front window and joined the man stationed there.

The man handed him binoculars. "I make two men for sure. I think I caught sight of the kid."

Lasky knelt, trained the glasses on the window across the street and focused for the short distance. The windows were grimy and it was hard to see clearly.

"I've got the men. I don't see—wait! There she is. That's Lillian."

"Right on the button," the other man said.

Lasky kept on looking. "Still only two men."

"Maybe the other two are coming later."

"We won't move till they do."

They turned at the sound of somebody approaching. A big, hard-looking man was moving toward them in a half-crouch. "Lieutenant Gurley," he said.

Lasky thanked him for coming. "Seeing this is your precinct, I wanted to make sure we didn't tread on anybody's toes in the Department. Have you been briefed on what's happening here?"

The big man nodded. "How's it going?"

Lasky handed him the binoculars. "We're waiting for the rest of the group. Then we'll go in."

The policeman squinted through the glasses. "Those windows. I can't get a good look." He brought the glasses down and used his own vision. "What did you say that number was again?"

"One fifteen."

"One fifteen West Twenty-eighth." He frowned over it. "I don't know, but that sure rings a bell."

Lasky looked at him. "You know it?"

"I've seen it on the blotter, I'm sure of it."

Lasky's offsider said, "They're moving into the other room."

Lieutenant Gurley brought the binoculars up again. "I got 'em," he said.

His next words were spoken a whole lot slower and with a great deal of astonishment.

"Holy Mother McCree!"

"What is it?"

"It's Syd and Errol, that's what it is."

Lasky looked confused. "You know those men?"

The lieutenant nodded slowly. "I knew I knew that address."

Lasky said, "They must have been hired to pick up the child."

Gurley's head movement changed from a slow positive nodding to a slow negative shaking. He said, "You wouldn't hire Syd and Errol to pick up the laundry."

106

"What?"

"They're cheap con artists. Hackers, more like it." The policeman coughed, embarrassed. "Mr. Lasky," he said, "I'm afraid you've got yourself a couple of ringers here."

Over in one fifteen West Twenty-eighth Street, Errol stood looking at Lillian, who was sitting in a chair. She sat straight, her arms folded, watching them silently.

"Smart kid," Errol said. "No noise, nothing."

"Knows when she's well off," Syd said darkly. He was scanning the newspaper again.

"Here it is, Bernie Silverman."

"Who he?"

"Used to own the kid's house. Got to be listed." He reached for the phone.

"Why?"

"I want to talk to the kid's old man. The ransom."

Errol didn't like the sound of it. "Aren't we gonna write one of them notes? You know, with the glue and the cut-out paper and stuff."

His partner had the phone in his hand and was dialing. "This is faster."

Syd got the number for the Nassau exchange, hung up and dialed it. "You got a number in Oyster Bay for Silverman? Bernie Silverman?" With the stub of a pencil he jotted down the answer on the newspaper. "Okay, great." He cut the connection and started to dial again.

Errol stopped him. "Hey, Syd."

"What?"

Errol jerked his head in the direction of the other room and moved toward it.

Syd followed. "What?" he said again.

Errol lowered his voice. "I don't like it, Syd. They could trace the call. They can do stuff like that."

"Naw, they won't have time. I ain't gonna chatter all day."

"Let's send a note, Syd. I like cutting things out."

Syd started back toward the other room. "Come on. Quit worrying."

Errol looked dubious but followed his partner, who picked up the phone. He glanced at Lillian. She hadn't budged; she still sat there like a piece of stone. If she was scared, she wasn't showing it.

Syd dialed, the phone buzzed in his ear and was answered immediately by a woman's voice that said quickly, "Mr. Lasky?"

"Lasky? Naw, you got the wrong—hold it. Lemme speak to Bergstrom."

"Who is this?"

"Put Bergstrom on."

A moment later a man's voice said, "Hello."

"Bergstrom? We got her. Your kid. You want to see her again you better find a million bucks in a hurry."

"What's that?"

"You heard. A million dollars. I'll call back tonight and let you know where and when for the drop. Get the money."

As Syd hung up, the door burst open and eight men with shotguns rushed into the room. Syd's mouth dropped open as the hands grabbed him. He looked in dumb amazement at the hard faces surrounding him, then looked over at his partner who was being similarly treated.

Errol looked back at him sadly. He shook his head and said, "I told you, Syd."

Chapter 15

"It was a fluke, that's all. One of those things that couldn't be foreseen." Lasky was doing his best to play it down. "It was nobody's fault. You can't protect against a freak thing like that."

Ella said, "The main thing is Lillian's back safe." She smiled delightedly at the little girl who was eating the bacon and egg sandwich that Hartley had just brought her. He was clucking around her like a hen. "The kid came through," he kept saying.

"There's no real harm done," Lasky said. "It's been kept from the press so we don't have to worry on that score. And it did prove that the system works. That bleeper led us to her like a neon sign."

Over by the window, Bunny mentioned something that had been bothering him. "If it happened once this way, it could happen again. What if it turns out to be open season on Lillian?"

"No, no. This was an isolated incident, a one-in-a-million shot. There's no doubt in my mind that the next people who try will be the people we're after."

"And if they're not?" Ella asked. "Even if your system is foolproof, she can't go on being kidnapped all the time." She turned back to the girl. "It must have been awful for you."

Lillian swallowed a mouthful of sandwich. "It got me off that goddamn bike."

"Believe me, Miss Brown, those men will come. And soon. The

best thing we can do is put this down as a trial run and get back to the game plan."

Ella kept at him; her mood was a mixture of happiness at Lillian's return and anger that it had happened at all. "You mean you're not going to take any steps to make sure we don't have another mistake?"

"That's impossible. But I'll tell you what we can do—step up the pace. Pile on the publicity. Maybe tomorrow you could take Lillian on an outing, just like any parents with their daughter. We'll make sure the press is on hand. It's bound to get a spread; you're still good news value."

"That's not bad," Bunny said to Ella. "The more coverage we get the more chance we have of attracting those people. And the sooner they'll act."

"How about it, Lillian?" Lasky asked. "It's your outing. Where would you like to go?"

"Aqueduct."

"I've got it," Bunny said. "The Central Park Zoo."

Lillian looked at him. "The zoo? What, do you want to see the bunnies humping?"

"It just so happens," Bunny replied, indignant, "that the reason I suggested the zoo is because it's very near the Plaza, and I thought you might like to have lunch in the Oak Room."

Hartley couldn't believe his ears. "You want to go eat at the Oak Room when you can have lunch here?"

Lasky was looking alarmed. "The Oak Room's pretty pricey. I like the idea of the zoo, but couldn't you all have lunch in the park?"

"You mean hot dogs? Come on, Mr. Lasky." Bunny got tough. "After what Lillian went through today you owe her. And we'll go in the Lamborghini, too."

"Oh no. I draw the line there."

"Okay, we'll settle for the Rolls."

Lasky said, "Mr. Calder, that raid today, with all those men, that cost us a lot of money. We're over budget now. You can have your lunch at the Plaza but you'll have to take the pick-up."

Bunny was scandalized. "We can't pull up at the Plaza in that thing. They may even throw us out of the Midtown Tunnel."

"Mr. Calder, you're forgetting that you're an eccentric millionaire."

"I'll look like a stark raving millionaire."

Ella cut the squabble short. "The pick-up will be fine, Mr.

110

Lasky." She raked Bunny with a scathing look. "Most of the world doesn't have any kind of transportation."

Bunny wearily acknowledged defeat. "I know, think of all the walking Chinese."

Lasky got up from his chair. "All right, tomorrow then. I'll set it up."

At one ten the following afternoon the car that glided up to the curb in front of the Plaza's carpeted steps was a Cadillac Eldorado with tinted, one-way glass. The doorman leaped to open it. The next car to arrive was a long-body Chrysler Imperial with an opera window each side. Then came a brand-new Lincoln Continental with a chauffeur up front. Then a forty-eight Ford pick-up with plant boxes in the back. The doorman pulled his hand away as if the truck were on fire. Bunny opened the door himself and went round and helped Ella and Lillian out. He handed the doorman a dollar bill and said, as they swept by him, "Keep an eye on it, will you?"

The doorman wasn't trying to be rude, he just didn't understand. "What am I supposed to do with it?"

"Water the plants," Lillian said.

They went up the steps and through the revolving doors, crossed the small foyer and followed the corridor round to the Oak Room. Bunny had called ahead for reservations and they were seated immediately. He'd used another name but he could see that the maître d' had spotted him, and a few of the other diners, too. Not that it mattered; they didn't have to put on their act till after lunch when they met the newspeople.

Bunny settled himself comfortably and took in the large baronial room. Waiters flittered to and fro, chafing dishes flickered, and there was a soft clinking of silver and expensive glassware. The place hummed with a mixture of brisk efficiency and cosy ambience. Bunny felt fine; partly because of where he was, partly because he'd had a good night's sleep at last. Lasky had had the chauffeur's quarters opened up for him and he'd been able to sleep in a bed again. It wasn't the bed he'd have chosen to sleep in—he glanced at Ella—he was still a long way from that. Still, he figured, ever the optimist, there was always tonight and the day's schedule looked promising: an excellent lunch, some mellow wine, a walk in the park, Ella unwinding all the time . . . yes, tonight could very well be the night.

A waiter broke into his reverie. "Would you care for a cocktail before lunch, sir?"

111

"Ella?" Bunny asked.

"Gin and tonic, please."

"A gin and tonic and a vodka martini."

"Make that two," Lillian said to the waiter.

The waiter, a fatherly type, smiled at her. "I'd bet you'd rather have a glass of milk."

Lillian, in her best Betty Boop voice, said, "I bet I'd rather have a hemorrhage."

Bunny closed his eyes. "Bring her the martini."

"She'll have a Coke," Ella said firmly.

The waiter went away, and Bunny opened the huge menu. He ran his eyes lovingly over the list of dishes. "Hello, fellas," he said.

Lillian, idly glancing through her own menu, brought a hand up to scratch at the Band-Aid on her arm. She was wearing another little-girl dress and Ella had once again worked a miracle with her hair.

Bunny said, "Hey Lil, don't scratch. Remember what Mr. Lasky said."

"He's another one," Lillian said to the menu.

When the waiter brought the drinks and took their order, neither of the girls turned out to have much appetite. Bunny tried to get a conversation going, but they didn't seem to have any appetite for that, either, and by the time the food arrived the table was shrouded in a stiff silence. The food was great, but Bunny didn't enjoy it much. Ella and Lillian did little more than push theirs around the plate, and Ella only drank half a glass of the wine he ordered. The only time the silence was broken was when Bunny had to again tell Lillian to leave the Band-Aid alone. He ordered dessert for her and called for the check, but the normally fine service was disrupted by a staff shortage and the check didn't appear. When Lillian had finished her ice cream, and there was still no sign of the check, Bunny started to get a little miffed; that plus the bad vibes he was getting from Ella served to fray his temper slightly, so that when Lillian started to worry the Band-Aid again Bunny spoke to her a lot louder than he meant to.

"Lillian," he said, shattering the repose of the tables around him, "would you kindly stop scratching your bleeper."

The check arrived instantly.

The photographers were waiting for them at the Children's Zoo the way Lasky had arranged it. The three of them played their parts exactly as they'd played them before: Bunny the confident, expansive multimillionaire, Ella the pretty, smiling wife and Lillian the darling little daughter, light of their lives. There were lots of questions and lots of photographs.

"You like the zoo, Sherrel?"

"Oh, my, yes," Lillian told the newsmen. She was hugging a piglet.

"We used to take her to the Bronx Zoo all the time," Bunny told them. "To ride the camel."

"You don't go there anymore?"

Bunny said, "She has her own camel now."

The newspeople grinned sickly and left soon after.

So did the Bergstroms. Bunny suggested they walk in the park for a while, seeing it was such a nice day. The heat had withdrawn, leaving one of those china blue skies that New York often comes up with in July; one of those days when the wind clears the pressure-cooker haze and blows away the city's hot metal smell. The trees looked ready to fall down under their weight of greenery, and, with the squirrels scampering around the paths, the ice cream carts, the kids carrying sailboats toward the pond, the park seemed a nice place to be for a change. It cheered Bunny up and he renewed his attack on Ella's stony indifference. Lillian was walking ahead of them out of earshot.

Bunny said, "Hey, I've got a great idea. Why don't we stay in town? We could have dinner somewhere, then . . ."

Ella froze him into silence with a single look. They walked on for another twenty yards and Bunny gave it another try. "There's a movie at the Beekman that's supposed to be fantastic. Not for Lillian, of course, but we could get a babysitter and . . ."

Again the icicles cut him short. They walked on for another twenty yards, then Bunny exploded.

"Ella. For God's sake! How long are we supposed to go on like this for? Are you going to keep treating me like a leper forever? Okay, I conned you. I rented your apartment and that wasn't honest. I never said I was honest. And those people wrecked it and I didn't mean them to wreck it. I've apologized for that over and over. Are you going to hold a grudge forever?"

She whipped round and faced him. "I'm no longer mad about that. I accept that you're a liar and a cheat out to make a fast buck, so I understand why you did it. And what's done is done."

"Then what?"

"It's your whole attitude to this thing here. You don't give a fig about a child who's risking her life. You don't even care about helping catch those men. All you care about is Bunny Calder."

113

"Now, wait just a second—"

Ella talked on through him. "Yachts and fast cars and fancy meals, that's the only reason you came in on this, because you thought you could lead the life of Riley."

"That's not true. I was coerced into this. I was—"

"And when it didn't turn out that way, boy, were you disappointed. So you moan and groan because of a little discomfort."

"A little? Have you ever spent two nights on a—"

"Look at that child," Ella demanded. "Have you ever seen a child as unhappy as that? And what are you doing about it? Nothing. Absolutely nothing."

"Listen, it was my idea to take her to the zoo. Nobody else's."

"You only wanted to come to the zoo so you could eat at the Plaza."

"It was her day. I thought the kid would like it."

"You thought *you* would like it. If you'd given a moment's thought to how Lillian would feel, you'd have realized that that's the last place she'd want to eat. Why do you think she spoke to the waiter the way she did? Because she'd never been to a smart place like that and she felt way out of place. It's not Lillian's day today, it's Bunny Calder's day, your favorite."

Bunny tried to protest but got nowhere. Ella was still in full flight.

"Why do you think she's doing this, anyway? Did you ever stop to ask yourself that? Did you ever wonder why a fourth grader is willing to risk her neck in a scheme as stupid as this one?"

"She volunteered," Bunny said lamely.

"And why do you think she volunteered? You don't know? I'll tell you. Money, that's why. She figures to sell her story to a magazine. And money will buy her some independence. How many nine-year-olds do you know who are thinking about buying their independence?" Ella's voice had grown progressively rocky and she turned away from him.

Bunny drew in a breath ready to reply with a burst of his own, then let it go and said nothing. He stared at the back of her head. "All right," he said quietly. "Okay." He left her, hurried down the path and caught up with Lillian. "Hey, Lil."

"Yeah?"

"Where would you like to go today more than any other place in the world? And don't tell me Yonkers Raceway or a gay bar or any of that stuff."

She looked at him, suspicious. "Who wants to know?"

114

"I do. Come on, Coney Island, The Cloisters, where?"

"This ain't a gag?"

"Scout's honor."

Lillian shrugged and tried to sound indifferent. "I don't know, rowing on the lake, maybe."

"Really? That's what you'd like to do, take a boat out on the lake?"

"It wouldn't bother me."

"Done!" Bunny said. He turned to Ella, who was walking up to them. "Come on, we're going boating. We'll grab a cab on Fifth. I'm buying."

"It's not that far, let's walk." Ella said it warily, not yet convinced of his sudden change of heart.

They set off up the Mall toward the lake. Bunny grinned at her. "You see? Bunny Calder Day is officially over." Ella still wasn't ready to believe it.

The lake looked cool and glassy when they got there, the rowboats moving over it in slow processions. They walked through the outdoor café and down the ramp where a man took the ticket Bunny bought and pulled a boat up for them.

"Lillian," Bunny said, "you're going rowing with the right guy. I just happen to be one of the top small-boat experts in the state."

Lillian wasn't impressed.

"I mean it. In my younger days I was a counselor at Camp Kahonomoka. I got so good with a canoe I could jump off the dock and land in it standing up. Never tipped once."

Lillian sighed.

"No kidding. Ask anybody who went to Camp Kahonomoka. You don't believe me, I'll show you." Bunny knelt down to the boat, turned it so it faced out into the lake, and gave it a gentle push. Then he ran back several yards, set himself, and when the boat was about six feet from the dock, started to run. He gathered speed, sprang from the edge of the dock, landed with both feet astride the center seat and fell sideways into the water as the boat scooted from underneath him. He hit the water with a surprised cry and an arm-waving splash and went under completely.

He spluttered up to the surface and half swam, half waded back to the dock, hauled himself out and stood blinking water out of his eyes and breathing hard. His hair was plastered over his forehead and running water like a tap onto the shoulders of his light tan suit which was now the color and shape of soggy cardboard. He pulled a soaked handkerchief from a top pocket, wiped at his face and waited for the two girls to say something.

They stared at him blankly, as if waiting to see what other crazy trick he was going to try.

He threw the handkerchief down. "Come on." He sounded whipped. "Let's go home." He started to squelch away up the ramp but Lillian's voice stopped him.

"You promised."

"Huh?" He turned to her in a shower of spray.

"You promised to take me boating."

"You're joking. You want me to take you out *now?*"

Lillian's eyes hardened and her jaw jutted at him. "You said we'd do anything I wanted."

"But I'm soaked, drenched. I'm going to get pleurisy as it is. You can't expect me to swan around out there in this condition?"

"You promised."

Bunny looked up at the sky. "Kidnappers," he said, "where are you now that I really need you?"

He switched his appeal to Ella. "Please. Tell her she's being unreasonable."

Ella's face was no softer than Lillian's. "So it's Bunny Calder Day after all."

Bunny opened his soaked jacket to reveal a soaked shirt. "Does it look like Bunny Calder Day? Ladies, have a heart." He looked back and forth between the two unyielding faces, then gave up. "Okay," he said, "we'll go for a day on the lake." He said it as if he were humoring them. "We'll go out there and we'll have ourselves a ball."

He sloshed by them to the edge of the dock, pulled another boat alongside, motioned them in and sat them down on the rear seat. Then he sat down himself, pushed off, picked up the oars and began to row.

It started thirty yards from the shore. Ella, who, like Lillian, had been sitting like a statue watching Bunny work the oars, suddenly began to splutter. The splutter turned into a giggle which blossomed into full-scale laughter. Bunny looked at her darkly. "What's so funny?"

She tried to answer and laugh at the same time.

"Camp . . ." she said. "Camp Kahon . . ." She couldn't get it out.

Annoyed, Bunny said, "Camp Kahonomoka?"

Ella creased herself, dissolved in a fit of uncontrollable laughter.

116

Bunny set his mouth and went on rowing. He didn't see anything at all to laugh about.

Ella, on the contrary, was holding her ribs, tears in her eyes. "Oh God," she gasped. "I'm sorry, Bunny, but the brown suit and the hair . . . you look like, you look like . . ."

He had to wait out another paroxysm to find out what he looked like.

She took a deep breath and managed it all at once. "Like an Airedale that's gone in after a stick."

This time she nearly fell off her seat.

Later, lying on his bed thinking about the incident, Bunny had the distinct impression that, despite looking like an idiot, he'd made some progress with Ella. It was something she'd said. But for the life of him he couldn't remember what it had been.

Chapter 16

From that point on, life for Don Ray Bergstrom should have taken a definite turn for the better. But somehow it didn't. The chauffeur's room was far more comfortable than the billiard room but it also had its drawbacks. There were no pinups in the billiard room and there were hundreds in the chauffeur's room. They papered the walls from floor to ceiling. There were blonde, brunette and redhead nudes, Fourth of July nudes, Christmas nudes, nudes on water skis, on motor bikes, in parachutes. Nudes standing, sitting and lying. There were a whole lot of them lying. The chauffeur was obviously a man who appreciated a trim ankle. Being surrounded by all this pulchritude only served to remind Bunny of the slow progress he was making with Ella. It was true that there'd been a noticeable relaxing in attitude toward him—a partial thaw—but he was still light years away from even the thought of getting her looking like the girls on the walls.

His relationship with the other lady of the house had shifted very little, too. Lillian still regarded him with a hostile suspicion that he'd been unable to make much of a dent in. But, then, Lillian seemed to excel in hostile suspicion. Even with Ella she kept herself contained, hardly ever speaking unless in answer to a question. Yet Ella, far from being discouraged, seemed very content to be with her and was in no way rejected by an attitude many people would have returned with their own indifference.

Through the day they only saw each other at mealtimes, Lillian having to spend the rest of the time on the drive with the bike. But after dinner they'd watch TV together—Lillian liked *The Twilight Zone*—and after that, Ella would often read her science fiction and fantasy, the only kinds of books Lillian cared for. Another thing that hadn't improved much was the food. Bunny had convinced Hartley that he'd mastered knockwurst and beans and suggested he move on to something else. So Hartley had switched to perfecting hash. It would still have been sent back at a Route Sixty-six truck stop, but it was either that or go hungry. But, for all the non-improvements, the days that followed—warm, sunny days with a breeze coming in from the bay at night—passed pleasantly enough and very uneventfully. And it was this last condition that was bothering Lasky. The second burst of publicity they'd received with their trip to the zoo hadn't produced the result that Lasky had hoped for, and five days after their outing he came to see them. He arrived after lunch, which proved to Bunny that the man was smarter than he thought, and joined them for coffee in the small sitting room. He got right to the point.

"Frankly, we're disappointed. We really did think we'd have some action by now."

"You sure those men are still around?" Bunny asked.

"Positive. They went to a lot of trouble to get here; they're not going to leave just because they find all the bank vaults closed. And I'm pretty sure that's what's happened. It's more than likely they came here thinking to rob a bank, but nobody has vaults like this country. Some of them are real feats of engineering buried in solid bedrock. I would have thought they'd have checked them over by this time, seen the impossibility of cracking them and started thinking of an alternate means of getting the money."

"Then you still think they'll go for it?"

"Personally, yes," Lasky replied. "It's my superiors in Washington who are getting impatient. They're talking about phasing things out here and coming up with another way of flushing those people out."

Ella spoke. She said exactly what Bunny and Lasky expected her to say.

"I think they're right. With all the coverage we got, those men must know about us by now unless they're hiding in a cellar. So it stands to reason that they're just not thinking of a kidnap. Not the Bergstroms' daughter, at any rate."

"That's exactly what my boss thinks."

"But you disagree."

Lasky took a long time stirring his coffee. "I can see his point. It's just that I hate to give up on this. If this plan works, it's going to work beautifully. But meantime, if those men are hatching something else, something that could cost lives, well, we obviously can't just hang around waiting for a disaster to happen. That's why everybody's getting anxious."

"Then what's the decision?" Ella asked.

"We're going to give it one more try. But this time we'll make it absolutely clear to those people. We'll give them a hint so broad they won't be able to miss it. If they ignore it, then we'll know for sure that they're not coming."

"But if it's going to be that broad," Ella proposed, "it's going to look like a trap."

"I don't think so. Not with what I've got in mind."

They waited for him to tell them what that was, and Lasky took his time. By the slow way he finished his coffee and put his cup and saucer down, it was pretty clear that he wasn't looking forward to explaining.

"It's my idea," he said, "and if it doesn't work, I'll probably find myself transferred to the Sanitation Department." He looked away from them, still stalling. "It's pretty wild, I warn you." He fiddled with his glasses, set them more securely on his nose. "You know those two men who took Lillian . . . ?"

Bunny snapped his fingers to revive his memory. "You mean whatshisface, Laurel and Hardy?"

"Syd and Errol, yes. Syd Reiner and Errol Breakstone."

"Sure. What about them?"

"We're, er, we're going to have them do it again."

Bunny and Ella traded fast uncomprehending glances.

Lasky repeated it in a braver voice. "We're going to have them kidnap Lillian again."

While the two astonished faces stared at him, Lasky burbled an explanation.

"I warned you it was wild, but it's got a great chance of coming off. You see, in my opinion, looking at it with hindsight, I think we made a big mistake hushing up that kidnap. I think we should have done the exact reverse, played it up for all it was worth. Milked it for publicity. So I figure that if we restage it, but this time make sure it makes headlines and play up the ransom angle and how you were ready and willing to pay it, those people can't fail to get the message, and maybe they'll be tempted into trying the same thing."

120

He stopped and tried to gauge the effect his words were having on his audience. They were hanging on every unbelievable word. He shifted his body uneasily.

"Well, what do you think?"

Ella didn't need any further prompting. "I think it's the stupidest thing I've ever heard of."

Lasky gave her a sad little smile. "That's what my boss said."

Bunny, chewing it over, wasn't quite so negative. "It's wild all right, but that's not what bothers me."

"What is it, then?"

"I assume the attempt is going to fail. I mean, those two guys are going to be caught red-handed, right?" Lasky affirmed it and Bunny continued. "Then why should those guerrillas be attracted by something that's gone down the drain? I would have thought they'd be scared off."

"Not these people. They're not after personal wealth, remember, they want the money to further their cause. If the kidnapping appeals to them, it wouldn't matter if a dozen people had failed trying it. They'd figure to be smarter and braver."

"I guess," Bunny replied. "I'll have to admit it's a smart way of nudging those men in the ribs."

Ella came in fast. "It's also a smart way of nudging a lot of other people in the ribs. It'll only increase the possibility of somebody else coming along." Lasky admitted that she had a point. "That's true, and we'd be unrealistic not to face it. But I still think the odds are against a repetition of that. But if by some freak lightning does strike twice in the same place, we've proved we can move in fast and correct the mistake."

"For God's sake, Mr. Lasky"—Ella was mad—"we're not talking about a bundle of newspapers delivered to the wrong address. We're talking about Lillian. How can you honestly consider a plan that involves men desperate enough to kidnap a child when you know full well that another slip-up is entirely possible? That was only supposed to have happened once. Well it happened once and we're damned lucky it turned out the way it did. This whole thing was a crazy idea from the start and it's steadily getting crazier."

Lasky glanced at Bunny, trying to round up some male support in the face of an emotional argument. But the trouble was, what Ella had said made sense, too, and both he and Bunny knew it.

To give the air a chance to cool, Bunny asked what he thought was a harmless question, but it backfired on him.

121

"Those two guys, Reiner and Breakstone; they're going along with this in return for leniency, huh?"

"Well, not exactly."

Ella's voice was as sharp as an ice pick. "And just what does that mean?"

"It means," Lasky answered, trying to toss it off lightly and having no success, "that they don't know about this. They're going to have to come to the decision by themselves."

Incredulous, Bunny said, "They're not in on it?"

"As a matter of fact, no."

"Insane," Ella said. "Stark, raving insane."

The government man squirmed in his chair. "Miss Brown, you have to understand our position here. Those two are in jail for a federal offense. You don't make deals with people on a charge like that. The last thing we could do is walk up to them and ask them to commit the very same crime that landed them in jail in the first place. So we have to use other methods." Nobody asked what kind of other methods because Lasky didn't give them a chance to. He plowed on. "There are certain strings we can pull. We can plant the idea in their heads. And we can fake a jail break for them. All completely unofficially, of course."

"Look," Ella said. "Those men tried a kidnap, which is inexcusable. But the fact remains that you'll be using them, taking advantage of them. And that's hitting below the belt."

"They'll benefit in the long run. As I intimated, we can't get their sentences reduced, but there are ways we can make things easier for them. Believe me, if this thing comes off, everybody's going to benefit."

"Everybody except Lillian," Ella shot back. "She's the only one who'll be in danger."

"No." Lasky shook his head firmly. "No danger. These men aren't desperados, just small-timers out of their league. Ask Lillian; she wasn't frightened of them. It wasn't a traumatic experience for her. That's why we chose her in the first place. She doesn't scare easy."

"In other words, you went out and got yourselves a block of wood." Ella was on her feet now and in full sail. "Well, let me tell you she's not a block of wood. Nor is she a poker chip to be gambled with. She's a nine-year-old child and just as scared and frightened by all this as any child would be no matter how tough a front she puts up. And you're going to have to stop playing with her life or, so help me, I'll turn the whole thing over to the newspapers. And I mean it."

122

Watching her standing there, her eyes on fire, her mouth like concrete, neither of the men doubted it for a moment. But Lasky still tried to appeal to her.

"Miss Brown, you wouldn't do that. Those men we're after—"

"I don't care about those men. I don't know them, I've never met them and for all I know they don't even exist. But I know Lillian does and I think it would be nice if she went on existing. And that's more important to me than a bunch of gunslingers who are here because you didn't ask them for their passports."

Lasky said nothing, not wanting to reply into the teeth of her anger, but waited till she'd turned away and crossed to the window. Her outburst had upset her and he gave her a minute before he spoke.

"I understand how you feel, Miss Brown. But this thing isn't as hairbrained or as dangerous as you're making out. Those two men didn't hurt her before and they won't hurt her this time."

"And if it succeeds in attracting the other people, can you guarantee the same thing about them?"

"I can guarantee that we'll get her out just as quickly."

Bunny had kept out of the exchange, not wanting to risk a broadside from Ella, but now that he saw she'd reluctantly accepted the situation he spoke up.

"You didn't tell us how you're planning to plant the idea."

"With Reiner and Breakstone? By putting a man in their cell who'll talk it up."

"But they got burned the first time. What makes you think they'll be eager to try again?"

"Ah," Lasky said. "We're not certain they will, of course, but I'm betting on it. Those two are criminals, admittedly junior ones up to now, but criminals nevertheless. And most people who work outside the law are terrific egotists. It's in their nature. When they're caught on a job they kick themselves for slipping up, but if given the chance, most of them would go back and try the same thing again to prove it can be done. I'm pretty sure those two will react the same way."

In a dull voice Ella said, "You'll fill Lillian in on all this . . . ?"

"Yes, indeed."

She asked him when all this was supposed to happen.

"Well, now that we have your approval we can move very quickly."

"When?" Ella persisted.

Lasky, caught out again, addressed his reply to the Oriental carpet.

"It's already under way," he said.

Chapter 17

The next morning found Syd and Errol in their cell at Rikers Island, which wasn't much of a surprise. Syd was lying on the lower bunk reading an article in *The New Yorker* about rheumatism among the Aztecs, while Errol was standing, feet astride, fists one on top of the other, practicing his batting swing.

"Hey, Syd."

"What?"

"You figure it'll be Sing Sing? I hope it's Sing Sing."

"Why?"

Errol took a cut at an imaginary ball. "I hear they're looking for a designated hitter."

"Hey, you guys." They looked round at the guard who was unlocking the cell door.

"Out."

"What's up?" Syd asked.

"New cell for a bit."

Errol was dismayed. "What's wrong with this one?" He didn't want to leave; he had his gum parked under the bed rail.

The guard motioned them out. "We're decorating." They moved down the corridor and stopped outside a cell in which a bulky, gray-headed man was sitting on his bunk. "Okay, Johnson," the guard said, "you got company awhile."

The man on the bunk responded, although Johnson wasn't his real

124

name. His real name was Howie Mott and he worked for Lasky. "Hey," Howie Mott said, launching himself into the role of tough old prison con, "what is this, Boys' Town? Three in one cell. You guys looking for a riot?"

The guard opened the door and shoved Syd and Errol in. "Can it, Johnson, or you and me'll have a little riot of our own." He locked the door and went back down the corridor. Howie helped him on his way with a high sign.

"Watch out for that guy," he confided to his new cellmates. "He's a real bastard."

"You been here before?" Errol asked.

"I practically got a lease on the place. You know what they got me for this time? Manslaughter. How about that? I mean, I wouldn't hurt a fly and they stick me with manslaughter." He socked a fist into his hand. "If I ever get my hands on that judge I'll kill him." He brooded about it for a minute then asked the other two what they were in for.

Syd told him. "Talking on the phone too long."

"Jesus," Howie said, "they'll get you for anything these days." He stood and indicated the bunk. "Go ahead, sit down. May as well get comfortable. I'm Rudy Johnson."

"I'm Errol Breakstone and this here's Syd Reiner."

Syd nodded at him but the other man didn't nod back. He was looking at them funnily.

"Reiner and Breakstone?"

"That's right."

"I heard about you. You two are the guys snatched that rich kid."

Syd was surprised but kept his guard up. "How'd you know about that?"

Howie spread his hands. "In the papers."

"I never saw nothing about it."

"You seen a paper since you been here?"

Syd said no.

"Well, there you are then. Sure, it had all about it. Out on the Island there, right?"

Errol looked delighted. "Those papers, they have our pictures?"

"Naw," Howie said. "Only the kid's." He looked back and forth between them. "You guys had a real sweet idea, you know that? Too bad you got hooked. That guy had the dough in his hand when the cops got there. A million bucks. In his hand."

An expression of extreme anguish spread over Syd's face and the noise he made reflected it.

Howie shook his head and sucked at a tooth. "I tell you that was some smart idea. That rich guy went straight to his safe and got the money out. Frantic, he was, so the papers said. He claimed he would've paid twice as much. Devoted father, you know? One of them."

Syd made the noise again, which Howie didn't seem to notice. He went on with his tale. "But here's a funny thing: This guy says that even after his kid was snatched and all, he still ain't gonna hire any guards or things like that. He said he wants the kid to have a normal life. Can you tie that? Christ, if it was my kid, I'd get a couple of starving Dobermans. No offense meant," he said quickly.

"None taken," Errol said gallantly.

Howie crossed the cell and absently drummed on the bars. The ring on his finger clanged against them. "You guys came up with a beaut. But, as the man says, you can't win 'em all."

The guard appeared and began unlocking the door. "All right you two, out."

"Where we going now?" Errol asked.

"Back."

"Should think so, too," Howie said. "Three guys in one cell. I'll write the Red Cross."

"You want it, Johnson? Keep it up, you'll get it."

The guard took Syd and Errol back to their cell, locked them in, and left.

Errol looked the place over. "I don't see nothing different."

Syd wasn't interested in the decor. He got straight onto his bunk and lay down. He looked awfully ill.

The reason why Errol hadn't spotted any alterations inside the cell was because all the alterations had been made outside the cell. But that didn't become apparent till that night.

Syd was still lying on his bed, looking very gray. He said for the seventeenth time, "He had the money in his hand. Our money. In his hand."

"Yeah," said Errol.

"A million bucks." Syd raised himself a bit. "Half of it yours, you understand what I'm saying?"

"Wow," Errol said. "Three hundred grand."

Syd lay back again. He felt terrible.

126

From somewhere near the door there was a dull metallic click.

Errol looked up and saw the door swing silently open a few inches. He stared at it, puzzled, waiting for it to close again. When two minutes had passed and the gap between the door and the frame still showed, he said, "Hey, Syd."

"What?"

"I think the door just opened."

"Huh?"

"The door. It's open."

Syd swung himself into a sitting position and took a look. He dropped to the floor, crossed the cell and gently slid the door back. They didn't stop to take a vote on it; they slipped through and into the corridor. They had an end cell, and the one opposite was empty, so none of the inmates saw them leaving. Nor did anybody spot them sneaking through the gate that closed off the corridor; it was slightly ajar, too.

"Somebody's gonna get into trouble," Syd whispered.

They stopped at a corner and peered round it. Ten feet away, the same guard who'd moved them from the cell was slumped in a chair, his feet propped up on the table in front of him, soft snores coming from beneath the newspaper that covered his face. Other than the snores, and the low hum of the night lights burning in the ceiling, there wasn't a sound.

They sneaked up to the desk. On top of it, in clear plastic wrappers that bore the name of a local dry cleaner, were two pressed and folded guards' uniforms.

Syd and Errol sneaked on by.

From under the newspaper one of the snores sounded a lot like a groan.

Ten feet farther on, Syd stopped and looked back at the parcels. He crept back, picked them up and rejoined his partner. They found a store room and slipped inside and changed into the uniforms.

"Our lucky day," Syd said.

Outside the main gate, Lasky, the prison warden and the chief guard crouched in the darkness of a parked car.

"What if they don't go for it?" the warden said. "What if they smell a rat?"

The chief guard answered him. "Those two couldn't smell a fire at Goodyear."

"They'll come," Lasky said. "It's only a—" He cut himself off as the door in the main gate opened and splashed out a pool of light.

Two uniformed guards emerged and the door closed again and left them in darkness.

"Is it them? Can you see?"

The warden peered ahead. "It's too dark to make them out. Damn it, we should have left the overheads on."

"I think it's them," the chief guard said. "That looks like Errol's shape."

"We'll know for sure if they make for the car," Lasky said. He was referring to the prison Plymouth they'd invitingly left in plain sight. The keys were in it.

"Hold it," the guard said. "I don't think it is them. They're moving toward that laundry truck." They could just make out the truck parked alongside an outer guardhouse.

The warden cursed the light again. "Can you see what they're doing?"

The guard, who seemed to have the best night vision, squinted his eyes. "I'm not sure but I think they're getting into the back."

A moment later a man came out of the outer guardhouse with a bundle under his arm. He got in behind the wheel, started the truck, honked the horn and, as the prison gates opened wide, drove the truck in.

"It's them," Lasky said.

Three minutes went by, then the door opened and the same two figures came through it again. The chief guard resumed the commentary.

"They've stopped. They're looking round. They've spotted the car. They're moving toward it. They're walking round it." He paused.

The warden, impatient, said, "Well?"

"They're walking around it again. Wait, I think . . . yes, they're getting in."

"Boy, they're slick," the warden said.

The three of them heard the car start up and saw the lights come on. As it started to move off the warden relaxed. "You know, for a moment there—" He quit speaking as the car pulled to a stop.

"One of them's getting out," the guard said. "Could be Errol. He looks like he's signaling to someone."

"Signaling?" Lasky echoed.

"No, wait. I'm wrong. He's wiping the windshield."

The warden put his head in his hands.

"He's getting back in . . . there they go."

They watched the car's lights move off again.

128

The warden, still in the same position, said, "The only possible mistake they can make now is to take the infirmary road," the guard said.

Five minutes later the car had returned, found the right road and disappeared toward the causeway to Astoria.

The warden watched the rear lights wink out of sight. "One of the most daring prison breaks in history," he said. He turned to Lasky. "Good luck with those guys."

"They'll come through," Lasky said.

The chief guard spoke. "I put the bleeper under the rear seat. That okay?"

"Sure. I doubt we'll need it anyway. Breakstone's mother has a house in Corona. We're pretty sure they'll head for there."

The warden looked in the direction of the vanished car. "Watch out, Corona."

Errol's mother lived in a neat, white-painted frame house two blocks away from the western perimeter of Flushing Meadows. It could hardly have been more convenient to the penitentiary, being just over three miles away as the crow flies, so it didn't take Syd and Errol long—after ditching the car in Jackson Heights and taking the IRT to Corona Plaza—to get there.

Errol's mother answered the door, and it was a moment or two before she recognized her son.

"Why Errol! I didn't know you. What a lovely surprise. Hello, Syd, how are you?"

"Hello, Mrs. Breakstone."

Errol gave his mother a big hug. "Hi, Ma."

"Why didn't you call me and let me know you were coming? But don't just stand there, come on in. Oh, this is wonderful." She twittered around them, ushered them in off the porch and into the hall, where she got a good look at the uniforms.

"But what's all this?"she asked,

"We got new jobs," Syd explained.

Mrs. Breakstone was a tiny woman, birdlike and happy, and it was clear where Errol had gotten his sunny disposition from. It was also clear that Mrs. Breakstone was the block off which Errol was a chip.

"Oh," she said to her son, her eyes dancing, "your poor dear father *would* be proud. A pilot for Pan American."

129

Syd shuffled his feet. "Uh, no, Mrs. Breakstone, not pilots. Bank guards."

Errol confirmed it. "I'm a bank guard, Ma."

"Well, that's an important job too, guarding all that money. Come on into the kitchen and tell me all about it while I fix you something."

Syd nudged his partner who spoke up. "Ma, would it be okay if Syd stayed the night?"

"Why of course. You're always welcome here, Syd."

"Thanks, Mrs. Breakstone. We got the painters in the apartment."

"Come into the kitchen and tell me all about it."

Syd nudged Errol again.

"You still drive the old Dodge, Ma?"

"Yes sir-ree. Runs like a top, too."

"Okay we borrow it tomorrow, Ma?"

"Have it as long as you like."

"Thanks, Mrs. Breakstone. We got an important job tomorrow."

"Come into the kitchen and tell me all about it."

They went into the kitchen and told her a bunch of lies.

They found that the cop had gone from outside the main gates of the Bergstrom mansion, not that he would have bothered them; they weren't going in the front way, they were just checking. They turned round, drove back and took the same side road they'd taken before, and parked the car in the same spot they'd parked in before. There on the drive, riding the same bike she'd been riding before, was the same little girl they'd snatched before.

They waited till Lillian slowed and was turning around, then Errol ran through the gate and grabbed her and tucked her under the same arm he'd tucked her under before.

When he sat her down in the rear seat Lillian said the same thing she'd said before.

"She say something?" Syd asked.

Errol told him the same thing he'd told him before.

When they got back to the house at Corona Mrs. Breakstone was surprised by the small addition.

"Well hello there, angel," she cooed. "How nice of you to come and see me." She smiled up at her son for an explanation.

"She got lost at the bank, Ma."

"We thought it'd be better if she waited here, Mrs. Breakstone. That okay?"

130

"Why of course that's okay. Awww, lost are you, Precious? What's your name?"

Deadpan, Lillian let her guess.

"I got her number, Mrs. Breakstone. I'm going in now and call her dad."

Mrs. Breakstone put an arm round Lillian's shoulder. "Come into the kitchen and tell me all about it. Would you like a cookie and some lemonade?"

When Lillian looked as if she were perfectly willing to starve to death, Syd put a hand on her arm. "Go have a cookie," he said. Lillian went with Mrs. Breakstone. The two men darted into the front room and Syd closed the door. He walked quickly to the phone.

"Now, remember, Syd. No gabfest this time."

Syd picked up the phone and dialed a number. "You think I'm gonna make a mistake like that again?" He asked for the Silverman number, wrote it down and hung up. "Right," he said. "Here goes one million clams."

He lifted the phone and began to dial.

Errol looked concerned. "Just tell him we got her and hang up, huh?"

Syd waved an impatient hand. "Will you quit? I know what I'm doing."

He completed the dialing and held the phone with both hands. A few seconds went by. There was an electric tension in the air. Then Syd's knuckles turned white as they clenched the phone closer to his mouth. Syd spoke into it. "Bergstrom?"

The door burst open and eight men with shotguns rushed into the room.

Chapter 18

As Lasky had promised, the kidnapping got a big play in the morning newspapers; two half columns on the front page of the *Times* and all of the columns on the front page of the *News*. Bunny, sitting with Lasky in the wrought-iron gazebo in the formal garden, read both reports and tossed the papers aside. "Okay, so much for the preliminary. Question is, are we going to have a main event?"

"We have five days to find out," Lasky answered. "That's all Washington has given me."

"Five days." Bunny thought about it, then got up and walked over to the railing and stood looking down at Ella and Lillian. Lillian had a pad in front of her and a crayon in her hand and, with the tip of her tongue protruding from her mouth, was painstakingly trying to draw a rose. She stopped abruptly, tore the page off, crumpled it and added it to the pile beside her. Ella said something to her softly and Lillian started on another outline. Lasky joined Bunny at the rail.

Bunny said quietly, "If you told me a week ago that that kid would sit still for art lessons, I would have said you were crazy."

"You're right. Ella's done wonders with her."

"Miracles," Bunny said. "I've never heard her say anything to Lillian about it, but I just don't see Lillian with a cigarette anymore. And she's swapped that racing form for *The Secret Garden*."

The subject of their discussion tore off another sheet of paper, screwed it up and threw it down. "Goddamn sonofabitch!"

"She's leaving that till last," Bunny said.

"You notice she never gets impatient with Lillian," Lasky said. "Never gets mad."

Bunny nodded. "I guess women make the best mothers."

Lasky glanced at him and allowed himself a tiny cough. "Has your personal relationship with them improved?"

"Uh uh. It's still the girls against the boys. Lillian won't give me the time of day."

"And Ella?"

Bunny gave him a look. "I'm still sleeping in the chauffeur's room."

This was more of an answer than Lasky had bargained for, but he rode it nicely.

"Well, it would have been nice if you two had been able to emerge, um, friends from all this, but still, you've both worked out amazingly well."

"It's those two that amaze me. Look at them. Lillian's been snatched twice and Ella's suffered through them both, and they've got the big one hanging over them and they're sitting round the garden like it was Sunday in Vermont."

"I think they're both happier now," Lasky said. "Lillian because she doesn't have to ride the bike anymore, and Ella because she feels Lillian's not so exposed."

"That's true," Bunny admitted, "but she's going to worry a lot more at night. Still, I think you were smart taking Lillian off the drive."

"It wouldn't have looked right if we hadn't. Not right after a kidnap that made headlines."

Bunny turned and looked back at the house, running his eyes over the eastern wing where the bedrooms were. He could see how easy it would be for somebody to climb up on top of the arcaded section, then haul themselves up the lattice work to any of the windows. He said, "I just hope they're quiet. If Ella heard them coming for Lillian she might react instinctively and maybe get herself in trouble."

"That's why we put Hartley there. In case of such an emergency."

"Hartley," Bunny said. "You know, I'd forgotten he was a gunman."

"And a judo expert. He can kill a man with his bare hands."

"I know. He's been practicing."

Lasky consulted his watch and said that he'd better get going. He reached into a pocket and came up with a card. "I won't see you again until this thing's over, one way or another. But if you need to contact me at any time, call this number and they'll transfer you."

"Where are you going to be?"

"We have a trailer parked next to the bleeper van. I'm sleeping in that."

They went down the steps of the gazebo, and Lasky checked the weather. The heat was still holding off. "It looks like it's going to be a nice afternoon. Why don't you take the ladies out on the Sound?"

Bunny gave him a tired grin. "Thanks, but we went boating already."

"I mean sailing. There's a small sailboat you can use. It belongs to the chauffeur."

"The chauffeur? I wouldn't have thought he went in for outdoor activities." Although, when Bunny considered it, maybe the chauffeur saw something in two white bulging sails.

Lasky said, "I'm sure it would be all right if you borrowed it. You could take them for a barbecue supper at one of the beaches. Who knows," he said, the trace of a rare smile on his face, "you might be invited to join the art classes."

Bunny watched him walk away and thought about his suggestion. A swim and a moonlight barbecue—not a bad idea. He switched his attention to Ella. She was a nice sight: she'd drawn her hair back in a short ponytail which accented the high cheek bones and the full mouth. And she was wearing a shirt and pants again, and kneeling down the way she was . . . damn it, she was a great-looking chick, and here he was living under the same roof and he hadn't so much as held her hand. Okay, there were mitigating circumstances. But still! He'd let her buffalo him, that was the problem. Lillian, too. They'd both taken away the initiative. It was time to recapture it.

He went down the steps to the garden and sauntered over to them. Lillian looked up at him, and he gave her a short bow.

"Good morning, Madam."

"What? You watch your mouth."

The smile he was wearing became a loop of surprise. "What did I say?"

Lillian slitted her eyes at him. "I heard. You called me a madam."

"I didn't mean that kind of madam. I meant Madam."

"It's a form of address, dear," Ella told her. Then she looked at Bunny coldly. "Couldn't you have said Señorita?"

Bunny was floored. "I just came out of the gazebo and already I'm in trouble for using the wrong foreign language."

134

"I know the kind of madam he meant," Lillian said. "He's got it on the brain."

"I have not either got it on the brain."

"Yeah?" Lillian grunted. "I've seen your room, buster. Boobs everywhere."

"They're not my boobs," Bunny said hotly. "They're the chauffeur's."

Ella directed Lillian's attention back to the drawing, and Bunny was left standing there, shot to pieces. He wondered what he was doing wrong. He took a deep breath and took another stab at it.

"Ladies." He checked Lillian to see if that appellation was acceptable. "As the weather's so nice, and as we now have the day free, I was wondering if a spin on the water might appeal to you. Apparently there's a sailboat we can borrow."

Lillian left off drawing. "Sailing?"

"Sailing. Unless you're scared of the water."

"I'm not scared of anything."

"Of course she's not scared of the water," Ella said. "I think we proved that in Central Park."

"All we proved in Central Park," Bunny replied, "is that I'm not scared of the water."

Bunny wasn't sure, but he got the impression that a smile flickered on Ella's mouth for a brief instant.

She turned to her charge. "How about it, Lillian, would you like to go sailing?"

Lillian went on drawing. "I don't mind."

Bunny said, as if it had just occurred to him, "Hey, why don't we take some hot dogs and things. We could have a picnic lunch and make a fire on the beach and have a barbecue supper. We could go swimming, too."

Ella again consulted her charge. "That sound like fun?"

Lillian shaded in a rose petal. "I don't have a swimsuit."

"You could go in in your underwear," Bunny suggested.

"I told you he had it on the brain."

Ella said, "We could ride into the village and buy you a swimsuit."

Bunny, forcing himself to overlook Lillian's remark, concurred. "Sure. We could pick up the franks at the same time. Come on, Lil, what do you say?"

"I don't care."

Ella caught Bunny's eye and gave him a fast nod, and Bunny slapped his hands together. "Let's do it, then."

135

He went back to the house, got out the pick-up, and drove every-body into the village. Ella took Lillian into a store and Bunny bought groceries, then they returned to the house, changed and drove down to the water. They found the boat bobbing at the jetty, its sails low-ered and loosely furled.

Lillian said, "I want to see him jump into it."

Bunny lowered himself into it instead, rigged it, helped them in and got under way. They moved through the neck of the bay into Cold Spring Harbor and out into the Sound. He handed Lillian the jib sheets, explained their function and left her to it. She didn't look displeased. Bunny let the wind take them in a line toward Greenwich. It was a perfect day for sailing; there was enough breeze to skip the boat along without making it too exciting, and the sun beat down and came off the water in bright flashes. There were quite a few sailboats out; a Coronado, her sails stiff, ran by them close. Bunny cupped his hands to his mouth and hailed it.

"Have you seen the white whale?"

The only laugh he got on board was his own. Undaunted, he offered Lillian the tiller. She came down the boat and he sat her down beside him and gave her a short course in seamanship. Lillian grasped the tiller in both hands and scowled at the sails as if daring them to slacken. The wind whipped through her hair and she blinked at the spray and tasted the salt on her mouth. It was clear that the whole experience was totally alien to her, but she was determined not to let it show. It was also apparent that she was enjoying herself, al-though she was trying to hide that, too.

Halfway across the Sound Bunny helped her take the boat about, and they headed south and made for the beach at Bayville. It was crowded when they got there, with splashing kids and mothers tan-ning on beach towels. The girls went off to find a spot, and Bunny followed with the gear. As he put it down and straightened up, Ella was slipping off her beach dress. She was wearing a white bikini, and while it wasn't a particularly skimpy one there was still an awful lot of Ella on view, and all of it very lush. Bunny marveled at how she could look so full and ripe yet not look an ounce overweight. He swallowed and hoped the water was cold. Next to her, Lillian had shed the shirt she'd been wearing over the tank suit Ella had bought her, revealing a figure as straight as a stick.

"Come on, Lil," Bunny said, "last one in's a rotten egg."

"Go ahead," Lillian said, "I'm safe."

Bunny was all set to come back at her, but held off when he saw

Ella just waiting for him to try. Instead he asked Lillian if she could swim.

"Sure I can swim. What am I, a rock?"

Ella chose that particular moment to stoop and pick up a towel and Bunny decided that it was time for that cold plunge. He gabbled something about racing everybody into the water, turned, ran down the beach and dived into a wave. He swam out a way and came back to find the two girls at the water's edge. Lillian was regarding the water as if she suspected crocodiles. She put one foot in, then the other, then waded out to her waist. She took a look at how the other kids were doing it, took a deep breath, then belly-flopped in.

From the start it was obvious that she'd never been in the water in her life. With her eyes clamped shut and her mouth tight she thrashed at the water with her arms and legs, beating at it as if she were trying to drive it away. Very quickly and very steadily she began to sink. Bunny beat Ella to her and pulled her up.

"Take it easy, Lil. You're trying to swim the medley all at once."

With Ella supporting her, Bunny showed her a dog paddle and the two of them spent the next half hour keeping her afloat. When they came out and dried off, Lillian let Ella put some suntan oil on her, then went off by herself down the beach. Ella tipped more oil into her hand and started on her own skin.

"May I do that for you?" Bunny offered.

The reply was distant, polite and negative. Bunny got tiredly to his feet and went off to give Lillian a hand. She was kneeling some distance away digging what Bunny assumed were the foundations of a sand castle. She attacked the sand with the same fierce purpose with which she'd tried to swim, scooping up each handful as if it were an enemy to be conquered.

"Hi, Lil. Help you with the castle?"

"It ain't a castle."

"What's it going to be?"

"What it looks like. A hole."

"Okay then, I'll help you with the hole."

Lillian left off digging to ask him a guarded question. "What do you know about digging holes?"

"What do I know about digging holes? You know that national monument out in Arizona, the Grand Plain?"

Lillian bit. "You mean the Grand Canyon."

Bunny shot a finger at her. "Now it's called that."

Lillian, who'd never heard it before, looked pained. "That's got

137

cobwebs on it." She resumed digging and Bunny helped her. They worked in silence for a good five minutes till Bunny couldn't resist it anymore.

"Lillian?"

"Yeah?"

"What are we digging this hole for?"

"I want to try something."

They dug for another five minutes, then Lillian stopped. "Okay, it's ready. Get in."

"Me?"

"Sit with your arms round your knees."

It was the longest conversation he'd had with her and Bunny didn't want it to end by refusing. He did as he was told. It was deep enough so that his shoulders were below the level of the sand. Lillian carefully and methodically started to fill the sand in.

"Lillian?"

"Yeah?"

"What am I doing in this hole?"

"Experiment."

The sand rose around him and pressed in on him tightly. Lillian patted the last handfuls into place just under his chin, and Bunny found that he was sealed in like a mummy, unable to move an inch. He began to feel very uncomfortable.

"Hey, Lil . . ."

But Lillian was walking back up the beach to the picnic bag Bunny had brought off the boat. She came back with a jar in her hands, opening the lid. When she knelt down beside him Bunny caught the unmistakable smell of peanut butter. He gave a nervous chuckle. "I bought that for you, Lil. I never was that—*Lillian!*"

She was smearing the peanut butter on his face. Bunny struggled in his tomb but the sand held him helpless.

"Hey thanks, Lil, that'll sure stop me from burning. Now would you please dig me up?"

Lillian was busy searching the sand.

"Terrific gag, Lil. Be a sport and dig me up, huh? And what the hell are you looking for?"

"I can't find any."

"Any what?"

"Ants."

"ELLA!"

Ella sauntered down to them. "What's the problem?"

138

"What's it look like?"

"It looks like you started lunch before us."

"Lillian smeared this guck on me. Dig me up will you, she's looking for ants."

Ella said, "Is that right, Lillian? You looking for ants?"

"Yeah. I read about it in this book. The Indians used to do it, only they used maple syrup."

Ella considered it. "I always thought they used honey."

Bunny rolled his eyes wildly. "Maybe they used Cream O'Wheat. *Will you get me out of here!*"

"Hey," Lillian said, "I found a crab."

"YAAA!"

"Must you yell," Ella said. "People are staring."

"I don't wonder. This is very embarrassing for me."

"Embarrassing for you? How do you think I feel standing here talking to a head?"

"Ella. Please. Tell Lillian to get me out of here."

Ella started walking back up the beach. She said, "Dig him up, Lillian, before the gulls pick his eyes out."

They spent the rest of the day swimming and tanning and gathering driftwood, and by the time they started to build a fire the day was getting ready to slide into dusk. Out on the Sound, sailboats, pinked by the last of the sun, headed home toward Greenwich and Port Chester, and the beach had all but emptied except for a few evening fishermen.

Bunny sat with Ella watching Lillian toast a frankfurter in the flames. "Wow," he said quietly, "nine years old and I think this is her first day at the beach."

Ella said, "There hasn't been anybody to take her."

"It's funny, but it's the kind of thing you just take for granted. Kids and beaches, I mean. But I guess there must be thousands of kids who never get away."

Ella nodded. "Just in Manhattan alone. I did some work with a group of children once, a little older than Lillian. A lot of them hadn't even been out of their neighborhoods."

A breeze blew up, cool suddenly, and Ella reached for a towel for her shoulders. Bunny started to help her.

"I can manage, thanks," she said.

Bunny waited a beat then said softly, "There's just no way I can get my hands on you, is there?"

139

Ella's head came round fast, but her face softened and she relaxed. "I'm amazed you'd want to."

"How come?"

"Well, I haven't shown you much in the way of charm, have I?"

"You've shown me you're a warm, intelligent, kind and beautiful girl." They stared at each other, both surprised by his words.

Ella dropped her eyes and got to her feet. "Let's eat. Lillian must be starving."

The breeze had died but there was enough to get them round Centre Island Point and into the bay, although it was dark by the time they reached the jetty. Bunny did a quick reefing job on the boat and secured it and they walked to the pick-up. It was only a three-minute ride to the house, but when they got there Lillian was yawning roundly and close to dropping off.

Watching her climb the steps, Ella said, "She had a big day. All that sunshine and salt air, I'm feeling sleepy myself."

"So am I. What do you say we break into Silverman's booze collection and have a nightcap?"

Ella took a long time replying. "It sounds nice. But I don't think so."

"I'll replace it if you're worried about that . . . ."

She smiled and shook her head.

Bunny didn't press it. "Another night, then. I'll see you in the morning." He moved toward the truck, but Ella called to him.

"Thanks for today."

"You bet."

They stood there for a moment longer, then Ella went quickly up the steps and into the house.

Bunny put the truck away and went back to the chauffeur's room, took a shower and got into bed. He turned the light out and stared at the ceiling, arms locked behind his head. The light from a three-quarter moon bounced through the open window and illuminated the pinups on the walls.

"Girls," Bunny said to them, "tomorrow night you may just have to get along without me."

Chapter **19**

Hartley, putting down coffee cups at the breakfast table, looked around at the empty doorway. "Kid's sleeping her head off. She's usually down way before this."

Bunny poured coffee. "She had a big day yesterday. It was all I could do to get out of bed myself."

Hartley said, "You people missed a great dinner last night."

A look of concern crossed Bunny's face. "We didn't miss it, did we? The perfect hash?"

"The hash was good, but the Royal Chocolate Pudding . . ." Hartley kissed his fingers.

Ella came into the room and flashed a smile which Bunny was happy to see included him. "Good morning. Lillian not down yet?"

Bunny got up and held a chair out for her. She was looking tanned and terrific.

"Not yet. Too much sun, probably."

"I guess," Ella said.

The three of them chatted for a while, Ella telling Hartley about the day at the beach and Hartley telling Ella about his culinary achievement. When breakfast was over and Lillian still hadn't appeared, the three of them found themselves looking at each other and wondering about it.

Ella said, "I think I'd better go and shake her awake."

She scraped her chair back, but that was as far as she got.

Lillian was coming through the door yawning, the normally pale white skin of her face a glowing pink.

"Hey," she said. "My face feels funny."

Lillian's sunburn ruled out any repetition of the previous day which, much to Bunny's chagrin, ruled out any advancement with Ella. The relaxed, informal atmosphere induced by the sailboat and the water and the warm sand was hard to duplicate indoors, and indoors was where Ella was keeping Lillian till her burn went away. So Bunny, figuring that the next day might be possible, drove into the village and stocked up on groceries again. He planned a long sail to Bridgeport, weather permitting, and another late barbecue and a nightcap to follow for sure this time.

But once again he didn't get the chance.

When Lillian failed to appear for breakfast for the second time running, Bunny went up to her room. Her bed had been slept in but was empty. And there was no answer when he knocked on the bathroom door. He went back downstairs, avoiding the breakfast room, and called the number Lasky had given him. A moment later he was speaking to him.

"Mr. Lasky, I can't find Lillian."

"Hold it." Lasky was back in thirty seconds. He sounded more relaxed. "She's there, Mr. Calder; we're getting her loud and clear. We're too far away to pinpoint her but she's on the grounds somewhere."

Bunny relaxed too. "Sorry to panic, Mr. Lasky."

"Forget it. We're still here."

Bunny hung up and rejoined the breakfast table. He said, "I'm getting like a little old lady. I can't find Lillian so I rush to the phone and call Lasky."

Ella said, "She's not in her room?"

"Nope, she's around somewhere, though. Shooting pool maybe."

Ella got up. "She always had her breakfast first. I'd better check."

Bunny poured himself some coffee and stirred it, waiting for it to cool. When Ella came back into the room, the color of her face and the way she moved stopped the cup halfway to his mouth.

"She's not there." Her voice sounded like somebody else's. "I found this."

Bunny looked at the thing in her hand. It was a small, flat piece of plastic the size of a postage stamp.

He could practically hear it bleeping.

142

Chapter 20

There were four cars pulled up in front of the house; two men examining the drive, a man high up on the lattice work under Lillian's window, and two other men poking round inside the room itself. Downstairs, in the main living room, there were six people: Bunny, Ella and Hartley, and Lasky and two other men. One of them was busy with a telephone and a tape recorder. The other was sitting beside Lasky, waiting. Nobody was saying anything. Bunny was standing over a chess table, a carved ivory piece in his hand. He examined it without seeing it then placed it carefully back on its square. He felt more like slamming it down.

"It's my fault. I should never have taken her swimming."

Lasky answered him. "We can't be sure that's what it was. Lillian was scratching that thing long before you went to the beach. We should have put it under her skin where it couldn't be moved."

Since he'd arrived there five minutes ago, Lasky hadn't said much to Ella and had avoided looking at her. But now he couldn't put it off any longer.

"Miss Brown, you warned me that this could go wrong. I should have listened. It's my fault."

Ella was sitting straight-backed, looking at her hands, her face tight and expressionless. When she spoke her voice was normal but her words sounded frayed round the edges.

"It's none of our faults and all of our faults. But I don't want to talk about that part. I want to know what we do to get Lillian back."

Lasky, relieved to talk about something practical, indicated the man next to him. "That's Mr. Daniel's department. He's had a lot of success with cases like these, and I'd like him to fill you in."

Daniel, whom they'd met briefly when the government men had arrived, was a serious-looking man, younger than Lasky and a lot bigger. His hairline receded over a clear, open face marked by strong, precise features—firm, straight lines to the jaw and nose, eyes that leveled at you steadily and reflected the confident manner and his forceful way of speaking. He looked like the president of a small, go-ahead company. He stood and launched into it without any preliminaries.

"For a start, let me say that I think our chances are very high. Far more so than in most cases of this type. And that's because the odds are stacked heavily in our favor. In the first place there are three government departments involved in this plus the police, should we need them, so we outnumber those people by thousands to one. Secondly, we're on home ground. There are no resources that aren't available to us, while those men are strangers in a foreign land with no organization to fall back on. And thirdly, and this is probably our biggest advantage, we know who we're dealing with. We know their names and what they look like and, most important, how they think. So we're going to be able to predict, in some measure, how they'll react in any given situation."

Bunny jumped in fast with the same point Ella was about to raise. "Mr. Daniel, just a moment. You don't know for sure that it is those guerrillas. Unless you've found something you haven't told us about."

"We've found nothing. But there's no doubt who took the little girl. I know the trap hooked the wrong fish before, but kidnappers aren't like burglars who'll go back to the same house they've robbed the next night. Nobody would try stealing the same child who'd been stolen a few days earlier. Kidnapping carries too high a penalty to go against odds like that. So it follows that the only people who could have done it is somebody who ignores odds. Like a politically motivated group who are driven to take bigger chances."

When neither Bunny nor Ella answered straight away, Daniel told them that, at any rate, they'd know for sure when the kidnappers contacted them, and Ella asked what the next step would be then.

"That depends on what they say. The disadvantage in a ransom case is that the other people call the shots. But they have a disadvantage, too. They have to pick up the ransom. Sooner or later they have to expose themselves to get their hands on the money."

144

"But they protect themselves when they do that, don't they? Make the—" Bunny glanced at Ella and changed the sentence "—warn you about being interfered with?"

Daniel said he was right. "They'll warn you not to go to the police, or else. And if we're smart they won't have any reason to think you have. They won't find out till we hit them." He switched his eyes to Ella. "And we don't do that till we're certain we can get the little girl out. As Mr. Lasky just told you, we've done this kind of operation before and had a lot of success."

"But not one hundred percent . . ." Ella's voice was flat and colorless.

"Not one hundred percent, no."

The admission was followed by a heavy stillness which was at last broken by the man who was working on the telephone.

"Mr. Daniel, ready for a run-through."

Daniel told him to go ahead, and the man dialed a number, murmured into the phone and hung up. A few moments later it jangled, and as the man lifted the handpiece the reels on the tape recorder started to revolve. The technician listened at the phone, spoke into it, hung up again. The tape stopped and he pushed the rewind button, halted it, then pushed Play. He adjusted the volume and a voice said through the speaker, "Testing, testing." Then came the technician's answer. Bunny watched the reels reverse and stop. He asked Daniel when he thought the call would come.

"I don't think they'll waste any time. With the amount of money they're going to be asking, they'll have to give you time to get it together. And when they do call, remember, your child is missing but she may have wandered off somewhere. You don't think for a moment that she's been taken. It happened once but you can't believe it could happen again so soon. So your first reaction should be disbelief. From there on you'll have to play it by ear."

"I suppose I should ask them to prove they've got her," Bunny said. "Unless they let Lillian speak."

"I doubt they'll do that. They won't call you from where they're holding her and they won't risk riding her around. Tracing a call through an automatic exchange is next to impossible and they probably know that, but they'll be playing it safe anyway. But you're going to have to be convincing. You'll have to go along with them. When they tell you not to contact anybody, agree to that. Agree to anything they ask just as long as it gets you your daughter back. Don't let your answers be too pat. They have no reason to suspect anything and we don't want to give them one."

They spoke for a few minutes more, then Daniel and Lasky left them and went upstairs to check on Lillian's room. From a corner where he'd been sitting quietly, Hartley got up and came over to Ella.

"It's a tough break. But that Daniel, he's a good man. He'll get her back."

Ella said, "He's convinced me it is those men. She must be terrified."

Hartley said no. "She's all moxie, that kid. She knows we're coming for her."

Ella wasn't fooled; she knew Hartley was just as worried as she was. She put a hand on his arm and smiled her gratitude. It was an awkward moment for him, knowing she'd seen through him, and he mumbled something about making coffee and left the room.

Bunny inherited the uncomfortable atmosphere. Outside of discussing the practicalities, there wasn't much he could say to Ella. Brave, confident words weren't going to do much good; they wouldn't hide the fact that Lillian had a knife pressed to her throat. And for all his expression of high hopes, Daniel had only increased the fears, like a doctor who wanted you to know the truth. He was thinking about what Daniel had said when the phone rang.

The first thing he was aware of, apart from the sudden cold shock that reached up inside him, was the casual unhurried way the technician picked up his ear phones and adjusted them on his head. A professional. Then Bunny grabbed for the phone.

"Hello?"

Lasky and Daniel appeared at the door. Ella sat forward in her chair. Everybody watched him. But Bunny's body relaxed.

"No, I'm sorry. Mr. Bergstrom is in the West Indies. Why don't you call in about a week. Fine. Thank you." He hung up. "A reporter after an interview."

Daniel said, "Better get used to the false alarms. You may have a couple more."

But he was wrong. The phone didn't ring again for another half hour, but when it did it was the call they were waiting on.

Bunny knew it by the slow, calculating way the man said his name.

"Mr. Bergstrom?"

"Hello?"

"We have something that belongs to you."

"I'm sorry?"

146

"We have your daughter, Mr. Bergstrom."

"What? Who is this?"

"We're holding your daughter, Mr. Bergstrom." The voice had a studied English accent, spoken with the correctness and precision of somebody who'd learned the language formally, but so affected as to sound almost comical.

Bunny let his own voice rise a notch. "Sherrel? I don't—Listen, whoever you are, this is the rottenest gag I've—"

The voice spoke on, smooth and insistent. "Naturally you'd like proof. There's a small birch tree under your daughter's bedroom window. You'll find something buried beside it. We took it with us when we took her last night. When you find it you'll conclude that I'm telling the truth."

"Wait—"

"I will call you back in ten minutes. You'll tell nobody of this, of course."

The phone clicked in Bunny's ear. It took him two tries to replace the receiver, which surprised him; he hadn't known he was that nervous. The reels froze and the technician spun them back, stopped them, then set them moving forward again. Bunny heard the conversation again, his own voice sounding strange to him. Before the tape had finished Daniel hurried from the room.

Bunny looked over at Lasky. "That's them, isn't it?"

"No doubt about it. Only one of them speaks English, and from what we know about him, that's the way he speaks it."

They both expected Ella to ask about the birch tree, but she remained silent.

She'd seen Daniel leave and she preferred to wait and see what he found. He didn't keep her waiting long. He came back into the room, something clutched in his hand. He held it out. It was a pink plastic doll.

"Buried where he said it was. You recognize it?"

Ella stared at it. It wore a foolish smile, as if it were embarrassed about its arms and legs, which were pointing every which way, and the smudges of dirt on its clothes.

Lasky supplied the answer for her. "It's one of the dolls we got for Lillian. For the press conference."

"Charming piece of symbolism, a buried doll." Daniel turned it over. The doll grinned up at him. "I don't know if these people have ever tried a kidnap before, but they certainly understand the psychology."

147

"The evil bastards," Bunny said.

Daniel looked at Ella. "I'm sorry you had to see this, Miss Brown."

Ella tore her eyes away from the doll. "Please, I don't want you to keep anything from me. I want to know what's happening so I can help. You don't have to worry about me going to pieces."

Daniel smiled, pleased with her answer. Then he asked to hear the tape again. When it had finished he congratulated Bunny.

"Nice, Mr. Calder. Just the right balance."

"That guy's voice gives me the creeps," Bunny said. He asked Lasky if it was an Oxford accent.

"Something like it. That man's the leader of the group, comes from one of the rich families. He was educated in England, then returned to his own country and joined the army. They sent him back to England to Sandhurst, the officers' training school. When he returned home again he joined the liberation group, then started a small army of his own."

Daniel glanced at his watch. "If he's punctual, and I'll bet you a year's pay he is, you'll be talking to him again in a minute. This time he'll spell out the threat and hit you for the money. He's bound to ask for a fortune, so you'd better resist at first. Try to find out as much as you can about the delivery arrangements but don't make it obvious. I don't think he'll tell you much, but it's worth a try."

Nobody said anything after that, but stood or sat where they were, waiting in an edgy silence for the phone to ring. It was the worst thing they could have done. When it sounded it was like a bomb going off.

"Hello . . . ?"

"You found it?"

"Listen to me. I want my daughter back. Don't hurt her. I'll do what you want, but don't hurt her."

"You haven't heard our price yet, Mr. Bergstrom. You may balk."

"Whatever it is, I'll pay it. I just want Sherrel back."

"The price is twenty million."

"Twen— You're joking."

"On the contrary, Mr. Bergstrom."

"Look, I know the papers said fifteen million but they were just guessing."

"I told you you might balk, Mr. Bergstrom. So we have nothing more to say because I'm not prepared to bargain."

"Wait." Bunny waited himself. He took a breath and spoke more slowly, putting a duller quality into his voice. "I'll get the money."

"Ah . . ."

"But it will take time."

"Naturally. You have forty-eight hours."

Bunny heightened his voice again. "That's not enough. I can't raise a sum like that in two days. Not cash. I'll need four days at least."

"Forty-eight hours."

"Look, I could get half the money by then."

The voice came back a fraction slower but with the same painful enunciation.

"Mr. Bergstrom, if you only pay us half the money, we can only give you back half your daughter "

Bunny brought his words tumbling on top of the other man's. "Don't hurt her."

He waited. "All right. Forty-eight hours. I'll try."

"I'm sure you'll succeed, Mr. Bergstrom."

"How do I get it to you?"

"I'll let you know tomorrow. Incidentally, Mr. Bergstrom, should you decide to bring in the police or try to trick us in any way, our business will be automatically concluded and, I'm afraid, to our mutual dissatisfaction."

There was a click in his ear and Bunny was holding a dead phone.

While the tape was being rewound, Daniel told him he'd sounded very convincing.

But Bunny shook off the compliment; he'd found it very easy to be convincing.

They ran the tape.

"Forty-eight hours," Daniel said. "That should be plenty of time."

"To get the money?" Bunny said.

"To make it up."

"You'll have it run off? Printed?"

Daniel was slower in answering this time. "I don't think you understand. We're going to have to fake that money."

Daniel was right; Bunny didn't understand. And neither did Ella.

"We couldn't get our hands on a sum of money like that. It's impossible."

Ella said, "But it's been done before. There have been lots of airline hijacks with large sums of money involved. I'll admit none of them were this big, but the airlines always got it ready."

Bunny backed her up. "That's right. Remember that Queen Mary scare? That guy asked for a fortune and they had the money all ready to go."

"Totally different situations. You have a couple of hundred people on a jet. On that ship there were a couple of thousand. And that kind of thing hits the headlines, so as well as their passengers, companies have their good names to protect. They have no alternative but to raise the money."

"I see." Ella bit the words off. "And because you don't have to look good, and because there's only one little girl involved, you're willing to take the risk, is that it?"

Lasky tried to explain how it was.

"Miss Brown, as Mr. Daniel told you, we have enormous resources we can call on here. There are very few avenues closed to us. But asking a bank or the mint or some other agency to lend us twenty million dollars cash is out of the question. Faking the money is the only thing we can do."

Bunny pointed at the tape recorder. "But you heard what Sandhurst said, any tricks of any kind. And you can just bet that what he was talking about was a fake payoff. If we try to give him Monopoly money, it'll be all over."

"Not if we handle it properly," Daniel said.

"How? What's your idea?"

"I can't tell you that till we find out what Sandhurst, as you call him, has in mind. He said he'll call tomorrow. That'll be just to keep the pressure on. When he calls the next day it'll be to tell you the arrangements for the drop-off. Once we know what they are we can formulate a plan of action. Until then, we wait."

Daniel could see that they didn't like the idea of that, but he didn't have anything better to offer. He recapped the situation, trying to sweeten it without being too obvious.

"As I said, the pick-up is their weak point and that's where we'll attack them. If we're smart enough and we move fast enough and we get the breaks, we'll end up winners. We'll get the little girl out and we'll get those men. But I want you to know that the only possible way of handling this is the way we're handling it. The money is a problem, I grant you. But I still think our chances of success are better than good."

Ella received this without comment, and Bunny kept silent too. For all Daniel's confident manner and careful choice of words, the man was still telling them that they were going to try a bluff. And the trouble with a bluff was that if it didn't come off, you were dead. The "you" in this case being Lillian. Bunny didn't agree with Daniel. Their chances weren't better than good at all. They were downright terrible.

150

Chapter **21**

For the rest of the day, and most of the next, there was nothing for Bunny and Ella to do but sit around and worry. Bunny did his best to make the situation sound better than it was by telling Ella the obvious things: that Daniel was clearly a man who knew his job and re-iterating his arguments about the odds being heavily in their favor. But all of this was negated by the knowledge that Lillian was hidden somewhere in a city of eight million, guarded by a group who'd kill a hundred people if it would do them any good.

Ella found it difficult to accept the fact that there was nothing to do but wait, but Bunny saw the point of Daniel's argument there—they had to let Sandhurst make his move, then counterpunch. But that still left them just hanging around waiting for the clock to move; waiting for the evening and the promised call. The call wasn't sup-posed to be important—Sandhurst had said himself that it was just to keep in touch—and yet it was contact, in a way, with Lillian, so Bunny was keyed up.

As it turned out, too keyed up. He made his first slip.

The call came just after 9:00 P.M., Lasky and Daniel in the room, the technician at the tape recorder, Hartley hovering in a corner, Ella unable to sit still.

"Bergstrom."

"Good evening, Mr. Bergstrom. No problems I trust?"

"No problems. The money's coming together. I'll have it by tomorrow afternoon."

"Fine, then we'll meet tomorrow night."

"Where?"

"I'll let you know in plenty of time. You bring the money, and two hours later you'll have your daughter."

"No. We'll swap at the same time. You take the money, I take Lillian."

It was a natural enough mistake; he'd been talking about Lillian, thinking about Lillian—it was out of his mouth before he could stop it. He tried to rush over it. "I'm not handing over twenty million dollars unless I see her there."

It didn't work. There was a small pause and Sandhurst said, "Who did you say you'll take?"

Bunny put a note of anger into his voice. "Don't play games with me."

The man's answer chilled him. "I think you might be the one playing games, Mr. Bergstrom. You called your daughter Lillian. Her name is Sherrel."

"What I call my daughter doesn't matter. What does matter is—"

"I'll call you back in thirty minutes." The man hung up.

Bunny did too, slamming the phone down. "God*damn* it!" He turned to face them. "I was thinking Lillian instead of Sherrel." He made a helpless gesture. "I'm sorry, Ella."

The replay started. When Bunny heard himself make the slip he swore and slapped his hand against his leg. He was the first to speak when the tape ended.

"What a dumb thing to do. Now he'll be looking for something."

Daniel said, "It all depends on what Lillian says. That's where he's gone now, to ask her if her father ever calls her Lillian."

"She's bound to say no. I blew it."

"Let's wait and see how he reacts," Lasky said. "It may not have been such a vital slip."

So they waited. But it was a long half hour. When the phone rang, and Bunny picked it up, the man's voice was like a shower of nails against his ear.

"Mr. Bergstrom, your daughter says you've never called her Lillian in her life. What's going on?"

Bunny chose the classic defense and came right back at him hard. "Look, she's nine years old and she knows what's happening to her. I wouldn't be surprised what she said. What's the sudden hold up? Are you trying to stall me?"

"I find it very strange that you'd call your daughter by a name that's completely unfamiliar to her and it leads me to wonder if things are exactly as they seem."

"You don't fool me. You're trying to make something out of nothing so you can raise the ante. I had to pull every last string to get that money ready and I couldn't get another dollar if I wanted to. And I'm not prepared to try."

The man took a moment before replying. His voice was softer now. "I'm not talking about the price, Mr. Bergstrom. That remains the same. However, the conditions of payment will change. I'm now going to assume that you've brought the police into this."

That shook Bunny and he had to force himself back into the role.

"The police? Just because I called my daughter a different name?"

"It remains unexplained, Mr. Bergstrom."

"Let's understand something. I don't care about you, I only care about Sherrel. And I'm prepared to pay for her. That's the deal we had."

"We still have it. But the transfer arrangements will be a bit more complicated now. The money, I assume you're having it delivered by armored car?"

Bunny didn't commit himself. "What's wrong with that?"

"Have them deliver a second armored car. An empty one. It's to be left in the parking lot at Haberman Station, make a note of this, Haberman Station in Maspeth. I want it parked, locked, and the key left beneath the left rear wheel. Have you got that?"

"I've got it."

"Have it there by 8:00 P.M. I'll send a man to pick it up. We'll be in radio contact with this man. If there is any attempt to interfere with him, or if he suspects that he's being followed, or if the armored car has been tampered with in any way, the deal is off and your daughter will be executed."

"Please. I'll see that the truck is delivered. When do we meet?"

The man told him that he'd call him when he had the truck, and cut the connection.

Bunny hung up and sagged into a chair. "We're still in business."

The technician reversed the tape and played it, and the room listened to the exchange.

"Why two trucks?" Ella asked. "What's he planning?"

"He's playing it cagy," Daniel answered. "He's not suspicious

153

enough to call it off, but he's on his guard. He wants to give himself as much protection as he can."

"You figure a switch?" Lasky asked.

"Probably. Lillian in one truck, the money in the other. Good protection all around. He's not dumb, but we knew that."

"What burns me," Bunny said, "is that he wouldn't have bothered with the trucks if I hadn't flubbed my lines. Now we've got a problem we don't need."

"Don't feel bad, Mr. Calder, that was a fine recovery you made. And the armored cars aren't necessarily a problem. They're pretty formidable things, it's true, but they have their drawbacks. For one thing, you can shoot a tire out with a high-powered rifle; then it's just an iron box going nowhere."

Ella had reacted to Daniel's mention of shooting and he saw it and shook his head at her. "Don't worry, we're not going to get into any shoot-outs. Not tomorrow night, at any rate."

"How can you be so sure?"

"Because we won't be there tomorrow night." He forestalled Bunny and Ella's surprised comeback by hurrying on. "Let me tell you what I think's going to happen. As I see it, he'll have one of his men pick up the truck just as he said he would. And I believe him about being in radio contact. They'll move it somewhere and we won't know where, because if we tried to follow it we'd risk blowing the whole thing. Then he'll call you and tell you where the truck is and that Lillian is inside it. He'll tell you to drive your truck there, with the money of course, and trade trucks. You'll drive Lillian away, he'll drive the money away. I'm only guessing, but I think that's what he's going to tell you."

"It can't work," Ella said. "He'll check the money before he turns over Lillian."

"I don't think so. I don't think he'll be there tomorrow night, either."

Ella, bewildered, looked at Lasky, hoping he'd disagree, but Lasky backed his partner up.

"They'll want to see what they're getting into before they commit themselves. They'll have Mr. Calder drive to a spot that they've staked out, someplace where they can watch without being spotted themselves. They'll be looking for us, which is why we're not going to be there. When they're satisfied that Mr. Calder's alone then they'll do the whole thing for real the next night probably."

"A dummy run," Bunny said.

"Exactly."

Ella wasn't satisfied with it. "What if you're wrong? What if they are there? With Lillian."

"Miss Brown," Daniel said, "you've got to realize something. There are no guarantees. We have no way of knowing for sure what those people are going to do. We have to rely on guesswork. And it's my guess that they won't try an exchange tomorrow night. They've got twenty million dollars and their freedom on the line. They can afford to wait. If you were in their position, what would you do, rush in or tread carefully?"

Ella's unspoken reply seemed to say that she'd never be in those people's position in the first place, and in the second place she didn't see how anybody could predict how those men would respond—a dedicated group of extremists who might do something completely reckless. By Daniel's own admission the whole plan was structured on guesswork; guesswork that might prove to have nothing whatsoever to do with real events. But she kept these opinions to herself. She could see that she wasn't going to sway Daniel, and if he was the best man for the job, as Lasky insisted, then he was the only man for the job. He was either going to be right or he was going to be wrong. The trouble was, if he was right he'd be one hundred percent right.

But he only had to be the tiniest bit wrong to be very, very wrong.

Chapter 22

The armored car arrived the next afternoon. It was a blue and red Wells Fargo truck, squat and massive, and the pebbles on the drive squished under its weight. Daniel produced a key and opened the rear doors. The inside was like the outside, cold bare steel. Apart from the two padded seats that hinged down against the far side, it was just an empty metal box.

Daniel said, "These things are designed to carry one or two armed men. The doors lock from the inside, and, as you can see, that's the only way in and it's a pretty tough way. The outside lock is really only to keep the doors from banging when there's nobody inside."

"First time I've seen inside one," Bunny said. "Those security people don't like you to get too close. I've often wondered what would happen if you accidentally stumbled against one of those guys with the drawn guns and the sacks in their hands."

Ella ran her eyes over the armor plating. "The truck you're getting for those men, is it the same as this?" Her voice was quieter than usual, flatter. There was a thin, pale look to her face, and the tightness around her eyes was evidence of a bad night's sleep.

"It's a Brink's truck, different firm. But it's similar, yes."

"Lillian will be able to breathe all right? It looks airtight."

Daniel pointed a finger. "There are ventilators in the roof. That used to be a weakness of the armored car; still is, I guess. More than one bandit knocked one over by dropping gas in there. But most of

156

these trucks carry gas masks now." He indicated something in a top corner. "That's a mike so the guards can talk to the driver. They can keep in contact without leaving the gun slots."

Bunny was impressed. "Whoever designed these things thought of everything."

Lasky, walking up, caught Bunny's remark. He tapped the studded steel body.

"I guess you could say Leonardo designed it. He designed the tank and that's all this really is." He looked all set to expand on the subject but didn't get the chance. A long black van drew their attention as it rolled toward them down the drive.

"The money," Daniel said.

He went over and conferred with the two men who jumped out of it. They unlocked the rear doors and began transferring its cargo to the armored car—twenty fat bulging sacks. Bunny said that it looked like all the money in the world and asked Daniel if they'd made everything themselves. Daniel told him that the sacks had been borrowed and offered to show him what they had made.

He picked up a sack and put it down at his feet. The bottom was reinforced with leather and underneath the handles a punched leather strip was sewn around the mouth of the bag, a padlocked chain threaded through it. There was a Manhattan bank's name and emblem stenciled on the white canvas sides.

One of the men handed him a bunch of keys and he chose one at random and inserted it into the padlock on the sack.

"Six keys, all standard. The padlocks are all the same."

The lock clicked open, Daniel unhooked the chain, spread the sack and brought out a fat bundle. It was the same size and shape as a wad of newly printed bills, except the bills were just plain brown paper. A white paper seal held the bundle together.

Ella took it and rifled the wad through her fingers. "Couldn't you have used something that at least looked like money?"

"Mr. Lasky's the expert on that," Daniel said.

Lasky filled her in. "There's no real way of faking money except by using the best counterfeit you can make, and that means using the right kind of paper and ink, the right processes, and an almost perfect engraving. It costs a lot of money and takes a lot of time, way longer than we've got. Anything less than the best is easy to spot. So you may as well use stiff brown paper."

"Which means you'll have to act before they get a look inside these sacks."

"That's right. But don't forget, when it does come to an exchange, examining the money will come pretty late in the piece. They have to unlock the truck, get into it and unlock a sack. Not a big production, I grant you; it'll only take a few minutes. But a few minutes should be all the time we'll need."

Ella didn't have anything to say to that. She handed the bundle back to Daniel and watched him drop it back in, relock the sack and place it in the armored truck. It was the last one, and the men swung the doors closed and Daniel turned the key in the handle. He told Bunny and Ella that they'd be back at seven thirty, and he and Lasky got into their car and followed the van down the drive. Ella watched them go and said something, thinking out loud. Bunny caught the words but made no reply. He knew what she was thinking and was glumly thinking the same thing. Ella had said, "Twenty sacks of brown paper."

The call came through just after eight, and they played the tape back two minutes later. Once again the clipped, plummy accent sounded in the room. Bunny was beginning to loathe the man as much for his speech as for what he'd done.

"Mr. Bergstrom? We have the armored car. I trust you have yours? And the money?"

"It's all ready. What about you?"

"Everything is in order. Now listen to me. Drive the armored car to the parking lot of the shopping center at the corner of Warner Avenue and Broadway in Roslyn. I'll repeat that once. The shopping center at Warner and Broadway in Roslyn. There is a phone booth there. I will call you there with further instructions in exactly forty minutes' time."

There was no need to play it through a second time. Daniel looked pleased.

"Good. He's still not taking any chances. The more suspicious he is now, the less he'll be next time."

Ella stopped herself from making the obvious comment here. It was too late to change anything anyway.

"He may call you at that phone box or he may not. He might just leave you there in the parking lot while he sees what's happening. If he does call you, it'll probably be with a new address. He'll want to move you around and see if you're being tailed."

Lasky was spreading a road map on a table. "Right here," he said.

Bunny went over and looked at it. It was a map of Nassau County, the streets marked in red and yellow. Lasky's ballpoint traveled a line along it.

"Down Shore Drive to Oyster Bay Road and the Turnpike. Stay on that all the way to Broadway turnoff and you'll hit Warner right here. What's that, about thirteen miles? You'd better get going."

He folded the map and passed it to Bunny, and Daniel handed over the truck's keys with some final instructions. "If he does call you, drive wherever he tells you. He'll probably say he'll meet you there. Wait there thirty minutes then come on back. You're only going on a milk run but good luck anyway."

Lasky added some encouragement, too. "I'm sure everything will be fine, Mr. Calder. We have complete confidence in you."

Which was a lot more than Bunny had in himself right then. He'd spent hours, days just sitting around waiting to do something, and now that the opportunity had arrived it seemed to have snuck up on him and found him unprepared. He wasn't afraid, just nervous, and he hoped it didn't show; Ella was worried enough as it was. He turned his eyes to her and caught her watching him intently. He smiled and took her hand in a quick squeeze and said the silliest cliché ever invented for tight situations. "Don't worry." Then he went out the door and headed for the truck.

It was strange to drive, thick and ponderous, the suspension hard as a rock, but after he got used to the slow gear shift and the heavy response of the wheel he drove it pretty well.

Coming up onto the Turnpike the traffic was light and he moved into the inside lane, held it at a steady fifty. He had nothing to do for the next ten minutes but watch the turnoff signs and think. He wondered what the odds were on Daniel being wrong; if Sandhurst was there with Lillian, how in hell was he going to explain the bundles of brown paper? Another thought occurred to him: Sandhurst had insisted that he drive the truck. Why? Why not an ordinary driver? Because they knew what he looked like and a driver could be a cop? Or could it be that if Don Ray Bergstrom's daughter was worth twenty million, Don Ray Bergstrom himself would be worth twice that? That would be perfect—instead of coming home with Lillian, they might take him as well. They might be waiting for him with guns —they'd discover the fake money and then there'd be two people to ransom. He put the disastrous thought from his mind and concentrated on the overhead sign that was coming up. The Jericho turnoff. He checked the map then checked his watch; he was making good time.

A car went by him fast, cut into his lane in front of him, slowed then shot off again. Kids fooling round? Or somebody who wasn't fooling round? He wondered if Sandhurst and his group weren't already watching him, driving along behind him somewhere, checking to see which cars followed him when he made his turnoff. He glanced in the wing mirror. That car behind him, a Pinto wagon; that had been there for a while. Christ! The sacks of paper he was carrying were starting to seem like a load of dynamite.

The Broadway turnoff, Route Seven, almost surprised him. He swung off the turnpike and down the ramp and followed the road past a green park that fringed the southern tip of Hempstead Bay. Warner should be the first on his right. He slowed at the beginning of a downtown section then spotted the spire of a supermarket. He took a right at the corner and guided the truck into the entrance of a shopping plaza. He rolled into the parking lot and parked in the middle of a group of cars. On the sidewalk in front of the supermarket, the phone booth stood like a beacon, somebody in it.

He checked his watch again: eleven minutes. He stayed in the truck and wound both windows down to get a better view. The plaza was a small one with just the one row of stores built in an el shape. A bake shop started them off, then a drugstore, still open, then the supermarket windows running down to the center doors. He could see a checker inside with the last of the customers lined up, somebody sweeping with a broom. The windows extended on the other side and then a news agent/card shop, a beauty shop, an ice cream parlor, a children's shoe store and a dry cleaner's. Along the bend of the el was a laundromat, a donut shop and a liquor store, a record store at the end, loud pop blasting out of it. There were maybe twenty cars parked round him. All of them looked empty, but it was hard to tell, the lights from the stores falling short here. Bunny saw that Sandhurst had picked a good spot; he could be in one of those parked cars and keeping an eye on things without appearing obvious. Or hidden up on the flat roof above one of the stores, high up where he could see if the truck was alone.

He sat there watching, letting the minutes tick by. The lot was starting to empty now, people getting into cars. Somebody killed the music in the record store and, in front of him, the market switched to its sentry lights. Nobody gave him a second glance, used to seeing armored trucks parked outside supermarkets.

He checked his watch: three minutes before the call. If there was going to be a call. He got out of the cab and strolled toward the phone booth, empty now, and dark. He didn't see the woman who came bouncing out of the drugstore and beat him into it by a couple of steps. She scowled at him as she shoved the door closed in his face, turned her back and took a long time putting her pocketbook down and digging for change. Then she dialed and started talking almost immediately, one hand flapping with a life of its own.

Bunny gave her three minutes exactly then tapped on the glass. The hand flapped on. He pushed the door open and smiled as the woman turned.

"I'm sorry to intrude, ma'am, but would you mind. I have an urgent call to make. She returned his smile with a look of outraged indignity. She was a short, plump flower pot of a woman with an iron slit for a mouth.

"Your call's urgent? My call's urgent. You wouldn't believe how urgent." She shoved the door closed and turned back to the phone to report the atrocity.

Normally there were at least six ways Bunny could have conned her out of the booth, but he had no time for the subtle approach, the sweep hand of his watch had passed the twelve. He pushed the door open again and got rid of her with an old-fashioned straightforward appeal.

"Lady, hang up or I'll kick your slats in."

The woman's eyes got big and she gabbled a fast excuse into the phone, threw it down, edged past the rapist-mugger and kept going.

Bunny wedged himself into the box and turned to close the door.

Behind him the phone rang.

"Bergstrom."

"The phone was engaged, Mr. Bergstrom. You weren't calling anybody, surely?"

"There was somebody in here, I had to wait. Where's my daughter?"

"She's waiting for you not far away. You have the armored car?"

"Yes. I told you before."

"And you're quite alone?"

"I'm alone. Come on, where do I go?"

"Drive west on Warner to Mineola Avenue, turn left, then take the third street on your right. Have you got that?"

"Warner to Mineola, left and third on the right."

"Our armored car is parked there. Your daughter is inside. The keys are under the left rear wheel. Park behind it and leave your keys in the same place under your truck. Get into our truck and drive it away immediately. Is that clear?"

"Clear."

"One more thing, Mr. Bergstrom, and this is most important. You'll find a tape recorder on the seat. Play it as soon as you drive away. Now I wouldn't waste time getting there. You'll find out why."

"What do you mean? What's on that tape?"

For an answer he got the steady buzz of the dial tone. He got out of the phone booth and into the truck in a hurry and swung out of the parking lot into the avenue. He wondered what Sandhurst was going to tell him on the tape that he wasn't willing to tell him on the phone. And why getting there fast was important. If it was a straight exchange, why all the mystery? It was all wrong. He went back over the conversation. "Our armored car is parked there. Your daughter is inside." A thought struck him, ice cold inside his head, colder inside his stomach.

He put his foot down and drove faster.

He hit the traffic on Mineola and made the left, counted off two streets and turned into the third. The street stretched in front of him, quiet. There were cars parked in driveways, a few at the curb but nothing that looked like an armored truck. A flood of relief burst over him; Daniel had been right. Sandhurst was just moving him around, making him sweat so he'd be all the more malleable the next time. The road started to curve. It wasn't straight after all, it was a crescent. And at the far end of the curve, as the street unwound, something different came into view. Something thick and high and boxy.

His headlights hit it and lit it up, and a fine tremor of shock stabbed through him. Daniel hadn't been right at all. He'd been insanely, crazily wrong. His first impulse was to just keep on going; to drive right on by the truck. He could think up some excuse for Sandhurst later. But if he stopped, what excuse could there possibly be for the cargo he was carrying?

Then he noticed something: the street ahead looked deserted; no parked cars even. Doors open to the summer night, TV sounds, no evidence of men with guns hiding anywhere. But that didn't mean there weren't any.

He jammed to a stop behind the truck and grabbed for the flashlight clipped under the dash. He got out of the cab and slipped under the other truck and stabbed the light at the rear wheels. It shone on the metal of a key ring, and he reached for it and pulled it out. Two keys. There should have been three: Ignition, cab door, rear door. He had a good idea which key was missing and he didn't

162

want to think why. He scrambled to his feet and checked the sides of the truck. The gun slots, two of them high up, were open on the curb side and he flashed the light in but the angle was wrong—he needed to get higher. He climbed up on the fender and had one foot on the roof when he thought of it: a perfect hiding place for four men with guns. He waited for the doors to burst open but nothing moved. He clambered up the rest of the way, flattened himself on the roof, leaned over and directed the flashlight through the gun slot.

The truck was empty except for a sleeping bag on the floor, a mop of brownish hair peeking from the top. The sleeping bag was very still. Whether she was drugged or, God forbid, dead, one thing was certain: this was the switch. Sandhurst had been telling the truth.

He dropped to the street, fumbled a key into the cab door and hopped in. As he knew it would, the other key slipped into the ignition and the engine roared. He took the truck away fast, followed the street round and started back on his tracks. There was no pursuit, no cries, no bullets shattering the windshield. He'd made it! If Lillian was alive, and something told him she was, he'd got her out of it and given Sandhurst the shaft at the same time. Lasky wouldn't get him this time but he only had himself to blame. The important thing was the bluff had worked. But the feeling of elation didn't come. Bunny knew it couldn't be that easy, just as he knew he'd find out why when he played the cassette tape recorder that lay on the seat beside him.

He dropped a reluctant hand onto the machine and punched a button. Sandhurst's voice sounded loud in the enclosed cab, almost as if he were sitting there.

"I'm going to assume three things, Mr. Bergstrom: one, that you've left your truck where you were instructed to leave it; two, that you've realized you don't have the key to the back doors; and three, that you've seen your daughter in there. Let me assure you she's fine. A harmless drug. As to the key, I didn't forget it. It's hidden somewhere in the truck you're driving. Unless you know where to look for it I doubt you'd find it inside of thirty minutes. If you have played fair with me and there is indeed twenty million dollars in the truck you left, drive to the telephone booth where we spoke earlier. After verifying the money I shall call you there at exactly nine o'clock and tell you where to find the key. If, however, you have not carried out your part of the bargain, there is no point in your going to the phone booth. I told you that if you tried to cheat me, your daughter would die—and I meant it. There is a bomb in the back of the truck, Mr. Bergstrom, timed to explode at nine oh three. I may add that any attempt to force the doors will set it off. However, let us assume that you have acted in good faith and that we'll be speaking shortly. Till then, Mr. Bergstrom."

Bunny was numbed by the words, stupefied. He watched the road in the headlights and listened to the hum of the tires and drove stolidly on, his mind immobilized. It was the sight of the shopping plaza that brought him out of it, and the thought of the phone that wasn't going to be ringing at nine o'clock. And the fact that three minutes later there'd be nothing to talk about anyway.

He snapped his arm up. He had exactly nine minutes to get Lillian out of a booby-trapped armored car. Think: the key was in the truck somewhere. His eyes darted round the cab—there were a hundred places it could be: inside the doors, under the mats, in the seats, taped underneath the truck or under the hood. Forget it. Call the house? Call Daniel? Two minutes to get to the booth and make the call, seven minutes left for him to come thirteen miles, call it eight miles if he met him part of the way. Eight miles in seven minutes through suburban traffic—too tight. And there was no guarantee Daniel would have a spare key anyway. He needed that key. He couldn't open the doors without it. A firehouse could open it but that was no good the way they'd do it. Could he get to the bomb without touching the doors? Spray something through the gun slots. Water, maybe. Defuse the bomb with water. A garden hose maybe—one of those houses back there. No, he needed a flood of water. Christ! He was only a few hundred yards from a whole ocean of water, Hempstead Bay. Bunny jammed on the brakes, skidded into the curb and reached for the map, then thumped a fist on the steering wheel. The map was in the other truck. He squinched his eyes shut and forced the image of the map onto his mind's eye. He needed a yacht marina, someplace where he could get the truck into the water. He remembered those little sailboats drawn on the map, half a dozen in Manhasset Bay, but how about Hempstead Bay? Yeah, Glen Cove! Straight up Route Seven where he was pointing now. He slammed the truck into gear and roared away. What was it, about four miles? He had six minutes. He could make it if he could find it. He floored the gas pedal and shot through the Turnpike interchange.

The bay opened up on his left, lights bouncing off the water. A small town came up ahead, and he leaned on the horn and ran a red light and kept on going. He sped by a sign that pointed to a beach and he started to brake then rammed his foot back on the gas. A

164

beach was no good; he couldn't risk getting stuck in the sand. He needed a ramp he could get the truck down.

The road moved away from the bay then, a mile later, bent sharply and took him through another town and on along the edge of the water. A marker said it was a mile and a half to Sea Cliff, and a trickle of sweat started down his eyebrow. He wasn't going to make Glen Cove, but he couldn't just keep driving and wait for the doors to blow off. He needed a marina, but if he stopped and asked somebody it'd be ten to one they wouldn't know. The only thing he could do was keep going.

He belted the truck along and kept his eyes away from his watch.

The road went straight then bent to the right and straightened again, and he spotted the lights of a town ahead. He bore down on it, barreled into it. The road took him through the town then tried to swing him away from the water. He let it go and took another road when he caught its name, Shore Road. It twisted and curved and the tight bends slowed him. If there was no marina he'd have to try a beach, have to try something.

The sign jumped out at him as if he'd willed it into being. It hung in the headlights like a message from heaven. Hallelujah!

He dropped down a gear and wheeled the truck into the turnoff. It was only a hundred yards to a wooden fence, a small gatehouse beside it, a clubhouse beyond it. There was a striped wooden barrier lowered across the gate. Bunny hit the horn, braced himself. He caught a fast glimpse of a startled face behind the window of the gatehouse, then the truck bucked and checked as the fenders splintered the gate and tossed it aside like a rag. He didn't have to look far for the slip—it was dead ahead of him, several boats drawn up alongside it, a large crane on the right. Bunny stood on the brakes and the truck skewered and burned rubber. He gave the wheel full lock and turned the truck so that it was facing the ruined gate and the man who was running toward him. He battled the shift into reverse, stuck his head out of the window and began to back down the concrete ramp that disappeared into the water. He figured that the most logical place for the bomb had to be at the bottom rear next to the doors, probably attached to the vertical bolt bar that locked the doors closed. He just hoped there was a sufficient gap between the doors and the frame to let the water flood inside. He was hoping a lot of things just then.

He felt the rear of the truck hit the water, then push into it. He kept it going until the rear wheels were completely submerged, and

165

thanked God that Lillian was lying in the front of the truck. He cut the engine, jerked the handbrake on and jumped out into two feet of water. He ignored the man who was shouting at him and whipped up his wrist; if the bomb was going off, it was going off in thirty-five seconds.

Then he saw that Lillian might not have even that long. The truck was slowly and inexorably sliding down the green slime of the ramp into the black waters of the bay.

It wasn't a hard choice to make; the bomb might or might not go off, while there was no question about what the water would do. He jumped for the cab and wrenched the ignition key over. Overheated, the engine coughed and whined and turned over reluctantly. But Bunny was too anxious. He shoved the truck into first and gunned the engine. The wheels spun on the ramp and the engine stalled and the truck continued its slow slide into the bay.

It wouldn't start again.

Bunny yelled out of the window, "The winch. Get the winch."

The man on the ramp glanced backward at the boat winch that Bunny was pointing to. He looked round again, bewildered, and didn't move. Bunny jumped for the ramp, slipped, got up and splashed through the water. He ran up the ramp, grabbed the hook that trailed on the ground, back-pedaled clumsily, and was brought up short as the pawl clicked over the ratchet wheel, then bit and held. He tugged on the cable, yelled at the man again. "Free it, for God's sake. There's a kid in that truck."

He shot a fast glance behind him. The truck was half submerged.

The man finally got his feet moving, trotted to the winch and released the cable. Bunny hauled it down the ramp, dropped the hook over the bumper and jumped for the cab. He coaxed the engine to life and barely touched the gas pedal, and with the man working the winch, slowly eased the truck clear of the water.

He didn't bother to check his watch; there was nothing he could do now but get clear. He leapt out and ran to the winch, grabbed the man standing there. "Get down!"

Wide-eyed, the man crouched beside Bunny. "What's going on?" he kept saying. "What's going on?"

Bunny stared at the truck, waiting. He could almost see it happening in slow motion: the hand of the clock completing its circuit, the dynamite expanding, bursting open, the explosion ripping round the steel box, buckling the doors, catapulting them outward, the cloud of smoke blasting out at a thousand miles an hour.

166

Except it wasn't happening. Nothing was happening. The truck was just standing there, hooked to the winch, water glistening on its metal body, dripping down the tires, running in little rivulets back into the bay.

The bomb was twenty seconds late. Then thirty.

Dead or delayed?

And if delayed, for how long? Maybe long enough to find the key.

He reached the truck on the run and started on the cab first. He found a flashlight in the glove compartment and searched the seats, ran his fingers under the dash, poked in the wiring, ripped up floor mats, peeled off the pedal covers. He got out and wriggled underneath the truck stabbing the flashlight around, checked axles and springs and wheel rims. He hauled out the spare and searched its compartment then crawled out, released the hood catch and started on the engine. When he was down to shifting the battery he found the key taped in a recess underneath. It had taken him a long time to find it, so the thought that had occurred to him had had plenty of time to mushroom: if the water hadn't knocked out the bomb, and it had failed to function for some other reason, would the key, which was supposed to deactivate it, have the opposite effect? He knew what he should do—leave it alone and go call Daniel, who'd send a bomb-disposal squad. But he also knew, with the key in his hand, that he wasn't going to do that just yet. He went round to the rear of the truck, pressed the key against the lock, and slowly, gently eased it in till it was snug. He let a breath out and took in another, held it, and began to turn the key. It moved easily in the lock and had reversed itself before he knew it. Now the handle. The handle would shift the vertical bar that ran down the center of the inside door. If anything was going to activate anything, this was what would do it. He closed his fingers over it and tried to tempt it around. He increased the pressure lightly but the handle still resisted. It wasn't built to open at a touch.

Bunny took his hand away, wiped it on his sleeve, and took a fresh grip. He flattened himself against the door, the only precaution he could take, then, without thinking too much about it, wrenched the handle to the right.

There was a click from inside. The door was unlocked. He moved to the side of the truck, leaned across and grasped the handle and, as he jumped backward, jerked the door open.

There was no cataclysmic explosion, no searing amalgam of flame

167

and smoke and twisted metal. The door banged harmlessly back on its hinges and half closed again.

There was no bomb at all that he could see.

There wasn't any Lillian, either.

Chapter **23**

"The bastard," Bunny said, "the rotten lousy bastard. Boy, did he put me through the hoop."

They watched him pacing over the carpet, too mad to sit down, too dirty, too. His clothes were soaked, his hands were black with grease, and his hair was a matted tangle. He dabbed at his face with a towel, then slapped it hard against his leg. He stopped in front of Daniel. "When you said a dummy run you meant it, didn't you. Only there were two dummies in that truck. Wouldn't you think I could tell the difference between Lillian and a couple of pillows in a sleeping bag?"

Daniel made a vague gesture. "Don't be too tough on yourself. They knew you wouldn't be able to see too much. They knew what they were doing."

"Then maybe you can tell me what the hell they had in mind."

Ella echoed Bunny's question. "That's what I'd like to know. What were they trying to prove with all this?" She'd experienced a mixed reaction to Bunny's story; she hadn't really expected him to return with Lillian, but there'd been a spark of hope all the same, and that had been snuffed out five minutes ago. Mingled in with her disappointment was the feeling of relief that nothing worse had happened, although the macabre details of Bunny's trip—the fake bomb and the dummy and the mock threat of death—left her with a fear that nagged at her more than ever.

"I'd say they were flexing their muscles," Lasky replied. "Showing you that they aren't to be trifled with." He looked at Daniel for confirmation and got it.

"Exactly. They chose a particularly tough way of demonstrating that the next time around it's going to be for keeps. I told you that these people had the psychology down. What they did, as wild as it was, is a classic example of the art of extortion—scare the pants off your victim and keep him scared. They went to all that trouble with the tape and the dummy and the key hoping to reduce you to jelly."

"He damned near did," Bunny said. "He had me like a limp rag." He stretched the towel in his hands and snapped it hard. "I would really love to meet that guy." As far as Bunny was concerned, the guerrillas were only one man.

Ella asked Daniel how he thought they'd react to the fake money and the fact that they'd tried to trick them. As she saw it, it couldn't affect Lillian one way or another, seeing as how the guerrillas had tried to trick them, too. It had been the question uppermost in her mind since Bunny had returned, but she'd held off asking it, afraid that Daniel might think differently. To her intense relief he agreed with her.

"They expected a trial run as much as we did. Don't forget, they're dealing with a self-made multimillionaire, and nobody makes a fortune being dumb. It'd be natural to expect him to try a few tricks if he thought he could get away with it. We didn't lose any points tonight. You tried to be cute, they tried to be cute. It comes out even-stephen."

"In point of fact we've made a lot of progress," Lasky put in. "You can bet they were watching Mr. Calder at some stage, so they know he was alone, which is going to make it a lot easier for us. I think the whole exercise was very productive."

Bunny stopped toweling his hair long enough to give Lasky a tired look. He said, "Mr. Lasky, only you could describe driving an armored truck into Long Island Sound as productive."

Daniel smiled and came to his partner's rescue. "I know what Mr. Lasky means and he's right. We were behind them before, but now we're ahead of them." He looked at Ella, glad to be able to tell her something encouraging for a change. "We know their strength but they don't know ours. They'll still play it cautiously, but I'm pretty sure they're convinced they're only dealing with one man. They won't be looking for us when we hit them." He switched his words to Bunny. "When Sandhurst calls again you'll have to admit you tried to

170

pull a fast one, there's no way out of it. But so did he, so you can be suitably angry. A man like Bergstrom wouldn't like to be cheated even though he's perfectly willing to cheat himself."

Bunny nodded his understanding. "I guess we'll get down to the nitty gritty this time."

"Yep. No more fooling around. This time everything will be for real."

"Except the money . . ."

"Except the money."

"What do we use for money, seeing they've got it?"

"The same thing," Daniel said. "We had two lots made up."

"Brown paper again?" Ella asked.

"Exactly as before."

"Excuse me," Ella said, "I think I'll go make some coffee."

Hartley, who, like the tape technician, was sitting on the other side of the room, jumped up and offered to do it for her, but Ella declined and left the room quickly. She'd had to leave or tear into Daniel, and there was nothing to be gained by doing that. She banged open cupboards, pulled out cups and saucers and banged doors closed again. The man was unbelievable; they'd just shown those people what they had to bargain with and here he was preparing to use the same thing all over again. She was tired of him being so wise after the fact; that little speech about how extortionists work, for example. He'd been as surprised as any of them by the bomb and the dummy. It had jolted him, and it had shown, even though he'd tried to hide it. She reached for the sugar bowl and slammed another cupboard door. She was angry, frustrated and very scared. When she brought the tray upstairs the men weren't sitting where she'd left them but were gathered round the tape recorder.

Sandhurst had called.

The tape man clicked buttons and the conversation was reproduced.

"Mr. Bergstrom?"

"Who else?" Bunny's voice sounded sharp and irritated.

"Have you finished playing games?"

"Have *I* finished? You're the one with the dress up dolls and the messages. What the hell do you mean running me around like that?"

"And what the hell do you mean by the bags of brown paper?"

Bunny let a lengthy second go by. "Okay, we both tried it on and it didn't work. Now what?"

"Now we do it with no tricks. This time we examine the merchandise before we swap. Do you agree?"

"Damn right I do. I want my daughter this time, not a dummy."

"She'll be real, Mr. Bergstrom. But if the money isn't, she'll also be dead." Bunny took the indignation out of his voice and let it collapse on itself.

"All right. It'll be real. I'll need time to get it."

"Naturally. Although I rather think you can get the real money faster than the fake. Am I correct?"

"I'll have it by tomorrow night. Where do we meet, same place?"

"No, I'll call you tomorrow at eight and tell you then. Bring the money in the truck you took tonight. And, Mr. Bergstrom . . ."

"Yes?"

"That's all you'll bring in the truck. Playtime is over."

There was the click of a phone hanging up.

After the government men had left, and Hartley had gone to his room, Bunny and Ella stayed where they were, sitting opposite each other in the living room. Bunny's clothes had just about dried but he was still covered with grime and looked a mess. He was tired and angry and wanted nothing more than to fall asleep in a hot bath, but he was too wound up to relax. Like Ella he couldn't believe that Daniel and Lasky were planning to play this one by ear too; to wait till Sandhurst called tomorrow night and then take it from there. Their only plan was to plant a bleeper in the truck, follow it, then make their move when the time looked right. When Bunny and Ella had argued vociferously against this course of action they'd been met by bland assurances that everything would be all right. The point was everything could not possibly be all right if that's all they were going to rely on. It just wasn't enough. Bunny said as much to her again. He was long past the point of playing Mr. Confident; he was too tired and had fought too many battles and it was zero hour tomorrow night. Instead of pulling his punches he told her exactly what he thought.

"They're making a colossal mistake. I think Daniel's underestimating Sandhurst by a couple of country miles. He claims he knows the guy, but if anybody knows him, it's me. I'm the one who talks to him. Daniel only listens to a playback. Sandhurst is smart and shrewd and ruthless. Look at the way he ran me ragged with nothing at stake. What's he going to be like tomorrow night when he's playing for keeps?"

172

It was a rhetorical question and Bunny sailed on. "I don't think Lasky's any smarter either. I'll bet his boss in Washington knows nothing about this. A rookie patrolman wouldn't try using fake money again. That's the worst thing about this, we're taking something that didn't work once and trying it a second time."

"I know," Ella said, "and I don't understand it either. Daniel says if they'd bugged the truck tonight they would have got the driver and probably Sandhurst but not the other two and not Lillian. Fine, I can see why he held off. But how he can seriously think he'll get everybody tomorrow night just because those people aren't expecting anybody . . . I mean, they're sure to have built-in safeguards. We know what they're like; they haven't missed a trick so far."

They both fell silent; it was pointless echoing each other; not if it all added up to a string of negatives. Bunny got out of his chair, crossed the room and sagged into another one. He picked at the braiding around the cushion, frowning down at it. When he spoke again his anger had melted and been replaced by a cooler emotion.

"Ella, we've got to do something. You and me." His head came up. "We've got to think of an alternative."

Dully, she repeated his last two words.

"When I meet Sandhurst tomorrow I want something better up my sleeve than a bleeper in the back of a truck. I don't want to have to depend on Daniel arriving at the last moment like the cavalry. We don't know what Sandhurst is planning, but you can bet he's planning. I need a better edge. Something a lot better than wrapping paper."

Then very slowly, his eyes widening, he sat up straighter in his chair. "Ella . . ." he spread his hands; it was so simple. "What have I been doing? I should have my brains reblocked. If we had real money in the back of that truck we'd be home and dry."

"But you know what Lasky said about that."

"Lasky's not going to get it. Don Ray Bergstrom is."

Ella sat straighter, too.

Bunny said, "If that twenty million was real we don't have to depend on Daniel and Lasky. Not for getting Lillian back. And good old Don Ray could raise that kind of loot with one phone call. And he's going to."

Ella thought of ten different questions but condensed them all into one word. "How?"

"How do you usually raise money? You get a loan from the bank. I'll simply call Chase or First National and put the arm on them."

"For twenty million? You think they'd lend you a fortune like that?"

"Banks do it all the time. That's how they make money."

"To corporations maybe, not to one man."

"We're talking about Don Ray Bergstrom. He's a corporation in himself. What's a bank going to get, something close to nine or ten percent. On a twenty million dollar loan? They'll jump at it."

For the first time Ella seriously considered what he was saying. "It's a great idea, but you'll never swing it."

"Sure I will." Bunny got up out of his chair. "I've been conning people all my life off my own bat. There's an admission for you. If I can't con them as Don Ray Bergstrom I'll turn in my badge."

"But it sounds so"—she searched for the right word—"outrageous."

"Not as outrageous as faking the money a second time. I think it'll work but I'll have to shake Daniel and Lasky, that's number-one priority. I don't want them charging in and blowing it."

That bothered Ella. "I don't know. There are four of them and they have guns. It sounds awfully risky just by yourself."

"That's okay, I'll be armed with the money."

"And after Lillian's safe? You'll still have to get the money back somehow. Wouldn't you want to have Daniel and Lasky around then?"

Bunny was emphatic. "No, ma'am. I'm planning to come out of it with Lillian *and* the money."

Ella looked at him blankly and Bunny laughed. But there was a firm purpose in back of it. He said, "Sandhurst conned me and I'm going to con him right back. He's going to find out you can't fool with the master."

174

Chapter 24

They knew that if Daniel or Lasky suspected that something was up they wouldn't get very far, so when they had coffee with Hartley next morning they were careful to hide any new sign of confidence. They chatted to him briefly, going over the events of the day before and listening to him speculate about their chances that night. He saw nothing but success ahead. Then they left him to his chores—Bunny was happy to see him occupied; he didn't want him overhearing the phone call he was about to make.

He passed up the phone in the living room on account of the tape recorder attached to it, and guided Ella into a room that had an outside phone. He called Information and asked for the number of a bank in Manhattan, choosing the same bank that had supplied the sacks for the fake money. He wanted the real money to look exactly the same as the fake stuff in case Daniel got nosy. He got the number, hung up and dialed again. His call was promptly answered and he asked for Personal Loans. He waited to be put through and winked at Ella. She was still dubious about the whole idea, not sure that it would work or that it was safe. By contrast Bunny was his old confident self—and it felt good. It was a relief to be back pulling strings again.

"Hello," he said, "who am I speaking to please?"

His voice was crisp, efficient; polite but with a lot of authority in it. "Mr. Morris. Good morning, Mr. Morris. This is Don Ray Bergstrom speaking . . . that's right, Bergstrom. Mr. Morris, are you empowered to approve loans of a substantial size or would you prefer I talked to your boss? . . . Twenty million. . . . That's what I said, yes. . . . Certainly I'll hold." A minute passed then he spoke again. "Mr. Hoyt, is it? Good morning. . . . Yes, Mr. Morris is entirely correct. Twenty million on a short-term loan. Now, Mr. Hoyt, as I'd like to negotiate this by phone, this is what I suggest you do. Call Information and get my number from them. It'll be listed under Bernard Silverman, Oyster Bay. I just recently bought his. . . . Ah, you read about that. Fine. Call me back immediately if you'd be so kind. That way you'll know it's me you're speaking to and not some prankster fooling around. You can't be too careful these days. . . . Thank you, Mr. Hoyt, I'll be waiting for your call."

Bunny replaced the phone and slapped his hands together. "He's calling back. I told you they'd go for it."

"They haven't gone for it yet," Ella said. "What if Mr. Hoyt wants some collateral?"

Bunny looked at her, surprised. "Well, of course he will. Nobody lends millions of dollars just on a signature. He's going to want all kinds of collateral."

Ella said, "Maybe I'm extra stupid this morning but what—"

"Collateral? This house, the yacht, the cars, securities. I'm worth half a billion, remember?"

Ella's mouth opened but the words didn't come for a moment. "Bunny. You can't do that. You can't pledge other people's property. And what securities? They don't exist."

"Mr. Hoyt doesn't know that. Like the rest of the country, he thinks I'm a rich man. By the time the bank gets down to the evidence of that, all the paper, it'll be too late to stop the loan. Anyway, if things go okay I'll have their money back to them before they get too upset."

"You know what you're about to do, don't you? You're about to perpetrate a colossal fraud. Borrowing money on your signature would be bad enough, but putting up fake collateral . . . they're throwing the book at people for that these days."

"But I'm only planning to keep it for a few hours. The bank won't be out anything."

"They'll be out twenty million dollars if those men take the money and run. Then they'll put you in jail forever."

"That doesn't scare me," Bunny said. "I'm already used to the cooking."

176

Ella said softly, "You'd take a risk like that for Lillian?"

"Not Lillian, Sandhurst. I want a piece of that guy."

Ella said, "She buried you in the sand."

"Sandhurst almost buried me in the bay."

"She smeared peanut butter on your nose."

"Sandhurst rubbed it in the dirt. Look, I'm happy to take Lillian with me. Wouldn't dream of leaving without her. But the main reason I'm doing this is because Sandhurst suckered me and lowered my national ranking."

It suddenly became apparent to Bunny that Ella was looking at him in a different way. It made him wonder if he could offer her a nightcap at nine thirty in the morning. Then the telephone rang and snapped him back into his part.

"Mr. Hoyt? . . . Hello again. Sorry to put you to this trouble but I thought you'd want to . . . fine. Glad you understand. Now, let me say at the outset here that I'm coming to you rather than my regular bank because frankly I feel they've been taking me for granted lately and I thought maybe it was time to give you people a try." Bunny held the phone away from his ear till the man on the other end had completed his confirming sales talk. "Good to hear that, Mr. Hoyt. Now, as I told you I need twenty million on short term. But there's one stipulation. Two really. I have to have the money by tonight and it must be in cash."

From three feet away Ella heard the reaction. "Cash?"

"I know it's a lot on such short notice but I have a chance to put through a really good real estate deal and, frankly, Mr. Hoyt, the seller is a bit eccentric and deals only in cash. A good business man but doesn't trust banks. Can you imagine that in this day and age?"

In his office in Manhattan Mr. Hoyt couldn't imagine that in any day and age.

"However," Bunny went on when he got the chance, "since the loan will be amply covered by the kind of collateral I'm prepared to put up . . . well, I suggest blocks of some of my blue chips, say fifty thousand each of GM, Kodak and Woolworth"—Bunny caught a glimpse of Ella rolling her eyes toward the ceiling—"but I suggest you work out the exact terms with my business managers tomorrow. What I'd like to do now is give you my verbal agreement to your standard rate and wave the discount in view of the inconvenience I'm putting you to. . . . Not at all, Mr. Hoyt. Now this is how I'd like the money, and it's most important. I want it in twenty of your money sacks, exactly twenty. And I want it delivered to me here in an armored truck as close to six this evening as you can possibly make it. It can't be any later. . . . That's right. And, Mr. Hoyt, I'm going to have to keep the money here overnight and I think the best way to do that is to leave it in the truck. I'll supply my own guards . . . fine. I'll see you at six and sign all the necessary papers then. . . . Excellent. Looking forward to meeting you, Mr. Hoyt. Good-bye."

Bunny took the phone from his ear, held it delicately between two fingers and dropped it back onto its cradle. "See? If you want to withdraw twenty bucks you have to wait in line. But for twenty million they deliver."

Ella slowly shook her head at him. "Anybody else would have used a drill and nitroglycerin. All you use is a telephone."

"The mouth is mightier than the sword." He started pacing the room again. "Let's see how it plays. Hoyt gets here with the truck at six. We get rid of him fast and stash the truck down the side drive where nobody's going to spot it. Sandhurst calls at eight with directions. I get into the truck with the fake money, drive out the front gate, zip down the side road to the side gate and switch trucks. Daniel and Lasky won't spot me because they'll give me a quarter mile start before they follow."

"No good," Ella said.

"Why not?"

"Because they won't be following you, they'll be following the truck with the bleeper, which you'll have left on the side road."

Bunny stopped pacing and tapped his forehead. "Right. We need a driver for that truck." He looked at her speculatively, but Ella raised both hands.

"I can't even work the shift in a Volkswagen."

"Okay, somebody to drive the truck." His finger traced the inlaid pattern in the top of a side table, following the loops and scrolls as if they were part of a puzzle. Then his head came up. "The driver. The man who drives the truck out here with Hoyt. He can hang around for a couple of hours and drive it back again."

"Without Daniel or Lasky spotting him?"

"I'll arrange to meet him round the corner somewhere. I'll drive the truck out of the gate and hand it over to him. Then he drives it back to Manhattan, and Daniel and Lasky follow, which gets them out of my hair. It'll work."

Ella said, "You're still way ahead of yourself. If Sandhurst tells you to go back to the phone booth in Roslyn again and the truck goes sailing by toward Manhattan, they'll know something's wrong. And you can't lie about his direction because of the tape recorder."

Bunny had the answer before Ella had finished posing the problem. "I'll fake the phone call from Sandhurst. I'll call from my room at seven fifty, say. You'll answer the phone, put on an act, I'll give you some address in Manhattan and that'll be where Daniel and Lasky will think I'm driving to."

"But you've forgotten the tape again. They'll hear you on the playback."

"That's the whole idea." Then, in a close imitation of Sandhurst's accent, Bunny said, "Mr. Bergstrom, is everything ready?"

A smile started in the corner of her mouth. "I didn't know you were that talented. That's not bad."

"It'll get us by. Daniel and Lasky aren't going to be expecting a fake call."

"That's true, but you'll have to make it before seven fifty. You have to be back here for the real call at eight, which only leaves you ten minutes to drive the truck to the corner and get back again. That's not long enough."

"Right again. Stick around."

"Unless I took the call for you."

"Nope. Sandhurst might not like that. He might want to call it off till tomorrow night. The trouble is, if I call much earlier than seven fifty, Daniel is likely to smell a rat. Every time Sandhurst has called he's been right on the button. A minute either way. Ten minutes early would be all right but not twenty."

Ella saw the problem but had no immediate solution. Bunny went over it.

"Let's see, I call at ten to eight from my room, hotfoot it back here, listen to the tape, then get into the truck and leave. That's five minutes. Daniel and Lasky leave at the same time and head for the bleeper van, or wait for it to join them. I drive the truck to the corner and turn it over to the driver. So I have to find a way to get back here in about three minutes. I could leave the pick-up at the corner but Daniel would spot it for sure."

"Lillian's bike," Ella said. "You could leave it against the wall at the corner. Hide it under the ivy. After you hand over the truck you simply pedal down the side road and up the side drive."

"Can I ride that thing? Does the saddle come up?"

"Yes, sir."

"Then that's that problem solved. And if that's solved, they're all solved. Or are they?"

Ella thought about it. "We'll have to get Hartley out of the way when the money comes and again when the call comes."

"God, yes. I'd forgotten about old Hartley. When the truck arrives at six go ask him to whip you up a scrambled egg on a sword or something. And at eight o'clock ask for coffee and keep him down in the kitchen. You know," Bunny said, "it's really starting to come together. It's a damned good plan."

"Oh, it's a honey. You're going to steal twenty million dollars and go up against a gang of terrorists by yourself. You don't do things by halves, do you?"

The soft light that Bunny had seen earlier was back in her eyes, and she'd moved closer to him.

Bunny found that he'd moved closer to her, too. And then, somehow, there didn't seem to be much space between them at all. They seemed to melt against each other and stayed that way for a long minute.

Very slowly, Bunny took his mouth away from Ella's. "This can't be us."

"Must be two other people," Ella murmured.

They moved together again and looked like they might stay that way permanently, but a heavy footstep sounded behind them.

"Watch it," Bunny warned, "it's the chef who walks like a bear."

Hartley clumped into his room, two steaming mugs in his fists. "Bullyon," he said. "Midmorning bullyon."

Bunny peered into the mug he was given. A square bouillon cube sat neatly on the bottom, undisturbed by the hot water. Bunny sipped. "Say, you must give me the recipe."

"Nothin' to it. You want a piece of fruit with it? Banana, apple maybe?"

They both declined.

"Go ahead, drink it," Hartley urged. "It can't hurt." He turned and clumped back out of the room.

"Momma was a bodyguard," Bunny said.

Ella laughed. It was possible to laugh now that there was a real chance of getting Lillian back. It was a wild idea of Bunny's, but there was no reason why it shouldn't work; they'd covered all the angles.

Which was true. They had covered all the angles.

Except the one they didn't know about.

180

Mr. Hoyt the banker was not a man to take a client's request lightly, especially if it came from a very rich, very important new client, so he made sure that it was six o'clock exactly when he steered his Lincoln Continental through the gates of the old Silverman mansion. Twenty feet behind him a silver-gray Brink's truck followed him in, and behind that another automobile. They rolled in a stately convoy up the drive to the marble steps where Bunny was waiting for them.

Mr. Hoyt looked like a banker, large, effusive, conservatively dressed. He had a well-barbered, jowly face which split into a smile of relief when he recognized Don Ray Bergstrom from the photographs he'd seen.

Bunny welcomed him, shook hands and ushered him inside, his manner polite but distant; a man used to dealing with executive underlings; a man who rarely met his equal and never his peer. After a few fast preliminaries they got right down to it, and Bunny started signing forms.

"I appreciate the service, Mr. Hoyt, and I apologize for the short notice."

"Think nothing of it, sir. Service is our middle name. Naturally we're delighted to be doing business with you even if the circumstances are"—he permitted himself an admonishing chuckle—"shall we say, irregular."

"I don't conduct business in the established manner, Mr. Hoyt. If I did, I wouldn't be where I am today."

"Of course. Of course."

"I've always sworn by one simple formula, Mr. Hoyt. Keep them guessing, keep them on the wrong foot, then strike when they least expect it."

Hoyt listened with both ears, grateful for the advice of a financial genius. Then he said, getting back to the business in hand, "Regarding the collateral, Mr. Bergstrom . . ."

"Yes. As I said on the phone, I suggest you contact my business managers for the actual paper. That's Daniel and Lasky, Inc."

Mr. Hoyt scribbled their name. "And their phone number, sir?"

Bunny gave him the number of the Haverstraw Travel Agency then steered him toward the front door. "Sorry I can't offer you some refreshment but I have a conference in a few minutes."

"Quite all right, Mr. Bergstrom."

They stepped out onto the drive. There was a driver and a guard in the front seat of the Brink's truck and two uniformed men in the car behind it.

Hoyt said, "I've arranged with the Brink's people to leave the truck overnight as you requested. Are you sure you wouldn't like extra guards?"

Bunny told him he preferred his own.

They walked to the truck, and Hoyt nodded at the guard, who spoke into the mike above his head. The rear doors clicked and swung open and two guards with pump guns climbed down. For a half second Bunny thought it was the fake money he was seeing—the twenty white canvas sacks with the bank's name on the sides looked exactly the same. At another nod from the banker the guard reached for a sack and pulled it out of the truck. He fitted a key into the padlock, snapped it open and spread the mouth of the sack.

Inside it was a neat, stacked, bundled sea of green.

"It's all in hundred dollar bills," Hoyt said. "Twenty sacks, fifty bundles in each, two hundred bills to a bundle." He nodded and the guard closed and relocked the sack and placed it back in the truck. He handed the keys to Hoyt, who passed them on to Bunny. "There are six keys, each identical, as are the padlocks."

The guard slammed the rear doors and locked them and handed over those keys, too.

"Rear and side door keys and ignition keys, two of each, identical, of course."

Hoyt dropped them into Bunny's hand and Bunny pocketed them.

"I'm impressed, Mr. Hoyt. I like your bank's approach."

Mr. Hoyt gave him the slogan. "We mean business, Mr. Bergstrom. Is there any other way we can help you?"

"As a matter of fact, there is. I have another Brink's truck here, an empty one. I wonder if the driver would take it back to the garage for me?"

Mr. Hoyt, who seldom went in for eyebrow-raising, went in for it now. "Another armored car?"

"I'll be finished with it in a few hours. I'd appreciate it, Mr. Hoyt, if you could ask the driver to wait."

"I'll check with him," Hoyt said, still shaken. This cash deal of Bergstrom's was evidently bigger than twenty million. Forty million? With a touch of awe in his voice Hoyt called the driver over. He explained the request and the driver agreed.

"I'll drive the truck out of the gate," Bunny said, "and meet you at the corner. You can take it from there."

The driver tried to help out. "No need. I can come in and get it."

"No. I have to drive it out of the grounds. It can't be any other way."

"I don't know about that." The man glanced at Hoyt, not happy with it. "Only us drivers are supposed to drive the trucks, the insurance, you know? And then you ain't bonded, either. And you ain't union."

Hoyt caught Bunny's look and jumped in quickly. "I'm sure it will be okay, driver. I'll call your boss and square it with him."

Bunny brought out his wallet and came up with a ten dollar bill. "Mr. Hoyt will drop you off in the village. You get yourself some supper and get a cab back here to the first corner outside the gate, and be there by five of eight. You must be there by that time. It's very important."

The money seemed to salve the driver's conscience. "Well, if you're only going to be driving it as far as the corner . . ."

Bunny had a few more words with Hoyt, who dismissed the Brink's guards. They got into the other car and drove off. Then the driver got into Hoyt's car and Hoyt shook hands with Bunny and took his leave.

On his way out of the gate the driver said to him, "What's a guy like that want to drive a truck for, anyway? He get tired of Ferraris?"

"Mr. Bergstrom is a very eccentric man," Hoyt replied, with a note of superiority. "And a very rich one. And the rich are different from us." Mr. Hoyt loved that quotation.

"He may be rich but he ain't union," the driver insisted. "They find out about this, they could fine me."

"How much would a fine like that come to, do you think?"

The driver eyed Hoyt and his expensive suit and expensive car. "At least twenty-five bucks."

Mr. Hoyt reached into an inside pocket. "If they do, I wouldn't want you to be out." He darted his eyes at the driver. "Just as I wouldn't want you to miss Mr. Bergstrom at five of eight tonight."

The banker didn't want anything to go wrong with this transaction. Don Ray Bergstrom was one customer he wanted to keep happy.

As the driver rode by the corner where he had to be later on, the truck he'd just delivered was on its way down the side drive. Bunny took it down to the wall, reversed it over a flower bed and stuck it under the overhanging branches of a thick green willow. Then he ran back up to the garage and got Lillian's bike. Ironically, somebody had leaned it against the truck that had been housed in the garage from the night before. The salt water didn't seem to have marked it and there were only a few scratches where it had creamed the gate. Bunny found a wrench and raised the saddle on the bike. Then he pedaled it down the drive, out of the side gate and up the narrow lane almost to the main road. The wall here had been built in a series of recessed brick arches which had become overgrown with ivy. The ivy was tough but Bunny managed to tear enough of it away to slide the bike under. It wasn't completely covered, and in Manhattan it wouldn't have lasted two minutes, but Oyster Bay people had better things to do than rip off bikes. He figured it would be safe enough for two hours anyway. He strolled back down the side road, going over everything in his mind.

As far as he could see he'd covered all the bases. There was nothing he could do now but wait for Daniel and Lasky to arrive, fool them with the phone call, switch trucks, take the real call, then go bail Lillian out. Which was probably going to be the easy part.

Getting the money back was going to be the toughie.

It was pointless trying to formulate some kind of plan, seeing as how he had no idea what the arrangements were going to be. And even if he had known them, he wouldn't have bothered. Bunny wasn't a planner; he thought best on his feet. He only hoped he was going to end up that way.

Chapter **25**

The black van that Daniel and Lasky arrived with was the same one Bunny had seen before. And he'd seen its contents before, too: twenty bulging white canvas sacks. A man got out of the van and at Daniel's direction brought the armored truck around from the garage. Then he began transferring the sacks. Bunny, watching the procedure, asked Lasky how much it cost to fake twenty million dollars.

"It's not cheap. We have to run the paper in a print shop so we can cut it and bind it. There's a lot of man hours involved."

"Well, you won't be making it up again. It either works tonight or it doesn't."

"I know that," Lasky said. "You all set?"

"What for? All I do is drive. You're the ones who have to be all set."

"We're ready," Lasky told him. He turned to watch a man fiddling with something under the back of the truck.

"The bleeper," Bunny said. He didn't need any confirmation.

When the man had finished, Lasky went over to his car, picked up a radio phone, spent a minute with it and came back. "They're picking it up loud and clear." The last sack was put into the Brink's truck, the doors locked, and the keys handed to Lasky. Lasky pressed them into Bunny's hand. Then Daniel arrived with the tape technician and they all went into the house. Ella and Hartley were there and everybody murmured greetings but said little else. The atmosphere was tense. The small talk, the theories, the speculation weren't much use now that they were just an hour or two away from a final result.

Daniel spoke briefly but had nothing new to offer in the way of strategy, reiterating the same old plan of follow, wait, and pounce.

On a sideboard, set against the wall, an ormolu clock ticked with a steady patient cadence, its ornate hands shadowing each other at seven forty-five.

The tape man moved in behind his machine and began fiddling with things in the manner of a percussionist tuning up.

Bunny decided against drawing attention to himself with an excuse and simply drifted toward the door and moved through it. Then he hurried through the house, out a side door, and ran to his room above the garage.

He dialed the house on the outside line and on the fifth ring the phone was picked up. Ella said hello.

Bunny closed his eyes and summoned up the remembered accent. "Mr. Bergstrom, please."

Her voice came back to him, tremulous and thin. "He's in another part of the house. Is that . . . ?"

"Yes, it is, Mrs. Bergstrom. I assume that's whom I'm talking to?"

"We have the money. We've done everything you asked. Please don't hurt Sherrel."

"Your daughter is in perfect health, Mrs. Bergstrom, and will continue to remain so just as long as my instructions are followed."

"We'll do anything you say."

"Very well." Bunny only hoped he sounded half as convincing as Ella did. "Tell your husband to drive the truck to Tenth Avenue and Twenty-third street in Manhattan. I will contact him in the phone booth on that corner. Did you hear that address?"

"Tenth and Twenty-third," Ella repeated.

Bunny hung up, ran down the stairs, recrossed the drive, entered the house and made his way to the living room. He acted surprised when he saw them round the tape recorder.

"He called early," Daniel said. "You missed him."

Bunny began an apology but Daniel wasn't interested. The tape rolled.

Bunny cringed inwardly when he heard himself doing the accent, but it didn't seem to bother either of the government men. They listened intently to the conversation and started moving as it finished.

"Okay, there it is," Daniel said. Everybody moved for the door.

186

Hartley's gravelly voice said, "On the way back, Mr. Calder, tell the kid I got her favorite for supper."

"God bless you, Hartley." Turning, Bunny saw the uncertainty in Ella's face, but there was nothing he could say to her now. He went through the rooms quickly and out onto the drive and hopped up into the truck.

Daniel appeared at the window talking fast. "We'll stay a quarter mile behind you till you get where you're going. When it comes to the switchover, stall as long as you can. Don't play hero, but if you get a chance to grab the girl take it. And be ready to hit the deck when we come in. We're going to try to keep bullets out of it, but there's no guarantee."

Lasky joined him and thrust a map at Bunny. "I've marked the phone booth corner, Tenth and Twenty-third. If the Expressway's jammed take the Northern State then Queens Boulevard. Good luck, now."

The two men stepped back and hurried away to their car. Bunny revved the truck and took it down the drive and out of the gate. He shot a look at his watch; he would have to hurry. In the rear vision mirror he saw Daniel and Lasky's car come out of the gate and pull over, waiting for the bleeper van. The road curved ahead, which meant that he'd be out of their sight at the corner as long as they stayed where they were. He hurried the truck along, watching the road bend then straighten, and the corner came up at him.

For a moment he thought the driver had let him down, but then he saw him. Bunny drove the truck into the curb and jumped out. "It's all yours. Back to the garage and don't stop anywhere."

The driver, who, after two hamburgers, a coke and a cab ride, was still thirty dollars up on the deal, moved smartly. "Yes, sir, Mr. Bergstrom." He got in behind the wheel and drove off.

Bunny raced across the road, turned into the side lane, and dragged the bike out from under the ivy. He pedaled away, keeping close to the wall, down the lane to the side gate and up the drive, hoping that Ella had been quick getting Hartley out of the way. He left the bike near the door and ran silently into the living room, collapsed into a chair by the phone and sucked in deep breaths. He'd made it with half a minute to spare. He was pretty sure Hartley wouldn't be able to hear the phone down in the kitchen, but he rested a hand on it all the same.

When it rang, just on eight, he snatched it up immediately. "Bergstrom."

"Anxious, Mr. Bergstrom?"

"Only to get this over as soon as possible. Where do I meet you?"

"Same place as last time. I'll call you at the same time."

"That nonsense again? Why not tell me now?"

"Because I'm a very cautious man, Mr. Bergstrom."

Bunny listened to the other man hang up, did the same himself and retraced his steps to the side door. He mounted the bike and pedaled back down to the gate, opened both gates wide, then let himself into the truck. He maneuvered it out from under the willow, across the flower beds and stopped it on the edge of the drive. He figured that Daniel and Lasky had to be on their way by now, but he gave it a few more minutes before taking the truck through the gates and up the lane. He took a left at the main road and drove exactly the same route he'd driven the night before. Familiar with it, he was able to judge it so that he arrived in the parking lot with a good five minutes in hand.

Once again he swept his eyes over the parked cars and the stores. The place looked exactly the same, the drugstore, the ice cream parlor, the supermarket closing up; even the music coming from the record store sounded like the same record.

At eight thirty-seven the light came on in the phone booth as somebody entered it. Bunny couldn't believe he'd made the same mistake as last night, but that's what had happened; he'd been too slow getting to it again. He got out and ran toward the booth. He could see a man in there, the phone in one hand, the other fumbling for change.

Bunny pushed open the door and started to speak, but didn't get very far. The man had turned and Bunny saw that his other hand was not digging for change but holding a pistol. His eyes came up to his face; a small man, stocky; very dark olive skin, a short, thick moustache under a beaky nose, thick black hair. The skin was young and unblemished, the facial features a thousand years old. The man hadn't spoken, but Bunny knew how his voice would sound.

"Good evening, Mr. Bergstrom." Now that he could see the man, the correct, formal accent sounded more ludicrous than ever.

"What is this?"

"Instead of a phone call, the personal touch. Shall we proceed to your truck?"

"Where's my daughter?"

"You can drive me to her." Sandhurst flicked his gun at the door. "Shall we?"

188

Bunny held his eyes for a moment longer then pushed out of the booth and walked to the truck. Sandhurst searched the cab before allowing Bunny to get in.

"I was checking for a walkie-talkie. I thought you might be in contact with people you shouldn't."

Bunny gripped the wheel and looked at him with loathing. He was playing a part he found easy. "There's just me and the money. Now take me to Sherrel. And if you've harmed her, believe me, I'll kill you before you kill me."

Sandhurst didn't appear in the least affected by the threat. Either he'd sensed that the man he was holding a gun on wasn't a killer, or he was used to living with the possibility of death.

"Drive out of the parking lot and turn right."

Bunny did as he was told. Sandhurst directed him to Northern Boulevard.

"How far is it?" Bunny asked. "Where are you taking me?"

"You'll see your daughter in thirty minutes. As long as we're not being followed."

He glanced in the wing mirror, although his gun stayed pointed at Bunny. Bunny wondered about the gun; the guy had Lillian, why did he feel he needed anything else? It had to be because he still wasn't sure whether or not the police were in on it. He'd demonstrated that. And if they were—if they moved in on the truck—Sandhurst would have Bunny as a hostage. And that, Bunny concluded, was possibly the only reason why he wasn't lying dead back there in the parking lot. Five miles farther on a dark-colored car moved to pass them, slowed in front of them and winked its brake lights twice. Sandhurst ordered him to follow it. The car had obviously tailed them from the parking lot looking for any tag. The knowledge that he'd done the right thing ditching Daniel and Lasky buoyed him up, although, surprisingly, he felt good anyway. Even with the gun a foot away from him there was no parched mouth, no shirt-sticking sweat as there'd been when he thought a bomb was in the back. A time bomb was all cogs and springs and buttons, a mindless piece of machinery that couldn't be argued with. But a man had to shoot a gun, and a man could be fooled. And Bunny knew that the man sitting next to him had to be fooled if he was going to come out of this a winner. He had to beat the guy.

The car ahead flashed under an overhead sign and the reflected light lit up the interior for a brief second. Two men. That meant the fourth would be with Lillian. Which could mean that she wasn't drugged or tied up, which was a big plus for him. When the time came for it, whatever developed, things were going to be a lot easier if she were mobile. Then another thought occurred to him; a far more disturbing one: that fourth man could also be with Lillian as a hedge against things going wrong at the last moment. That was more likely; it fitted the pattern of Sandhurst's thinking—the two armored trucks, the scary run-through, the meticulous way he'd covered himself against being followed. He was playing a very tight game so far.

Bunny glanced at him. The man was watching the car ahead, his face unexpressive. The gun was resting loosely in his hand pointing down now. For the moment he seemed satisfied that there was no immediate danger.

They drove through Little Neck and Douglaston and kept going. In the sky above them a plane approached La Guardia. They rumbled through the crisscross of the Whitestone Parkway and came out at the edge of the Bay. They were getting close to Manhattan, and Bunny wondered if that's where they were headed after all. A few miles farther he found out. The car they were following turned off the highway away from the city approaches. Bunny caught sight of a sign that said Steinway Avenue. The car took a left and Bunny was lost; as near as he could figure it they had to be somewhere round Long Island City. They went through a drab, nondescript area, sad-looking red brick houses and some newer high-rises fronting the street. Something that looked like a freight terminal loomed up ahead. The car slowed and made a turn and drove through a double gate in a high cyclone fence. There was a long roofed-over construction that covered raised wooden loading docks stacked with crates, two truck-trailer containers standing at one end. They moved around to the rear of the building, bumping over the broken asphalt yard that was patchily lit by stanchion lights spaced at wide intervals along a side wall. The car's headlights lit up a dark opening and the car disappeared into it.

"Where are you taking me?"

"To your daughter."

Bunny slipped the truck down a gear and followed the car. The ramp dipped and curved down and around and came out in an underground garage. Jacketed lights blazed in the ceiling and bounced off the oil-spotted concrete floor. On one side was a repair shop with a large hoist, a tire machine, and a long work bench with spanners and wrenches mounted above it on the white tiled wall. There was an old-fashioned gasoline pump at one end.

The garage was empty except for the Wells Fargo truck that sat solidly on the floor near the rear wall.

Bunny brought the truck around in a tight circle and parked next to it, facing the entrance. There was only one way in and out of the garage and he wanted to be ready to leave in a hurry if he had to. And the way things were shaping up it looked like a definite possibility.

The two men had got out of the car carrying machine guns.

The men themselves, with tiny differences, seemed carbon copies of Sandhurst—same age, same build, same fierce, dark features. The guns were Garrard M-16s and had to be stolen U.S. Army issue.

Bunny turned a hard face to Sandhurst. "She'd better be in there."

Sandhurst opened his door. "Come and see for yourself, Mr. Bergstrom."

Bunny got out and watched as the man thumped on the rear of the truck and called out something in a guttural language Bunny had never heard before. There was a heavy click as a bolt was shot back and the doors were pushed open. Inside, illuminated by the small ceiling light, Lillian was sitting against the far wall. The man who'd opened the door held a machine gun pointed at her. Bunny said, "Sherrel!" and started forward, but was stopped by the gun which spun round to cover him. Bunny said, "Are you okay?"

"Yes." Lillian looked tired and pale but was clearly unharmed, and Bunny let out a silent breath. The possibility of her not being okay was something he hadn't let himself think too much about. He reached into his pocket for the sack keys and held them out to Sandhurst.

"Get your man out and I'll take this truck. You can check the money now."

He knew that once he could get that gun away from Lillian's head, and get her locked safely inside the truck, it would be a whole new ball game. But Sandhurst wasn't interested in the keys. He was a long way from making a trade yet.

"All in good time, Mr. Bergstrom." He barked another order and one of the men leapt up into Bunny's truck, got the keys and opened the rear doors. Sandhurst spoke again and the man guarding Lillian brought her out of the truck and stood with her a few feet away, and Bunny noticed the walkie-talkie hanging from his shoulder. The man at Bunny's truck was joined by his companion, and together they began to transfer the sacks into the Wells Fargo truck.

Bunny didn't get it, and said so.

"One last precaution, Mr. Bergstrom. While it's true we saw no visible sign of the police, they could still have followed you electronically. Planted a device in one of the money sacks."

That was too close to home. It shook Bunny and he gabbled to cover it. "I've told you a hundred times. There *are* no police. I've brought you the money, why don't you take it, for God's sake, and give me my daughter?"

"Very shortly, Mr. Bergstrom. In the meantime, you will please take our truck for a little drive. If there are any police they will no doubt intercept you under the impression that it is us leaving with the ransom. Your daughter will remain here as our security."

He signaled to Lillian's guard, who guided her over to Bunny's truck, which was now empty, helped her into it, followed her in, and locked the doors behind him.

"You're just wasting time," Bunny yelled. He sounded very angry but his real emotion was dismay; Lillian was out of reach again.

Sandhurst hadn't liked being shouted at, especially in front of his men, and the pistol in his hand swung up. But he checked himself and regained his composure.

"You'll find the keys in the ignition, Mr. Bergstrom. Drive toward the Queensboro Bridge, to the approach, then drive back here. If you're stopped, don't bother to return. There'll be very little to come back for."

Bunny said, "I don't understand you. You've got twenty million dollars right in the palm of your hand and you're willing to watch it drive away again."

"Because it's less important than our freedom. There are plenty of other rich men with daughters." He motioned with the gun and Bunny decided to get the charade over quickly. He took the truck over the floor and up the ramp to the outside yard. Going through the gates, he saw their car not far behind him; they were going to keep him in sight all the way.

He took a right, drove a few blocks, then took another right when he hit a main road. He drove south in the direction of the bridge, thinking hard. Daniel had underestimated Sandhurst even more than he'd realized. The guy had even figured the bleeper. He thought about the garage back there, and what he was going to do when he got back. He wondered how they'd got in and where the night watchman was. Probably tied up somewhere with a lump on his head.

He stopped for a red light and looked in the wing mirror. He couldn't see them but they had to be there; close enough to shadow him, far enough away to split if they had to. Only they wouldn't have to. The light changed and he rolled away again, spotted a bridge sign and followed it to the approach, went on by it, made a U turn and drove back toward the garage. One thing about this little jaunt, it was giving him time to think. He'd been in their ballpark and he knew the layout; and he knew the position, not that that had changed any. He still had the money and they still had Lillian. And he still needed to end up with both. He thought about the layout again and the germ of an idea began to stir. Coming up to the cyclone fence, their car appeared behind him, shot by and beat him into the garage. He followed them down the ramp and pulled up near Lillian's truck but farther back toward the wall and facing the entrance again.

Sandhurst was coming toward him and Bunny got out. "Satisfied?"

"For the moment." Sandhurst was joined by the other two whose guns, while not actually pointing at Bunny, were slanted in his direction.

"Then I'll show you the money and we can all get out of here."

Bunny, the keys in his hand, opened the truck, got up into it, and fished the sack keys out of a pocket. He said impatiently, "Which sack? I'll open them all if you want." Without waiting for an answer, he took hold of the nearest one and inserted a key into the padlock.

Sandhurst stopped him. "There's no need, Mr. Bergstrom. You wouldn't offer if it weren't real. And we're in a hurry now."

Bunny jumped down to the floor. "Get your man out of that truck and I'll drive my daughter home."

"Not yet."

"What?"

"I told you I was a cautious man. We'll take her with us and let her go when I'm absolutely certain nobody's waiting for us outside."

There were two reasons he couldn't let him leave with Lillian, one very obvious one. She'd no longer be any use to Sandhurst after he felt safe and he might feel that it was easier to put a bullet in her head and leave her in an alley than just let her go. And secondly, and not nearly as important except to Bunny, if Sandhurst left with Lillian and the money, he'd have ended up with all the marbles and Bunny would be left with nothing but a loser's grin. And he was getting very tired of jumping whenever Sandhurst rattled the chain. But he was in no position to argue as long as there was a man with a gun on Lillian. He had to get that man out of that truck in a hurry.

Which reminded him of how desperately he'd tried to get into that truck.

Which triggered the idea that had been building in the back of his mind. He set his face in a hard line and chose words to match. "Listen, kid"—his tone was scathing, contemptuous—"I was trading horses when you were still stealing hubcaps. I figured you'd come up with something like this so I came prepared."

Sandhurst hadn't expected this and he was shaken. He took a half step backward, joining his men, the guns pointing straight ahead now.

"What do you mean?"

"I took a leaf out of your book. I had a man rig incendiary bombs in some of those sacks. Real ones. I activated them when I turned that key just now. Unless I leave with Sherrel that money goes up in smoke." He glanced casually at his watch. "In ninety seconds."

Sandhurst couldn't hide the surprised anger that flared in his face. "I don't believe you."

Bunny took out the sack keys, six of them jingling on the key ring, and tossed them to Sandhurst. "The bombs have defuse switches. There are four of them, but there are twenty sacks. Unless you know which ones, the whole lot will go."

Sandhurst flipped his pistol around so that he was holding it by the barrel. He gripped it tightly. "I can force you to tell."

"Not in the time you've got left. We had a deal, mister. It's still on as long as I leave with my daughter."

Sandhurst hesitated for the briefest second then shouted a short burst in his own language. The door of the other truck banged open and the man inside came out on the run.

Bunny said quickly, "First four on the left, last row."

Sandhurst was pulling keys off the ring, slapping them into his men's hands, shouting instructions at them. The four of them jumped for the truck and tumbled inside. Bunny gave it half a beat then sprang in behind the wheel, started the truck, rammed it into reverse and shot it hurtling back toward the wall. It didn't have far to travel, twenty feet, but that was enough. It crunched into the wall in a squeal of brakes, and Bunny didn't have to look to know that he'd done it. None of the men had had a chance to get out; it had happened too fast and they'd been thrown forward by the sudden movement. The rear of the truck was flush against the wall, the doors opened back on themselves.

Sandhurst and his men were imprisoned inside like flies caught in a bottle.

Lillian *and* the money. Bunny thumped the wheel in victory. He'd beaten the bastard. Walked over him. And it had been so easy.

194

But his exuberance didn't last long. The speaker above his head crackled. "A smart idea, Mr. Bergstrom, but futile. Tell your daughter that if she moves, we'll kill her."

For a moment Bunny didn't get it. But only for that fraction of time. In his headlong rush, Lillian's guard had left the truck doors open. Bunny could see Lillian standing inside, eyes wide, waiting. And if he could see her, so could Sandhurst, through the gun slots in the side. He could kill her from there. Bunny shouted to her to stay where she was, then Sandhurst spoke.

"Drive the truck away from the wall, Mr. Bergstrom."

Bunny ran through the permutations: Lillian couldn't close the doors without moving. He couldn't close them himself without getting into the line of fire. And if they stayed open it was a stalemate only as long as Sandhurst held his fire. A few warning bursts and he'd have to move the truck.

This time Bunny thumped the wheel in bitter frustration. He'd been so close. If those doors had only swung a few feet more he would have swept the board. The speaker crackled again. "We don't seem to be moving, Mr. Bergstrom. Now I'll give *you* ninety seconds."

Bunny could see that whatever he did he'd have to free those men. But he could still make Lillian safe all the same. Doubly safe now that he thought of it. He reached above him and pressed the switch in the mike. "I'm thinking about it." He didn't hear the answer, he was already sliding out of the door. The side wall was about five feet away on his left, Lillian's truck was parked on the other side of him about thirty feet ahead. He couldn't be seen if he moved straight forward, which he did, hugging the wall, running. He crossed around the front of Lillian's truck, the angle obscuring him from Sandhurst's view, reached into the cab and pulled the hood release. He lifted the hood, propped it open with his shoulders, dug his hands in, and snapped off the metal clamps on the distributor cap. He slipped the rotor arm out, lowered the hood, and sped back to his own truck. He jabbed the mike button.

"Okay, I don't have much choice."

He started the truck, chunked it into gear, and raced the engine. Then he eased the clutch and floored the gas pedal. The truck shot forward and he swung the wheel, shouting out of the window as he bore down on the other truck. "Lillian! Lock the doors!"

He saw her startled face an instant before he slammed into the half-opened doors, belting them closed.

The impact bucked him out of his seat and he fell back again and shoved the gears into reverse. He knew the men would be spilling out behind him but he didn't waste time looking. He took the truck roaring backwards and jammed the brakes on ten feet from the wall, cut the engine and snatched at the ignition key. He tumbled out of the door and ran for the back of the truck.

There was the shattering noise of a machine gun and the dry popping of armored glass, then he was scrambling up into the back of the truck, jerking the doors closed, shooting the lock home.

He stumbled over the money sacks, slammed the gun slots shut and flopped down in the iron darkness and waited, listening.

Nothing.

He got up and cautiously opened the slot a half inch, wondering if the black muzzle of a gun barrel was going to be the last thing he'd ever see. But the men were clustered round Lillian's truck, pulling at the rear door and getting nowhere with it. When Bunny saw that Lillian had heard and understood him, he let out the breath that had been searing his lungs.

Lillian was the whole key; by putting her out of reach he'd taken away their best weapon. They still had him and the money, although they couldn't drive the truck away without the ignition key. Not immediately, anyway. But if they cannibalized Lillian's truck and made a jump wire, they wouldn't need the key. They could simply drive the truck someplace quiet and spend all night, if they had to, getting in to him. Then they'd hand him his head. But hot wiring the truck would take time, and Bunny was counting on the fact that Sandhurst had already stayed in one spot longer than he wanted to; he knew he'd start bargaining for the key by threatening Lillian.

And he was right.

"Mr. Bergstrom, we still have your daughter." He sounded furious; the subdued smoothness gone from his voice, replaced by a tighter, shorter sound. "Throw out the ignition key or we'll drive her into the river."

It occurred to Bunny that he'd shouted Lillian's name, and Sandhurst would have heard him, but the man had other things to think about now.

"No, you won't. Take a look at that truck's engine."

He'd remembered Daniel saying how an armored car relied heavily on its mobility. By taking the rotor arm he'd turned the truck into an immovable iron vault, and at the moment, a vault was the safest place Lillian could possibly be.

He watched the men poke into the engine and make the discovery. He saw Sandhurst slam a fist against the hood. Then they talked together for a moment, Sandhurst either explaining or outlining something.

The huddle broke up and Sandhurst came toward him, sticking his pistol into his belt. Bunny narrowed the slot and watched him warily.

"I underestimated you, Mr. Bergstrom. We concede partial defeat. We'll settle for just the money."

"What do you propose?"

"We'll swap keys. You give us the key to your truck and we'll give you the key to our car. You can drive your daughter home in it."

"I don't like it. The moment I step out of here you'll grab me and force Sherrel to open these doors."

"Very well then, we'll put our guns over by the wall where you can see them. I'll order my men to stand well away. You and your daughter can leave first. We'll follow and take a chance that you don't have any friends waiting outside."

"I'll have to think about it."

"We're running out of time, Mr. Bergstrom."

Bunny believed him on that score but wasn't sure about the rest. Either Sandhurst was being practical or he was trying another con. Bunny slipped the rotor arm out of his pocket and juggled it in his hand. The fact that they were willing to put their guns down probably meant that Sandhurst was on the level. But if he was, and they made the exchange, Sandhurst would still end up with the money.

"Mr. Bergstrom?"

"Give me a minute."

In the beam of light coming in from the gun slot Bunny stared at the rotor arm as a point of focus and mentally restated the problem in its simplest terms: one man, one child, two trucks, twenty money sacks, four men with guns. The man was locked in one truck with the money. The child was locked in the other truck. What he needed was the man and the child and the money locked in the same truck. And since Lillian was easier to move than the money, he had to find a way of getting her into his truck.

He was reminded of the old cannibals and missionaries puzzle that you played with coins. Three missionaries had to get three cannibals across an imaginary river without ever being outnumbered on either bank. The boat they had to use would only take two people at a time. Like all puzzles, you could work it if you made the right moves in the right sequence. But what were the right moves here?

"Do you accept, Mr. Bergstrom?" This time Sandhurst rapped impatiently on the side of the truck.

Bunny found that he was looking at the answer. The rotor arm he was holding. He jumped to the gun slot. "Okay, but this is how we'll do it. You and your men will put your guns up like you said. But you'll bring me the rotor arm of this truck."

Sandhurst was genuinely surprised. "You're joking. You want to hold both rotor arms?"

"No. I'll swap you rotor arms."

"I don't follow you. Where will that get us?"

He sounded confused and Bunny knew he had him going.

"It'll even up the bargaining. If we trade rotors you'll have control over my daughter and I'll have control over the money. We'll both have control over something the other wants."

"But you already have control over the money. You have the ignition key."

"That's not good enough. If you want to spend the time you can hot wire this truck and you know it. But if I have the rotor, something that you really need, I'll feel safe enough to come out and get my daughter."

"And then?"

"Then I'll hand you the rotor of this truck, and the key, in return for the keys to your car. Then we'll leave in that, just as you proposed."

Sandhurst examined the proposition. Bunny knew that there was only one possible thing he could be looking for—the catch. And if he thought long enough he'd spot it and realize what Bunny had in mind.

Bunny hustled him along and threw in a little misdirection. "Come on, it makes sense. And remember, I get the car in exchange. Backed up and ready to go."

Sandhurst retreated over to his men and conferred with them again. There was a brief argument which Sandhurst extinguished with a sharp order, and one of them detached himself from the group and ran to Bunny's truck. Bunny heard the sound of the hood being opened and watched Sandhurst come back toward him.

"Very well, Mr. Bergstrom, we'll try it your way. But it has to be fast and it has to be correct. No tricks. I warn you, I'm not going to be fooled again."

"Neither am I," Bunny shot back. "We're just going through with the original deal, the one you tried to renege on. Tell your men to put their guns against the wall where I can see them. Yours too."

Sandhurst did as Bunny told him and the men propped their guns against a far wall and moved away from them. The one who'd been under the hood handed Sandhurst something and Sandhurst gave him his pistol, and it was put over with the rifles.

"Hold it up," Bunny said.

Sandhurst held up a rotor arm.

"Now turn around."

Sandhurst complied and there was no other pistol that he could see.

"Move toward me. Keep your hands straight in front of you."

Bunny glanced at the men. They'd moved thirty feet away from the guns. It would take them maybe three seconds to reach them. It wasn't much margin but he hoped it would be enough.

"Now move to the rear of the truck . . . stop right there."

There was no way he could open the doors and still keep an eye on Sandhurst or the other three, so he made it fast. He slid the gun slot closed, jumped for the lock handle, wrenched it down and shoved the door open. Nobody had moved. Bunny stepped out, one eye on the men, one eye on their leader. He held the rotor out and Sandhurst did likewise, and they moved across the floor watchfully. They stopped opposite each other and simultaneously slapped the small cylinders into each other's hands.

"Now back off," Bunny ordered.

The man did so.

"Now have one of your men bring the car closer. Wait. You do it."

Sandhurst turned and went to the car parked near the wall. It was a mistake but it was too late to stop him now. The car started and backed toward him, then stopped, and Bunny tensed as Sandhurst got out. But he held nothing in his hands except the rotor arm and the key.

"Open both doors," Bunny said. He knew he'd been lucky; Sandhurst could have had a gun in the car. "Now move your men farther back."

Sandhurst said something and his men moved, but only a few feet.

Bunny looked over the area Lillian had to cover: ten paces, all of it in the open. This was the crunch; if Sandhurst was going to try something this would be when he'd try it.

It was also when Bunny was going to make his move.

He took a tentative step forward. "Now I'm going to call my daughter over. When she's sitting safely in the car, I'll hand you the key and the rotor arm and you'll hand me the key to the car. Then we're going out of here at a hundred miles an hour. Now move away."

As Sandhurst backed off, Bunny raised his voice. "Lillian. Can you hear me in there?"

Her voice came back surprisingly clear. "Yes."

"Listen to me. When I say so, I want you to come out and get into the car that's parked here. You got it?"

He got the same answer and he swept his eyes over the four men, fixed them on Sandhurst and held them there.

"Okay. Now!"

There was the snap of a lock and the truck doors swung open. Lillian jumped out and moved stiffly toward the car. She didn't look right or left.

"Around this side," Bunny said. "Rear seat."

When Sandhurst stayed where he was Bunny knew that he intended to play it straight; the man really was anxious to leave.

From the corner of his eye he saw Lillian come round the back of the car, then he heard the rear door open and close. He motioned to Sandhurst. "All right."

Sandhurst moved toward him, his hand holding the car keys extended in front of him. Bunny dug the truck's ignition key out of his pocket and added it to the metal cylinder in his left hand. He stopped Sandhurst two paces away from him. "That's far enough."

Sandhurst held out his other hand. "The rotor arm, please. And the key."

Bunny took a silent breath and set himself. He brought his hand up slowly, palm upward, and as Sandhurst reached out, he made his move.

There are some people who would have thought that it was unsporting of Bunny, who was four inches taller and thirty pounds heavier, to hit the other man, specially as Sandhurst wasn't expecting it and was wide open. That hardly made it an even contest. But Bunny had never thought of himself as sporting anyway. He'd suckered Sandhurst and everybody knows what suckers are never given. His fist thudded into Sandhurst's body just below the breastbone sending him staggering back and over the fender of the car. Bunny whipped round and dived for the car's rear door, jerked it open, pulled Lillian out and half helped, half threw her into the back

200

of the truck. He tumbled in after her as a cacophony of noise sent bullets spanging off metal and chunking lumps out of the rear wall. He banged the doors closed, rammed the belt down, and fell back onto the money sacks. He rolled off, waded through them and turned on the interior light.

"Hi, Lil," he said. "What's new?"

He tossed her the rotor arm.

Lillian, wide-eyed and breathing hard, caught it and turned it round in her hand.

She said, "I heard most of it. They need this doohickey to move the truck, right?"

"Right on."

"They can't get one from the other truck?"

"No ma'am. Different make of truck."

"Clever you."

"A compliment," Bunny said. "I don't believe it."

A torrent of words outside, delivered in a screaming rage, cut into their conversation. It didn't matter that they couldn't understand any of it.

"I think he's got his breath back," Lillian said. "What do we do now?"

"Sit tight. They can't touch us in here. They'll just have to fold their tents and steal away."

"Where's Lasky?"

"Manhattan. I'll tell you all about it later."

"So those guys get away?"

"I had them at one point. But we're still ahead of the game." Bunny looked at her closely. "They treat you okay?"

"Not bad." Lillian said it as if she were commenting on a vacation she'd spent in a mediocre resort.

"You weren't scared?"

Lillian shrugged. "I wasn't too happy when I found I'd scratched the bleeper off."

Bunny started to ask her another question but stopped. Somebody was getting into the cab of the truck. He heard the snick of gears, then whoever it was getting out again. More to himself than to Lillian he said, "What are they up to? They can't drive this thing anywhere." He slid the gun slot open a fraction and peeped out.

"What are they doing?" Lillian asked.

"I don't get it. They're putting the rotor back into the other truck."

201

"Then they're going to try towing us."

Bunny looked around at her quickly. It was a smart deduction. He'd left the truck in reverse. Is that what they'd done, taken it out of gear? He realized it didn't make sense.

"They'd have a hell of a time trying to tow this thing up that ramp. And what happens when they hit the street? One armored truck towing another, a different firm's? Not even any uniforms or anything. They wouldn't last two minutes."

"Then what are they thinking?"

Bunny watched them, unsure. They finished in the engine and slammed the hood back into place. He could see Sandhurst, his hand held to his stomach, hurrying two of his men into the truck. When the fourth ran to the car and moved it over against the far wall, Bunny knew the answer to Lillian's question.

"They're going to try and ram us."

It made sense. Their truck was parked at an angle to the wall and less than six feet away. If Sandhurst drove head on into them and sent them lunging back into the wall it just might spring the doors. They were steel doors, thick steel, but they still had to be by far the weakest part of the truck's design. It could happen.

Bunny watched the three men drive out in the truck, the fourth loping after it over the floor, following it up the ramp.

He reached for the door lock and shot it back. "Lock this after me. When you hear me yell, open it fast."

"What are you going to do?"

But Bunny was already out of the truck and running. He didn't dare move their truck, he'd have to replace the rotor arm and he didn't want to be caught with his head in the engine, but he thought he might be able to do something about the other truck. To build up speed, Sandhurst would have to come belting down the ramp and, because it curved, he wouldn't be able to see into the garage until he was in it. So he'd smash straight into the car that Bunny was going to move there.

Or would have had he been able to move it.

They'd taken the key with them.

He looked wildly around for something else he could use and his eye landed on some oil drums under the hoist in the repair shop opposite. He raced over to them wondering if they'd be heavy enough to stop the truck, but when he saw what they contained he had a better idea. They were resting on wheeled carts and the nearest one moved easily when he pulled it. He trundled it quickly back across the floor,

202

stopped it, put a foot and both hands against the drum and tipped it over. It fell heavily on its side and a couple of week's worth of oil changes splashed out onto the floor and spread in a thick black puddle just inside the beginning of the ramp. As he turned and ran he heard the rumble of the truck coming. At the same time he caught a fast glimpse, or thought he did, of something or someone in the doorway in the wall near the car—it opened onto steps that led up to the yard above. Instinctively he squinched his body in as he ran, shrinking against the tearing metal agony. He was amazed when it didn't come.

He shouted, hammered on the door. "Lillian!" He was through it and locking it a moment later.

"Get down behind the sacks. Hold on tight." He made it to the gun slot in time to see it happen. The heavy truck came charging out of the ramp, swaying round the bend. The front wheels swung toward them just as they hit the pool of oil. With nothing for its tires to grip the truck plowed straight ahead following its momentum. The driver tried frantically to correct, but with the truck's speed and enormous weight fighting against him he couldn't do it fast enough.

The truck missed them by three feet and broadsided with a tremendous crash into the back wall.

"Jesus!" said Lillian.

Sandhurst and two others came running down the ramp, stopped and took in the situation. Sandhurst looked at the oil, looked at the truck, realized what had happened and who was responsible. He shouted something, the pistol in his hand jerked up and he pumped three fast shots at the gun slot where he knew Bunny was watching. It was done in sheer frustration and the bullets pinged harmlessly off the truck's side. He snapped an order and the two men ran to the other truck and dragged out the driver. The man's head was bloodied and he looked unconscious. They carried him to the car, laid him out in the rear seat and ran back to Sandhurst. Then the three of them moved toward the repair shop and out of Bunny's vision.

Bunny closed the gun slot and filled Lillian in on what had happened. He didn't look happy.

"I was wrong, Lil. That guy's not going to go away at all. He's a sore loser." Lillian patted the sack she was sitting on. "He wants this."

Bunny pointed to his head. "He wants this, too. He's been here too long, and he knows it, but he's too mad to quit now."

"They going to try and ram us again?"

"Nope. I've spoiled that for them. But I think I showed them a much better way of getting to us. That oil I spilled out there. You know what oil's famous for, don't you?"

Lillian didn't need a diagram. "Burning."

As she said it the sound of something heavy being wheeled across the floor came to them. Bunny didn't have to look to know what it was: the other oil drum. They heard a clang and a clatter, then caught the thick cloying smell that was starting to rise from beneath the truck.

Bunny tried to figure the odds. "We may be okay in here, Lil, we may not. It's thick steel and maybe the heat won't get us if we lie on the bags. On the other hand, it might be like being inside a saucepan. If it gets too tough we'll have to get out and give up the money."

Lillian absorbed this without a change of expression. She asked blandly, "What'll happen then?"

"They'll probably break both my thumbs but they won't hurt you. I wish I hadn't hit that guy now. I wish I'd just given him a polite shove."

The lie was delivered effortlessly. Bunny knew very well that the best they could expect was a fast burst of gunfire. Sandhurst was long past playing the gentleman. Bunny opened the gun slot a fraction. Apart from the car across the floor and the truck against the wall there was nothing to see. He heard a metallic banging, then nothing for a minute; then a soft splashing noise. When he caught the unmistakable smell of gasoline he knew they'd smashed the lock on the gas pump in the repair shop.

They were pumping gas out onto the floor.

Lillian looked at him expectantly but Bunny was fresh out of ideas. The only thing he could think to do was wait and see how bad it was going to be.

It was a longer wait than he thought. Sandhurst was flooding the place. Then the pump stopped and there was a silence; a tight, nervous quiet that seemed to be expanding around them.

Bunny licked his lips. "Oh, I almost forgot. Hartley told me to tell you that—" The truck was rocked by the explosion, shaken by the shatteringly loud *baroomph* as the gas ignited instantly over its entire surface. A quieter, deeper noise followed it from beneath the truck as the oil went up, and the howling roar outside increased.

Perched on the money sacks, they felt the first fingers of heat starting up through the metal and running round and above them. Bunny thought fleetingly about the cannibals and missionaries game again. It

204

was being played all too literally now; he'd made a mistake and the cannibals had them in a huge iron pot. But he knew it wasn't the heat that would drive them out. Already it was getting tougher to breathe; the exterior heat seemed to be reaching through the sides of the truck, blotting up the oxygen inside. And even with the gun slots shut, the thick acrid smoke from the oil was seeping through the door jamb.

Lillian started to cough.

The fire, the fumes or the machine guns. It was some choice.

Bunny got up and stripped his jacket off. "Lillian, we're getting out of here."

He stood her in front of the door, unlocked it, tossed the jacket over her head, scooped her up in his arms, and kicked the door open.

It was as if he'd let something wild in. The heat slammed into him, clawed at his eyes and mouth, swamped the interior of the truck, and came back at him from all sides. He leapt into the fire, over and through it, landed awkwardly on the cement and went down, Lillian tumbling from his grasp. The floor, sloping to a drain in the center, had stopped the gasoline short of the wall and created a pocket of sanity. The rest of the garage was a madhouse, an inferno of noise and jumping flames and heat-warped air. Sandhurst had crazily spilled gas everywhere and produced a holocaust which had driven him and his men out, too. Their car was gone.

Bunny yanked Lillian to her feet, bundled her into the cab of the other truck, jumped in after her, and pushed her down to the floor. Whether or not the key was in it was something he didn't even consider; he just reached for it and started the truck, backed it clear, took it forward in a fast sweep and pointed it at the ramp. He gave the truck everything it had and reared it across the floor, a fiery bow wave of gasoline spurting away from the tires like a boat zooming across a flaming sea. The thought of the truck's gas tank going up didn't occur to him; he was too busy trying to breathe and see and not to yell out loud at the scorching heat that plucked at his face and tried to toast his hands on the wheel. The truck plowed through the oil slick in front of the ramp, skewered to the right, grazed the ramp wall but kept on going. Bunny belted it up through the long twisting curve, saw the entrance ahead, hunched down and hung on. They shot out into the sudden coolness of the yard, and on his right, through tear-streaked eyes full of stinging smoke, he got a fast impression of a car traveling parallel to them, men inside it.

He didn't hesitate. He jerked the wheel over and sent the truck careening toward it, but the car banked hard and he missed the doors, crunched into the front fender and bulled the front of the car halfway through the mesh of the cyclone fence.

He riveted his eyes on the car doors and desperately tried to get the truck started again, but it had been through too much. He knew it too, knew it wasn't going to start again, but he went on trying, watching the doors with a horrible fascination, waiting for Sandhurst to emerge and riddle the cab with bullets.

And a man did come out.

But it wasn't Sandhurst.

But Bunny recognized him all the same.

The man spoke and his words were preceded by a groan. "Look at that. More expense."

Bunny was in shock.

The bundle on the floor of the cab moved and Lillian rose. She sat up and looked out of the window. "I thought you were in Manhattan," she said.

"Are you all right, Lillian?" Lasky asked.

Lillian said she was fine.

Two men got out from the front seat of the car and another from the rear.

Flabbergasted, Bunny looked around him. There were more men and cars, including the car he'd thought he was ramming. Sandhurst and the other two were stretched out against it being frisked.

Bunny wiped a hand over his brow, knuckled the tears out of his eyes, and tried to select a single, clear, coherent question from the three hundred that were tripping over themselves inside his brain.

He didn't get the chance. An enormous concussion shook the ground as something down in the garage exploded. Bunny knew what it was: the gas tank in his truck; the one he'd just jumped out of, leaving the doors open on twenty million dollars. For the first time that night he started to feel very very ill.

He said with funereal slowness, "Mr. Lasky, do you know what that was?"

Lasky knew. "Probably your truck going up."

Bunny gave him a ghastly smile. "Do you know what was in it?"

"Sure I do. Now come on, get out you two before a firetruck runs you down."

Bunny got out of the cab like a zombie. He had news for Mr. Lasky.

But, as it turned out, it was Lasky who had news for Bunny.

Chapter **26**

On the ride back to Oyster Bay he delivered it to him bit by bit. For the most part Bunny's comments consisted of three You're putting me ons, two You've got to be kiddings and one extremely loud You rotten sonofabitch.

Lillian fell asleep against Bunny and she was still asleep when they arrived at the house. Bunny got out and scooped her up for the second time that night and turned to see Ella on the steps. She looked at the limp child in his arms and froze.

"She's fine," Bunny said. "She's just asleep."

Ella ran down the steps and reached for her. "They didn't hurt her?"

Bunny nodded at the knee she'd skinned jumping out of the truck. "That's the only scratch, and I think I gave her that."

Hartley appeared and had the same first reaction as Ella. Bunny calmed him. "She's okay. Just a little tuckered out."

Hartley let out a breath that would have inflated a balloon. He looked at Lasky. "You get those guys, Mr. Lasky?"

"All four."

Hartley beamed. "The kid came through. You too, Mr. Calder, way to go."

Ella put a hand on Bunny's arm and searched his face. "Are you all right?"

"I'm fine too. Mr. Lasky's fine, we're all fine. Just a little glazed, that's all."

Ella said she'd better get Lillian to bed, and Hartley took her and together they went into the house. Bunny and Lasky followed them up the steps and moved into the big living room where Bunny announced that he was going to broach Mr. Silverman's bar. Lasky didn't dare object.

By the time he'd returned to the room, carrying his second Scotch and beer chaser, Ella had rejoined them.

"She's dead to the world. I don't think she's had much sleep in the past few days."

It was plain that Ella hadn't either. She sat down quickly in a chair, the tremendous relief having a delayed reaction.

"Oh boy," she said. She blinked at them and took a few deep breaths. Then she sat up straighter. "Tell me what happened. How did you do it?"

As she said it, Ella seemed to realize that whatever had happened was supposed to have happened without Lasky. She tried to indicate his presence with a sideways movement of her eyes.

"Did you get the . . . the truck back okay?"

"The money? Yeah, it's safe." Bunny swigged at his drink.

"Then Mr. Lasky knows all about it?"

The glass jerked down from Bunny's mouth. "He knew about it before I did. Ella, as much as it pains me to say this, I've been conned out of my shoes." He waved his drink at the government man.

Ella, astonished, had to have it verified. "Mr. Lasky conned you?"

The man they were discussing wriggled uncomfortably in his chair and fiddled with his glasses.

Bunny said, "Alongside him, I am as a hick from Council Bluffs."

Ella demanded to know what had happened, and Bunny, briefly and very sketchily, described the scene in the garage. "The first hint I got that Mr. Lasky was around was when I rammed his car coming out. Incidentally," he said to the man, "where's Daniel? Too ashamed to show his face, I take it."

"He's downtown with those men."

Impatient, Ella said, "Then you followed Bunny tonight. We didn't think you'd do that."

Lasky nodded. "I know. You thought we'd follow the other truck."

"You know about that?"

208

Bunny asked the ceiling a question. "Does he know about it? Tell her, Mr. Lasky."

"Well." Lasky took a long time picking some lint off his knee. "At first we thought we could get away using fake money. But then it became more and more apparent that it wasn't going to work. That armored car arrangement was a very smart way of making the transfer and we began to realize that what we needed was real money."

"And he knew I'd get it for them," Bunny said, disgusted. "I may sue."

"I didn't know for sure, Mr. Calder. I just thought it was highly likely. I knew you'd never go for trying the fake money a second time, so I was pretty sure you'd come up with an alternative plan. And knowing your particular talent for, er, improvisation, I was confident you'd use your supposed wealth to get real money."

"I'm definitely going to sue."

Ella said, "In other words, you let him do your dirty work for you."

"Well, we couldn't get real money for him, Miss Brown, and that's what he had to have."

"Except," Bunny said, "what I ended up with was the fake stuff. They switched money on me, wasn't that sweet of them?"

"You must understand, Mr. Calder, we couldn't risk that money falling into those people's hands."

"Oh I understand all right. But that doesn't change the fact that I was up there in that truck tonight practically insisting on showing Sandhurst a sack full of wrapping paper."

Lasky said, "You had to believe it was real, Mr. Calder. That's why the bluff worked. Because you were convinced, Sandhurst was convinced."

Bunny held up a thumb and forefinger separated by a fraction. "I was that close."

"It was a game of inches all the way," Lasky said.

Ella spoke. "Please, you're ahead of me. How did you know Bunny had got that money? Did you count on him going to the same bank?"

"We thought it very probable, but it was safer to check with the security people. There are only a handful of armored car services; we put the word out to them, and when the Brink's people got a call from the bank for a delivery to the house here they contacted us."

Ella was nodding her head. She filled in the next part herself. "You found the truck hidden on the side drive. You took the fake stuff out of that black van of yours and put it into the truck, and put the real stuff into the van. Then you drove round the front and we watched you load it into the original truck. When Bunny switched trucks on the corner the real money was driven back to Manhattan. Am I right?"

"Yes, indeed. It went back to the Brink's warehouse, where it's locked up tight. We knew you were going to try a switch. You had to. We bugged the truck on the side drive of course so we could follow it."

Bunny rattled the ice in his glass and lowered the contents another half inch. He said, "When they sent me out in their truck tonight to see if anybody would grab me, why didn't you?"

"We almost did. We saw it heading toward the bridge, and that looked like the best place for us to move in. Only one exit to block. But when you turned round and went back we were glad we'd waited."

Bunny accepted that but was still uncomfortable. "You told me in the car that you saw most of that garage bit from the side door."

"That's right."

"Then why didn't you jump them when they had their guns down?"

"Too risky. They would have gone for them anyway, which would have started a lot of shooting, and you and Lillian were out in the open then. We knew we'd get our chance if we waited, and we did. It's hard to get out of a car door and fire a machine gun at the same time. When those men zipped out of the garage we collared them before they could get off a shot."

"They zipped out for a good reason. It was damned hot in there. Were you going to let us roast?"

Lasky looked wounded. "We were coming in to get you when you came out and got us."

"You cut it awfully close, Mr. Lasky."

"I know it. But then that gasoline fire surprised everybody. Us and them."

Bunny said, "Lillian and I were a trifle nonplussed, too."

"You must be feeling pretty tired, Mr. Calder." Lasky got up. "I'd better go away and let you get to bed."

Bunny rose too. "I'm more thirsty than anything. I'm going to have another drink on the house."

"We'll wrap up things out here tomorrow. I'll talk to you some more then."

210

Ella offered to see Lasky to the door, and Bunny went back to the bar. He made himself another drink, brought it back into the living room and had half finished it by the time Ella returned.

She sat down next to him. "Well, well," she said. "And all this time we thought Mr. Lasky was just a mayonnaise sandwich."

"Mr. Lasky's a dangerous man," Bunny answered, brooding about it. "I asked him what would have happened if their little scheme hadn't panned out. You know, if we'd got Lillian but lost the money. Do you know what he said? He said they would have done everything in their power to have my sentence reduced. Can you beat that? He would have let me take the rap for finessing that money out of the bank."

"But Bunny, you must admit it was your idea."

"I know, but goddamn it, he had it first."

"You're just peeved because he fooled you."

"I know why I'm peeved," Bunny said.

"Why?"

"Because he fooled me."

"He told me how you handled Sandhurst in that garage tonight. That was pretty smart, Bunny."

"He was from out of town."

"It was also pretty brave."

"It was also pretty dumb. I almost got Lillian and me barbecued."

Ella put a soft hand on his chin and turned his face towards her. "You look funny without eyelashes."

"Uh huh."

She took one of his hands and turned it palm up. "You've burned your hands, too."

"Yeah."

"You should put something on them. Come on, you're exhausted. You take the master bedroom tonight. I've hogged it long enough."

"No, hell. I'd just dream I was back on the snooker table."

"Go ahead. I insist."

Bunny got up, tired all of a sudden.

Ella said, "You go on up and I'll bring you something to put on your hands."

Bunny didn't argue. He took his drink and mounted the stairs and went down the hall to the master bedroom. He got out of his clothes and took a shower, letting the hot water soak into him. Then he dried himself and got into the big double bed. It was silky and soft and smelled vaguely of perfume, and was very, very comfortable. He'd almost dozed off when Ella came in.

"You bring it?"

"What?"

"Something to put on my hands."

"Oh sure," Ella said.

"What is it?"

The light went out and there was the soft noise of a zipper unfastening.

"Me," she said. Then Ella was lying next to him.

Very next to him.

Bunny was suddenly not so drowsy anymore. "Well," he said. A mixture of surprise and indignity. "How about that! You got me into your bed under the pretext of ministering to my wounds. You conned me. You of all people."

Ella kissed him, long and lingeringly, and curled herself around him. "Sweetie," she said, "everybody cons you. You're easy."

Chapter 27

One thing that the temporary inhabitants of the Silverman mansion could not possibly have complained about during their stay was the weather. It had been one sunny blue sky after another, and their last day was perfect, too. But the inhabitants weren't appreciating it much. They weren't appreciating anything at eleven o'clock that morning. An air of gloom hung inside the house as if a week of dull drizzling rain was continuing outside.

Hartley brought a suitcase up from the servants' quarters and put it next to Ella's in the front hall. He was wearing a blue suit and it was the first time she'd seen him out of his chef's whites. He looked like somebody else.

He said to Ella, "Lillian still not down?"

"No. She was still asleep half an hour ago."

"What time are they coming for her?"

"About eleven thirty." Ella looked very glum.

Hartley frowned. "She missed her breakfast. I had oatmeal for her the way she likes it."

"I left a glass of milk on her dressing table."

"The kid should eat."

They lapsed into a sad silence, then Bunny arrived from the chauffeur's room and added his suitcase to the other two. Ella smiled and kissed him and hugged him close for a moment, then went back to looking glum.

213

Bunny looked at the pair of them, standing forlornly by the luggage, waiting. He took in the hall, the black and white marble floor, the gilt-framed oil paintings, the delicate wall plaques, the elegant curving staircase that soared up, over and around.

"Well, it wasn't much," he said, "but it was home."

There were no takers. Ella played aimlessly with a tag on her suitcase, and Hartley frowned down at his shoes. Bunny decided to leave them alone and went into the house.

Then the doorbell rang and Hartley opened the door and Lasky walked in. They swapped good mornings, and Lasky noted the subdued atmosphere and ran his eyes over the suitcases.

"Lillian not down yet?"

"Not yet."

"I had eggs for her as well," Hartley said.

Lasky asked where Bunny was, then excused himself and went after him. He found him in the bar bent over an enormous humidor.

"Hello, there."

Bunny slammed the lid shut. "Mr. Lasky you caught me. I've been eyeing these Upmanns for a week now. Do you think the budget will run to two of them?"

"It looks as though it already has. How do you feel this morning?"

"A little stiff and crackly, but otherwise okay."

Lasky held out an envelope. "This is for you. A check."

Bunny took the envelope by a corner. "Notice how lightly I'm holding it."

"You can take a better grip than that. We made it out for a little more than the amount you owe Miss Brown."

"Oh?" Bunny slipped the check out. "Hey." His eyebrows went up. "This sure beats the employment business."

"You did a splendid job for us, Mr. Calder. We appreciate it."

"Lillian did all the work."

"We have a check for her, too," Lasky said. "Mr. Smathers, the lawyer, he's going to look after everything."

Bunny flicked the piece of paper in his hand, still tickled about it. "I expected a government calendar and a firm handshake."

"Well we wanted you to come out of this with more than a couple of burns."

Bunny grinned at him. "As a matter of fact, Mr. Lasky, I'm coming out of this with a lot more than that. I got myself a terrific girl."

It was Lasky's turn to be surprised. "Really? You and Miss

Brown? I'm delighted." Lasky looked it, too. He seemed to like the role of matchmaker.

"So am I," Bunny said. "Have a stolen cigar."

They walked together back through the house and heard the sound of a car on the drive before they'd reached the hall.

Lasky said, "That'll be the people from the children's home. Now comes the hard part."

"I know it," Bunny said. They were both thinking of Ella.

They went into the hall where Hartley had just admitted the hatchet-faced woman they'd seen on her previous visit. She dismissed Bunny and Hartley with a distasteful glance, barely tolerated Ella, and focused her attention on Lasky.

"Good morning. I've come for Lillian Phelan." She had a voice that matched her face.

"She'll be right down," Lasky said.

In a carefully controlled monotone, Ella offered to go up and fetch her. But there was no need. Lillian was coming slowly down the stairs, suitcase in hand.

The woman's voice hacked at the air. "Come along, Lillian. Let's not keep everybody waiting. We don't want to be late on our first day back, do we?"

Lasky said, "Hello, Lillian. How do you feel this morning? All recovered?"

"I'm all right."

"Fine. I didn't get a chance to say too much to you last night, you went out like a light. But I want you to know that we're all very grateful to you and we think you did a terrific job for us, and, well, anytime that we can do anything . . ." Lasky trailed off, unhappy with the way he'd put it.

"Sure," Lillian said. She moved by him and Hartley shoved a package at her.

"Brownies," he said. "I baked 'em for you. Case you get hungry later on."

Lillian took the package. "Thanks."

Hartley shuffled his feet, held out a giant paw for a handshake, then turned it into a pat on the shoulder. "Hang in there, kid."

Lillian looked at Ella, who had crouched down beside her and was closing a lock on her suitcase. She said busily, "I think everything's in there. Except the clothes you were wearing last night. I washed those but they're not dry yet."

"Thanks," Lillian said.

"I'll mail them to you. Or I could bring them myself, if you like."
Lillian shrugged.

"It wouldn't be any trouble," Ella said.

Lillian moved toward the door, and Bunny, last in line, tried to make it light. "Take it easy, Lil. And as they say in the theater, it was great working with you."

"Bye," Lillian said. She went out of the door, and the woman, with a fast professional smile at Lasky, followed her out to the car.

Hartley coughed and said that he thought he'd left something on the stove and left the room. Ella had her face turned away. Bunny examined the marble floor, and Lasky didn't know where to look.

There was the sound of a car door slamming and an engine starting, and the gravel scrunched as the car made a U-turn and rolled away down the drive.

Ten yards farther on it came to an abrupt halt. The rear door flew open and Lillian bounded out and came running back up the drive, took the steps two at a time and hurled herself into Ella's arms.

"You bring me that washing real soon," she said.

Ella just nodded over and over.

Lillian released her, ran to Bunny, hugged him too, then trotted down the steps and back to the car.

Bunny couldn't have been more amazed if it had been Miss Hatchet-Face who'd run back and hugged him.

He watched the car start up again and disappear round the bend in the drive. "Goddamn it," he said, "Lillian shouldn't have to go back to that place with that woman. There must be something we can do."

He stopped himself and swiveled his eyes at Lasky, but Lasky didn't appear to have heard him.

Good.

The next day a classified cable arrived on an executive desk in a government building in Washington. After it had been decoded it read like this:

HAVE RECEIVED INFO EX-NAZI GROUP ENTERED COUNTRY LAST 24 HOURS. APPARENT PURPOSE RAISE LARGE SUM MONEY. SUGGEST USING SAME TECHNIQUE CASE JUST CONCLUDED AND SAME TEAM. INFO RECEIVED BY PHONE. CALLER UNIDENTIFIED. MALE, HEAVY GERMAN ACCENT.

LASKY

216